BLOGGER GIRL

MEREDITH SCHORR

booktrope

Booktrope Editions
Seattle WA 2013

Cover Design by Loretta Matson
Edited by Gabrielle Roman

This is a work of fiction. Names, characters, places, brands, media, and incidents are either the product of the author's imagination or are used fictitiously. Any resemblance to similarly named places or to persons living or deceased is unintentional.

PRINT ISBN 978-1-62015-157-0
EPUB ISBN 978-1-62015-253-9

For further information regarding permissions, please contact info@booktrope.com.

Library of Congress Control Number: 2013946451

CHAPTER 1

I SLID MY MOUSE back and forth between 4 and 4.5 pink champagne flutes. I couldn't decide if the book, *Gladly Never After*, was 4.5 flutes worthy. The ending was a bit abrupt and the hero was kind of obvious from the beginning. At the same time, it was certainly an engaging story, so much so that I took every available opportunity to turn on my Kindle to see what happened next, even while squatting on the toilet between beers at happy hour.

"Long!"

I saved a draft of my review and stood up. "Yes, Rob?" I walked into his large fishbowl shaped office knowing he wasn't going to come to me. "What's up?"

Rob handed me two sheets of paper. "Can you scan this to Bartlett?"

Removing the papers from his hand, I said, "No problem. Should I include a message?"

He scratched his thick head of brown hair. "Nah. He'll know what it is."

Rob's recent takeover of a high-profile litigation was definitely getting in the way of my blogging. I had four books scheduled for review in the next two weeks and had received several more on my Kindle from publishers and authors in the past couple of days. Then again, it was my day job as a legal secretary at a mid-sized New York City law firm that paid my $1800 rent, not my voluntary – albeit immensely more satisfying – side gig as a chick lit book reviewer/blogger.

"Also, send an email to the team about squad drinks around the corner at Banc Café at 5."

My heart skipped a beat. "Who should I include in the email?"

Rob was now facing his computer and without bothering to turn around, he said, "The whole team, Lucy, David, Nicholas, Blah, Blah, Blah, Blah."

Rob probably didn't actually say, "Blah, Blah, Blah, Blah" but that was all I heard after "Nicholas." Ordinarily, I preferred the company of friends over the partners, associates and paralegals that made up Rob's team, but I'd make an exception if Nicholas was going to be there. I took stock of my outfit, exhaling a sigh of relief that I was wearing a flattering low-cut black top and form-fitting black skinny pants. I fingered my necklace, a platinum chain with an opal pendant that conveniently fell right in the line of my cleavage. "Sounds good. Uh, I forgot who else you mentioned after Nicholas." *Not that it matters.*

Rob waved me away. "Just the team. The usuals. Add a sentence at the end about inviting anyone I forgot."

"Gotcha."

When I got back to my desk, I emailed the team about happy hour, casually adding Nicholas' address somewhere in the middle. It was very short notice, but (a) it was free drinks and (b) Rob was the boss and by virtue of him being the boss, sufficient advance notice was not required. Once I confirmed that the email went through, I practically ran to the copy room to scan Rob's documents and quickly emailed them to Bartlett. I glanced at my Movado watch, a gift from my parents for my 28th birthday earlier that year. It was 4:42. After I grabbed my enormous leather pocketbook from the bottom drawer of my desk and told Rob I was stepping away, I headed to the bathroom and called Bridget.

She picked up after one ring. "Is everything okay?"

I ran a brush through my long light brown hair and shook my head from side to side to give it some bounce. "Why would you ask that? Because I called instead of texted?"

"Bingo!"

Bridget had been my best friend since the 7th grade. Text messaging often won out over actually talking on the phone, but it wasn't like telephone conversations were reserved for emergency trips to the hospital or anything. I removed the pink monogrammed makeup case I'd had since junior high school from the bottom of my pocketbook.

"Having drinks with the team tonight after work."

"The team, huh? Does that include your work crush? What's his name again?"

"Nicholas!"

Bridget snorted. "I know! Nicholas *Strong*," she repeated. "Rhymes with Long. I remember."

"Ha ha. Be nice." Mentioning the rhyming of my last name with Nicholas' wasn't one of my proudest moments, but it was after two flirtinis, and two flirtinis for a 101-pound girl were like five flirtinis for an average sized woman.

"Well, have fun. Don't do anything I wouldn't do," Bridget said dryly. Gun shy after an uncharacteristic one-night-stand generously left her with a case of crabs, she hadn't done anything with anyone in over a year.

"I'm not entirely certain he sees me as anything more than that 'chick' who occasionally connects him to Rob's voicemail, but he's serious eye candy. Chances are, we'll exchange less than four words, I'll end up extremely frustrated and regret going in the first place."

"There you go, Ms. Positive! Good luck."

"Thanks. See ya." I hung up the phone and wiped the corners of my lips before applying a shiny but translucent gloss. I dusted a little powder over my nose trying unsuccessfully to hide the constellation of freckles that appeared at the tip. I zipped the case and returned it to my bag. I wished I knew how to apply dramatic makeup but every time I made an attempt, I looked like one of those freaky pageant kids.

When I returned to my desk, I noticed that Rob's light was off. It was only 5:05. *Someone needed a beer.*

I opened my saved post to finish my review.

In closing, I would highly recommend Gladly Never After to all lovers of chick lit, particularly those who prefer books with more action/dialogue and less description/ backstory.
Rating: 4.5 Pink Champagne Flutes

I set my blog to post the review at 6 the next morning and logged off of my computer. At least I'd be fashionably late.

* * *

I spotted my crew immediately upon entering the dimly lit restaurant. They had taken over the left side of the semi-circular bar. I stood up as tall as my 4'11" frame allowed and approached the crowd. Although my eyes looked straight ahead towards Rob, always the center of attention at these events, I used my peripheral vision to confirm that Nicholas was in attendance. He was talking to Lucy, a junior associate in the group. Lucy was actually really nice, but her straight blonde hair was always pulled back into a tight bun and her daily attire consisted of stodgy business suits. She looked like a librarian and I couldn't imagine Nicholas being interested in her as more than a colleague. *On second thought, maybe Lucy is one of those stereotypical librarian types who's kinky in the sack.* I had often wondered if Nicholas had hooked up with any of the female associates in the office while pulling an all-nighter or after one of the many firm-hosted parties. As I glanced back at Lucy in jealous paranoia, I was surprised to catch Nicholas looking directly at me. Could he tell I was thinking about him? Bridget and I always said guys had radar.

"There she is. My right hand. What are you having?" Rob asked.

I tore my eyes away from Nicholas and focused my attention on Rob. "A glass of Prosecco. Thanks." I considered asking for a cocktail menu but wanted a drink in my hand too badly to spend the time considering my choices.

Rob raised one of his thick dark eyebrows and took a sip of his lager. "Beer isn't good enough for you?"

"Not when the firm is paying." I giggled.

Rob handed me my glass and I casually looked around. I caught Nicholas' eye again and prepared this time, gave him a friendly wave.

"Hey you," he said, smiling wide as his brown eyes darted down to my chest and quickly back to my face.

His appraisal of my rack, while subtle, was unmistakable. Not that a guy checking out a girl's chest was an indication of actual interest. It was probably merely instinct for them, but I was still thrilled. I would be the first to admit that I drew attention to my chest since, being so short, I needed to give people a reason to look down far enough to see me. I raised my glass and smiled back. "Hey," I said before turning back towards Rob. I wanted more than anything to go over and cock block his conversation with Lucy but I didn't have the nerve. Checking out a girl's cleavage was not necessarily an invitation for conversation.

"Did you send that email to Bartlett?" Rob asked.

Without batting an eyelash, I responded, "Did you ask me to?"

Rob offered a bemused smile. "Touché. I thought you might be too busy working on your blog to attend to such menial tasks like getting your work done."

"When has my blog ever gotten in the way of attending to your business, Rob?" Rob loved to give me shit about my blog, but I knew he was joking. I had only worked with him at our current firm for four months, but had been his assistant at his previous one for close to two years. He had left our old firm more than six months earlier, leaving me behind with a promise to use his influence to get me hired as well. We worked well together. Although in his mid-fifties, Rob had the energy of a teenager and was extremely high-strung. I knew how to take him down a notch without threatening his authority.

"What blog?"

I felt a flush creep across my cheeks as I turned around to face the source of the question. I wasn't surprised, since I blushed whenever I talked to Nicholas, even when the phone rang at work and I saw his name on my caller ID.

"You didn't know about Kim's blog?" Rob asked, his blue eyes reflecting amusement.

Nicholas shook his head, not removing his eyes from mine.

All I could think about was running my fingers along the dark stubble on his jawline. Never completely clean shaven, he currently looked like he hadn't touched a razor in several days. I held his gaze, willing my voice not to give away my crush, but the heat on my face suggested a crimson complexion that probably already had. "I have a blog where I write book reviews." I figured Nicholas didn't know about my blog since our opportunities to socialize outside of work had been few and far between in the four months we'd worked together. It was that unfamiliarity which I blamed for my chronic bashfulness in his presence. *Well, that and his overwhelming sex appeal.* Unable to maintain eye contact a second longer, I glanced back at Rob hoping he'd pick up the dialogue.

"It's incredibly popular. Publishers actually beg my secretary to read and review their client's novels on a daily basis." Rob beamed at me like a proud uncle as if he was somehow responsible for my blog's immense popularity.

I turned back to Nicholas and smiled shyly. "Every other day basis is probably more accurate but yes, it's a widely read blog. I have several thousand followers and get requests from authors, publicists and agents pretty often."

Nicholas looked at me with admiration. "Awesome. What types of books do you review?"

I hated this part of telling people from work about my blog. I never knew if the attorneys would raise their noses in the air and judge my taste in "literature." *Here goes nothing.* "Chick lit," I admitted.

Nicholas tilted his head to the side. "Like the gum?"

I giggled as if I'd never heard that one before. "Yes, it's called chick lit, like the gum. But it's also a book genre. Like *Bridget Jones's Diary, The Devil Wears Prada.* You know?"

Nicholas looked thoughtful as he rubbed his thumb along his chin. "My ex-girlfriend had a bunch of books with pink covers. Were those chick lit?"

Forcing myself to stay focused instead of wondering what his ex-girlfriend was like, how long ago they broke up and why, I smiled and said, "Probably." Although chick lit had certainly evolved beyond stereotypical pink covers, it wasn't the time to go into defense-mode.

Nicholas smiled wide. "Very cool, Kim!" Glancing at his empty glass, he said, "Time for a refill. Be right back" and walked towards the bar.

I tore my eyes away from the back of Nicholas' light blue business shirt and back to Rob. But Rob was now talking to Lucy about some guy she had deposed the previous day. *Boring work talk.* I downed the rest of my Prosecco and walked over to the bar. After quickly getting the bartender's attention, I ordered another glass, on Rob's tab of course, and observed Nicholas finish sending a text. As he smiled into his phone, I felt my Hanky Panky thong practically melting off. At only about 5'7", his stature might have kept him off of some women's top five lists but since I was vertically challenged too, he was currently number one on mine. I couldn't even think of who would follow him in second and third place.

"Penny for your thoughts, Blogger Girl."

I snapped out of my list making and faced Nicholas, silently praying he was not a mind reader.

He looked at me expectantly.

I swung my free hand in dismissal and lifted my drink towards him. "Nothing important. Cheers!"

Nicholas clinked his glass against mine, said, "Cheers" and took a sip of his drink.

Following his lead, I took a sip of mine.

Nicholas inched closer to me. Speaking in almost a whisper, he said, "Having fun yet?"

Very aware that we'd never stood this close to each other and that these were practically the most words we'd ever exchanged one on one, I replied with faux nonchalance, "Can't really complain about free drinks. You?" The cuffs of his shirt sleeves had been pushed up to his elbows and I pondered whether the dark hair on his arms was coarse or soft. I wondered what it would feel like to run my fingers up and down his arm. I also wondered if he could hear my heart beating through my chest.

"Definitely can't complain about that," Nicholas agreed. "And a break from work is always welcome, especially these days." He smiled. "Doing anything good this weekend?"

I had practically forgotten it was Thursday night, which was odd for me since I lived for the weekends when my secretarial duties did not get in the way of my reading. "Not sure yet. Probably drinks with friends. And I need to catch up on some reading. For the blog. What about you?" *Please don't mention a girlfriend.*

"Oh, this and that." His eyes glowed, almost like he was holding back a secret.

I bit down on my lip and without thinking, blurted out, "Do This and That have last names?"

Nicholas gave me a once over before shaking his head laughing. "I'll probably spend most of it at work actually. So, tell me more about this blog."

I tipped my head to the side. "What do you want to know?"

"I don't know. Like, what made you start it?"

"The condensed version or the truth?"

Nicholas cocked an eyebrow. "How long of a story is the truth?"

"Why? Do you have a date to rush off to?" I swallowed hard. *Nice, Kim.*

Laughing, he said, "It's just that your answer was rather mysterious, you know?"

I shuffled my feet. "Well, I usually tell people I started the blog because I've always loved to read, blah, blah, blah."

"Blah blah blah. Gotcha."

After he said that, he winked at me and when my knees wobbled in response, I grabbed the bar with my free hand. "The truth is that one day I was bored at home surfing the Internet and I found all of these blogs dedicated to romance books, like Harlequin stuff, and then I found some more devoted to science fiction, thrillers and so on. But I could barely find anything dedicated to chick lit and it pissed me off because I love it. I figured if I love it, there must be other girls who love it too and maybe if I started this blog, I'd find them and we'd bond." I paused. "Aren't you glad you asked?"

As his phone rang, Nicholas distractedly responded, "Yeah, that's cool," before bringing it to his ear. He whispered, "Sorry" before answering it.

I wondered if it was from "This" or "That."

Nicholas hung up his phone and frowned at me. "I knew it wouldn't last. I've gotta head back to the office."

"Oh that sucks." Of course, if he had to work late, there was less time for him to have sex with someone else later, except maybe Lucy the Librarian within the confines of one of their offices. Or maybe he didn't really have to go back to the office but all of my blog talk had bored him so intensely that he was happy for any polite excuse to be free of me. *Snap out of it, Kim.*

Nicholas shrugged. "The glamorous life of an associate. But it was nice talking to you, Kim! Don't be a stranger."

"You either. Don't work too hard."

"Tell that to him," he said, gesturing towards Rob. With one last smile and a light tap on my shoulder, Nicholas walked away. As I answered another co-worker's question about where I had bought my peep-toe bright red patent leather pumps, I saw him make his round of goodbyes and walk out of the bar.

Even though I was pleased that my banter with Nicholas had finally progressed beyond telling him that Rob was in a meeting or running late, I hoped I hadn't gone too far with the blog talk. It wouldn't be the first time. Served him right for asking, although he probably knew I wasn't prepared to converse with him about anything work-related. I looked inside my half empty glass. Rather than come out and chug almost two drinks, I should have used the time to read. I was too buzzed to concentrate on a book now and was positive I was incapable of writing a coherent review.

I grabbed my coat and walked over to Rob to say goodbye.

"You're leaving before my big announcement?" Rob asked, his shoulders dropping.

I pretended not to notice his disappointment. Rob had a "thing" for making announcements. I wasn't sure if the content of the speech mattered to him as much as the pleasure he seemed to derive from hearing his own voice against a backdrop of silence while he had everyone's rapt attention. "Are we all getting six figure bonuses? And by 'we all', I mean secretaries included?"

Rob smirked at me. "Yeah, right."

"Am I getting fired?"

"Not if you stay for my announcement."

I glared at him.

"No, you're not getting canned."

"Then what is the announcement about this time?" I bet he hadn't even written it yet.

Rob took a sip of his beer and looked down at the dirty floor. Looking back at me with a sheepish expression, he said, "I'm not quite sure yet."

Aha! I thought so. "Then I am going to excuse myself and you can repeat your brilliant announcement to me tomorrow." *Insert kiss ass comment here.* "And I'm sure it will be brilliant."

Rob gestured with his hand towards the entrance of the bar. "You're excused."

After I said my goodbyes to the rest of the squad, I walked out onto chilly 3rd Avenue. As I zipped up my jacket, it occurred to me that Nicholas had conveniently neglected to answer my question as to whether he had a date later. I walked back inside the first set of doors, removed my phone from my bag and texted Jonathan. I was as horny as a 15-year-old boy at a strip club.

CHAPTER 2

I ROLLED OFF OF JONATHAN and onto my back. Since I was almost always on top when I slept with him, I wondered if all of his pot smoking made him incapable of doing the work. When we dated in high school, cheap beer, not weed, was his drug of choice.

"So what's going on with you?" he asked, reaching one of his lean arms over to grab a cigarette from his midnight blue IKEA dresser.

I quickly got out of his bed. The smell of cigarettes made me sick. "When are you gonna quit smoking?"

"Hey, I don't complain when you text me for a booty call so no complaining about the smoking."

"Screwing me is not bad for your health!"

"That's arguable," Jonathan laughed as he scratched his unruly head of dark hair.

I swatted him with my pants before putting them back on. "Time for a haircut, Middleton!" Although I vaguely remembered being madly in lust with Jonathan when we were high school sweethearts from the ages of 16-18, we had been just friends for the past ten years. And friends with benefits off and on for the past two. I hadn't dated anyone I liked in a while, was uncomfortable taking home strangers from bars, and Jonathan was either too lazy or stoned to make the effort. We fell into bed occasionally out of convenience and, that night, out of mere sexual frustration on my part.

Still lying on the bed, one arm extended behind his head, Jonathan took a drag with his free hand. "How's *Black is the New Purple* going these days?"

"*Pastel is the New Black* is going very well, thank you." I chuckled. Jonathan never remembered the title of my blog but at least he always managed to ask about it.

"Did you hear about Hannah Marshak?" He sat up and tapped his cigarette into an ashtray.

"Ugh. What about her?" Hannah was bitch central in my high school class. Well, at least to me and Bridget. She had more personalities than Sally Field in the movie *Sybil* and some of our class probably thought she was cotton candy sweet.

"She wrote a book."

I felt my face drain of color as I remembered Hannah suggesting in front of my entire 8th grade Home Economics class that I should have an expert look at my Coach bag because the leather strap looked too dark to be authentic and she would feel *so* terrible if my mother had spent money on a fake. Hannah came off looking like a Good Samaritan while I looked like the poor little girl with the knock-off bag. I considered donating the bag to Goodwill but Bridget said that would be playing right into Hannah's hands and talked me out of it. "She *what*?"

"She wrote a novel. Some crap about a chick in Paris." Jonathan took another deep drag of his cigarette. "It's being published."

My throat burned as if I'd chain smoked a pack of Jonathan's Marlboro Reds and I was afraid I was going to regurgitate Prosecco all over his dirty wood floor. "I gotta go."

"You alright?" Even though the effects of weed had seemingly rendered Jonathan paralyzed in his relaxed position on the bed, I could hear a hint of emotion in his voice.

"I'm fine," I lied. After squeezing my feet into my shoes, I walked around to Jonathan's side of the bed and kissed his stubbly cheek. "As always, thanks for the good time."

"You can leave the money on the counter."

"Fuck you."

* * *

As soon as I got home, I called Bridget.

"Wow. Two actual phone calls in one day. How did drinks go? Did you and Mr. Strong go at it in the bathroom stall?"

"In my dreams. You're never going to believe what Jonathan told me."

After a brief hesitation, Bridget asked, "When did you talk to Jonathan?"

"At his apartment earlier."

"I thought you had drinks with work people?"

"I did. I went to Jonathan's afterward." I paced my studio apartment, still reeling from the news.

"Oh. Why?"

"Frustrated. Like I knew I would be. Jonathan is easy and available and after years of practice, he knows how to push my buttons. But this is not why I called!"

Sounding meek, Bridget asked, "Why did you call?"

I was dying to tell her about Hannah but she didn't sound right. "You okay, Bridge?"

I heard her take a drag of a cigarette. "I'm fine."

"Ugh, between you and Jonathan, second hand smoke is gonna kill me."

"Jonathan's still smoking too?"

"Yes. The smoking is one thing, but he's kind of gross in general these days. I don't think he's gotten a hair cut in six months."

"Last time I saw Jonathan, his hair was cut close to his head, practically shaved."

"I guess you haven't seen him in a while. Now he looks like the straggly kitchen mop I had before I finally discovered the genius that is the Swiffer."

Bridget let out a belly laugh. "I remember that mop. It looked like Bob Marley!"

"I made sure not to run my hands through it." Clarifying my statement, I added, "Jonathan's hair, not the mop. But back to you, for someone who recycles and eats practically all organic, the smoking is a bit ironic, don't you think?"

"I'm celibate, Kim. Let me have my nicotine." I heard her take another drag.

"Whatever. No one is forcing you to allow one bad experience to turn you into a nun. Not all guys have crabs."

Bridget exhaled loudly. "Have you ever had crabs, Kim?"

She knew the answer to that question. "No." I'd never even had a yeast infection.

"I didn't think so. Let me tell you, it's not pleasant."

"I can only imagine. Anyway, back to the reason for my call."

"Which obviously wasn't to tell me about the size of Nicholas' penis."

I pictured Nicholas naked. Although he was short, I had a feeling he was not short changed where it mattered. "No. It's about Hannah Marshak."

Bridget groaned. "Ugh. What about that piece of shit?"

I smiled slightly. Bridget hated Hannah as much as I did and was the only girl who stood by me, defending the authenticity of my Coach bag. "She wrote a book."

"What? No way!"

"Yes way," I said sadly.

"I'm sorry, K," Bridget said softly.

I wrapped my hair into a ponytail holder and kicked off my shoes. "Why are you sorry?"

"I know you wanted to be a writer back in high school."

"And you wanted to be an astronaut."

Bridget laughed. "Yeah. But I doubt Neil Armstrong tossed his cookies after riding roller coasters like me."

I walked over to my bed, pulled down the comforter and sat on the edge. "Writing blogs is about all this girl can handle." When I wasn't working, I was reading. When I wasn't reading, I was blogging. And when I wasn't doing either of those things, I was responding to emails from authors and publicists, maintaining my Facebook, Twitter and blog pages, corresponding with other bloggers about author blog tours and so many other tasks associated with running a successful site. "Between the day job and the blog, I barely have time to wipe my ass, much less write a book. But I bet Hannah's book sucks!"

"Definitely," Bridget eagerly agreed. "But she would never admit it. Just like when she insisted she was accepted to Brown University but chose to go to a state school out of loyalty to Plum and Marla who didn't get in. Please. I'd really like to see that acceptance letter."

I had to laugh. There really was no way Hannah had been accepted to an Ivy League school, but none of her minions dared to challenge her. "Maybe she's lying about writing a book too?" Bridget suggested.

"Yeah. I bet her rich parents hired a ghost writer," I said, although I doubted it.

"A what?"

"Never mind. I'm tired. Gonna pass out."

"Jonathan wear you out?"

To brush my teeth or not brush my teeth, that was the question. I climbed into bed and cradled the phone in my neck. "It just feels like it's been an unusually long day. Talk to you tomorrow, Bridge?"

"Of course. And no worries about the book. I'm sure it will crash and burn."

I hung up and went to bed feeling slightly better.

CHAPTER 3

THE FOLLOWING MORNING, I logged onto my computer at work and after making sure Rob hadn't sent me anything urgent, I shared my review of *Gladly Never After* on Twitter and the *Pastel is the New Black* Facebook page. When all of the clocks in my immediate surroundings - computer, work phone, cell phone and watch, promised it was past 9:30, I called to wish my younger sister Erin a happy 25th birthday. She was currently unemployed, having been laid off from her position in Boston as an Assistant Buyer at Lord & Taylor, and didn't wake up until at least 9.

When she picked up the phone with a froggy, "Hi," I adopted my cheeriest voice and said, "Happy Birthday!"

"Thanks. You're the first to call me."

"Didn't Gerry wish you a Happy Birthday?"

"Yeah, but he didn't *call*. He said it to me in person this morning when he woke up next to me in bed. Duh!"

I rolled my eyes. *Silly me.* "Aha. Yeah, well, I hope you have a great day. Anything fun planned?" I looked towards Rob's dark office. I knew he had an early meeting out of the office that morning but he would probably be in soon and I wanted to get in some reading time while I could.

"Gonna take it easy today. Maybe head to the gym later. Ger is taking me to Atlantic Fish Company for dinner." Erin yawned and I pictured her stretching lazily in her bed.

"How's the job search going?" Yes, it was her birthday and I probably could have refrained from being a nag, but the fact that she sat at home all day while I had to work irked me.

"It's going. But I was actually thinking it probably makes no sense to get a new job since I'll have to quit once I have a baby anyway."

I sat up straighter in my chair. "You're not even pregnant!" I knew I had said that very loudly when I heard a chuckle from Patti, the secretary who sat outside of the other partner's office. Lowering my voice, I said, "Are you?" I felt a headache coming on and rubbed my brow.

"No. But it's only a matter of time."

"I understand." I was proud of my restraint since I actually did not understand at all and *wanted* to suggest that the money she could make in the meantime could help pay for her child's college education or at least designer baby clothes, considering my sister's priorities. "Anyway, dinner at Atlantic Fish Company sounds fantastic. Get the lobster so I can live vicariously." Atlantic Fish Company was where Gerry's parents had hosted the rehearsal dinner the night before Erin and Gerry's wedding.

"I probably will. Or maybe the surf and turf."

I was happy we had moved on to a more agreeable topic of conversation. "Well, 25 was a great year. I'm sure it will bring all good things." Actually, 25 had been kind of shitty. I spent most of it as an intern at an advertising firm running around fetching coffee and making copies. I still made copies, but Rob never asked me to make his coffee. And since I'd started my blog over a year ago, my lack of passion for my job didn't bother me as much.

"I can't believe I'm 25 already and been out of college for three years. Speaking of which, are you going to your high school reunion next month?"

"Yeah." Bridget and I planned to go to the reunion only after getting wasted first. And I hoped to drag Jonathan too for some moral support. I didn't hate high school so much as tolerate it as an unavoidable rite of passage. I had no desire to go back but there were some old friends I actually wanted to see. "Why?"

"Someone wrote on Hannah Marshak's wall on Facebook that she was excited to see her at the reunion."

There were so many things I wanted to say to this. Firstly, why were Erin and Hannah friends on Facebook? They weren't in the same graduating class and, to my knowledge, didn't even know each other.

And secondly, in order for Erin to see what other people wrote on Hannah's wall, she'd basically have to stalk her. That part didn't really shock me. I opened my mouth to say all of these things but stopped short. It was her birthday after all. "Well, yes, I'm going to the reunion." *Fuck it.* "How did you guys become friends on Facebook anyway?"

"I saw her listed under people I might know and I friended her. She accepted immediately! I seriously cannot wait to read her book."

"Wait. You know about Hannah's book too?" I felt like I had been punched in the stomach.

"Of course, I did," Erin said enthusiastically. "What do you mean by 'too'? Who else knew? Well, besides everyone of course." I could picture Erin rolling her eyes as she said that last bit.

"Jonathan told me," I mumbled.

"Jonathan? You still see that pothead?"

"Yes, I still see him. And he's more than a pothead. He's also a graphic designer." A freelance graphic designer who worked from home and smoked dope all day, but since Erin disapproved of him I was more inclined to defend him.

"Anyhoo, you know I don't read chick lit, but if Hannah wrote it, it's probably great."

Normally I would defend chick lit, especially since Erin read almost all historical romances which did not exactly qualify as The Great American Novel either, but I was more bothered by the second half of her statement. "The book will be great because Hannah wrote it? Based on what? She wasn't even in honors English classes in high school and as far as I know, has no writing experience." She wasn't in honors English yet managed to get into Brown. Of *course* she did.

"Well, she majored in fashion design and spent a semester in Paris and her book is about a fashion designer in Paris. Why do you hate her so much? I noticed you guys aren't Facebook friends."

Raising my voice, I said, "I don't hate her, Erin."

"What? You still upset that she made fun of your last name?"

"It was your last name too."

"Yeah, but I'm not really short." Erin giggled.

"Okay, so I called to wish you a happy birthday and I did. I should get back to work."

"C'mon Kim. I'm only teasing. It was so long ago. She's a sweetie now. But anyway, thanks for the birthday wishes. I'll talk to you soon, okay?"

Although I doubted Hannah was a "sweetie" now, I didn't bother to argue the point with Erin. "Sounds good, bye." I hung up the phone right in time to see the back of Rob's head as he came rushing around the corner and into his office. Before he closed his office door, he gave me a little wave.

Good morning to you too, Rob. I took a deep breath and exhaled deeply. I squeezed my shoulders in an attempt to give myself a mini-massage. I glanced at my computer and switched from the Facebook blog page to my personal page. In addition to a notification that my friend Caroline liked my status, I had a friend request. I clicked to see who it was and sucked in my breath.

Hannah Marshak.

CHAPTER 4

WHAT THE FUCK. Hannah's ears must have been burning. Why would she friend me on Facebook? We hadn't exchanged a single word since the summer after senior year in high school when we attended some of the same graduation parties. And it wasn't like we did keg stands together at those or anything. At best, we exchanged fake pleasantries.

Without confirming the request, I clicked on her page. Although most of her information was private, I could see that she had 423 friends, also lived in New York City and called herself a writer. Leave it to Hannah Marshak to be confident listing herself as a "writer" before her first book was even published. Since her pictures were public as well, I took a look-see. Still disgustingly skinny with huge boobs. Okay, I had pretty big boobs too and wore a size 0 but it was my natural shape. Hannah was flat-chested and chunky until at least sophomore year in high school and I'd bet my next tax refund that she got a boob job and probably binged and purged to maintain her shape. And what was with the tan? She couldn't possibly maintain that complexion living in New York without sunless tanning. She was easily as fake on the outside as she was on the inside.

At least she was single. I'd assumed she married some CPA from Long Island and cheated on him with her tennis instructor. "Whatever."

"Whatever what?"

I looked up to see Nicholas leaning over my desk and his eyes bored into mine. Even in my annoyed state, I instantly felt my face flush as I wondered what it would feel like to kiss him. "Oh. I was just mumbling to myself."

"Any particular reason or is that typical for you?" Nicholas asked, wiggling his eyebrows.

"Ha ha. No, I got a friend request from some bitch I went to high school with and it took me by surprise."

Nicholas nodded as if he understood. "So what will it be? Confirm or ignore?"

I sighed. "I really want to ignore it. There's no love lost there. But my reunion is coming up and that would be kind of messed up, right?" I hoped he'd say no.

"If you want my honest opinion, the 'PC' thing to do is accept the request. You could always hide her newsfeeds or limit what she sees if you really don't want to engage."

I rolled my eyes to indicate that his honest opinion was not what I wanted to hear.

Grinning he said, "But being 'PC' is highly overrated. Ignore the bitch."

"I like that idea much better," I said smiling.

"I thought you might." Motioning towards Rob's office, he said, "Anyone in with him?"

I wished the answer was "yes" so I could spend more time talking to him. "Nope. Go on in."

Nicholas walked away but turned around before he reached Rob's office. "Let me know what you decide."

Even though I figured he was just being polite, I gave him a close-mouthed smile and nodded. "Will do."

As I picked up my phone to text Bridget, I heard, "Hey Kim," and looked up to see David, Rob's paralegal, walk by.

"Rob called me in," he said before pausing outside of Rob's closed door.

I motioned towards the door. "By all means. I'm not his bouncer."

"With your stature and all, you'd be a force though." David laughed and then turned bright red as if he thought I'd be offended.

I flexed my muscles. "Don't let the height fool you. I can take you down!" I liked David. Rob complained that he'd bill four hours for something that should have taken less than one, but Rob drank two Red Bulls every morning for breakfast after running four miles on the treadmill. And he and his 35-year-old wife had climbed Mt.

Kilimanjaro on their last vacation. Compared to him, everyone was slow. And besides, David was always eager to help out and never tried to pull rank on me. Not that it would have gotten him far.

Less than thirty seconds after David went inside, I heard Rob yell, "Long!" He acted as if he was the only one working on the floor. I hurried to his office, opened the door and sweetly said, "Yes?"

"I sent you an email with a document attached a moment ago. Can you accept the track changes and send it back to me?"

From the corner of my eyes, I saw Nicholas look up from his legal pad and over at me. I stood straighter, hoping he liked what he saw. "Of course. But did you need to shout at me from behind closed doors to ask me that? You could have called. Or sent another email." Rob gave me a mock dirty look while Nicholas and David snickered. "If that will be all?" I asked.

"That will be all!" Rob said. "Kindly let the door slam you on the ass on the way out."

Still laughing when I returned to my desk, I made the track changes as quickly as I could. I had some reading to do and still wanted to tell Bridget about Hannah's friend request.

* * *

I couldn't believe I had an advance review copy (ARC) of Olivia Geffen's new novel in my possession. Olivia Geffen had already written five *New York Times* bestselling women's fiction novels, the first of which had recently been made into a movie. Her books sold themselves, so I was surprised when her publicist asked me to review her latest for *Pastel is the New Black*. I loved her writing style and was excited to start reading. It was too cold to read outside in Madison Square Park which was a few blocks away from my office building, so I bought some lunch at the firm's cafeteria and found a table in the dining area. It was kind of loud but thankfully I was used to drowning out distractions.

I took a bite of my turkey and Swiss cheese sandwich and settled in. I got through three pages before I realized this latest book was not going to be like her others. And I wasn't sure I was happy about it. I put down my Kindle for a minute and took a sip of water. As I stared ahead, I saw Nicholas rush by with a tray. He was always in such a hurry. "The Glamorous life of an associate," like he said. I was about to resume reading when he looked my way. We locked eyes and he stopped walking. He approached my table and I smiled.

"Hey there. Taking a break from the boss?" he asked.

"Yup. I always take advantage of my lunch hour. I suppose you're working through lunch?"

"I was planning to." He glanced at my Kindle. "Am I disturbing you?"

"Not at all! Sit." I would so much rather read between Nicholas' lines than a book.

Nicholas sat down and put a napkin on his lap. He looked at my Kindle again and back to me. "You reading for the blog?"

"Yup. I would have read this book anyway, but the author's publicist asked me to review it so I have double incentive now." As I felt my blood pressure rise, I figured it was my body's reaction to having lunch with my office "lust man" and tried to breathe normally.

Nicholas raised an eyebrow. "Impressive!"

I felt myself blush. "Thanks." I took a dainty bite of my turkey sandwich and a sip of water.

"I checked it out, you know."

I put down my sandwich. "Checked what out?"

"Your blog."

I gulped. "You did?"

Nicholas smiled. "Yeah. I wondered what all the hoopla was about."

"What did you think?" I held my breath.

"Seriously impressive. Your reviews are really great. Very honest."

Nicholas paused to eat some soup. I counted three hearty spoonfuls of what looked like lentil. Then he ate several forkfuls of salad. I watched him in amusement. When he finally came up for air, he smiled. "And some are kind of brutal."

"Not brutal. Just honest. I always try to say something nice about every book, to balance out the constructive criticism." Drawing to mind a book completely lacking in story structure that I had reviewed earlier that month, I added, "Sometimes it's not that easy, let me tell you."

Nicholas smiled softly. "I also read a few of your regular posts. I especially liked the one about juggling your day job with the blog. You're a great writer. "

And the blushing continues. "Thanks."

Pointing to my Kindle, he said, "What do you think of the book you're reading now?"

"Well, I've only read three pages but..." I crinkled my nose. "I don't think I'm gonna like it, which surprises me because I loved all of Olivia Geffen's other books."

"Yeah, she's great!" Nicholas said in delight.

"You've read her stuff?" I found that surprising since Nicholas hadn't even heard the term "chick lit" until the Squad happy hour and also, well, because Nicholas was a guy.

"Of course, I have! What was that one?" Nicholas scratched his chin. "The one with the pink cover?"

"*Swimming Upstream*! That was my favorite!"

"Mine too!" Nicholas said.

"I love the way she..." Noticing the twinkle of mischief in his eyes, I stopped talking and studied him. "You never read *Swimming Upstream*, did you?"

Nicholas shook his head. "No."

"Have you read anything by Olivia Geffen?"

Nicholas pursed his lips and shook his head again. "That would be another no."

I reached over and slapped him lightly on the hand. "You've never even heard of her, have you?"

Chuckling, he said, "No, I haven't."

"You suck!" I giggled.

"Sorry, but I couldn't resist. Are you always so gullible?"

Feeling myself blush again, I said, "Not usually, no. You must be really good."

Nicholas locked eyes with me. "I am."

Blushing harder, I took a sip of my water.

Gesturing towards my Kindle, he said, "So, why don't you like this one?"

"Too serious. Her other books were more light reading. Not completely frivolous, but more escapism. I like books that make me laugh, not cry. Unless I'm crying tears of happiness. I'm only on the third page and one of the characters has cancer." I shrugged. "I feel like many of the well-established authors in the genre are moving away from fun 'chick lit' towards deeper women's fiction and I don't like it. There are already plenty of authors who write deeper fiction very well like Jodi Picoult and Anita Schreve, but there are few who can write with a humorous tone like Geffen and it bothers me when they change their style." I stopped, realizing I was babbling about chick lit *again*, but Nicholas had not removed his eyes from mine the entire time I spoke and he appeared to be genuinely interested.

Nicholas gazed at me with focus. "Wow. You sure are passionate about books, huh?"

"I guess." I laughed. "Much more interesting than litigation, no offense."

"None taken." Nicholas' eyes scanned the length of my face. "So, three pages in and already thumbs down? Do you always form opinions so early?"

I smiled at him coquettishly. "Are we talking strictly books here?"

Nicholas grinned. "I actually was. But I can already tell you're an opinionated person. Wouldn't want to get on your bad side."

"How do you know you're not already?" I flirted.

Raising his eyebrows, he said, "Um, don't think you'd let me infringe on your lunch hour and precious reading time if I was."

"You got me! But a girl can change her mind, so don't mess with me." I smiled and our eyes locked but I couldn't bring myself to hold the gaze and quickly looked down at my sandwich. I took a bite even though I could barely taste what I was eating.

"I wouldn't dare." Nicholas looked at the empty plates on his tray and stood up. "I should get back to work. Thanks for letting me crash your lunch hour."

Damn him for being such a fast eater. "Anytime," I said. *Really, anytime.*

"If I don't see you beforehand, have a great weekend."

"You too," I said, a little sad that I wouldn't see him for two days. I wouldn't go as far as to say I was dreading the weekend, but I doubted I'd have my usual case of the Sunday night blues knowing I'd see him again on Monday.

"Use the time to make a decision about the high school bitch. In the meantime, make her suffer."

I winced at the mention of Hannah. "Somehow, I doubt she's giving it much thought at all."

Nicholas winked. "You never know. Don't sell yourself short. See ya." And with that, I watched him walk away.

Usually when people used the word "short" in front of me, it turned into a tease-fest, but Nicholas didn't seem to make the connection. I wondered if he was as nice as he seemed or if it was an act. Part of me hoped it was an act because if he was as nice as he was sexy, he truly was the perfect guy and he probably wanted the perfect girl. I definitely did not qualify for that position. His ex-girlfriends were probably all gorgeous super model types or really brainy heart surgeons. I was merely your average secretary-next-door with a nice rack.

Don't sell yourself short, Kim. I looked at my watch. I still had ten minutes to finish my sandwich and read a few more pages. Too bad I wasn't very hungry anymore and already didn't like the book.

CHAPTER 5

I TOOK A SIP of my pinot grigio and scanned the menu. I already knew I wanted to share the artichoke pizza and the avocado and artichoke salad with Bridget. We had both been "artichoke whores" since junior high school, when Bridget's mom made roasted artichokes for a party she was hosting for her mahjong group. The addiction grew even stronger once we moved to the city and tried the famous artichoke and spinach dip at Houston's restaurant. The name of the restaurant had since changed to Hillstone but to our relief, the dip recipe remained intact.

"What time is she getting here?" my friend Caroline asked.

I put down the menu and looked toward the hot pink entrance of Gina La Fornarina, a very "girls' night" friendly Italian restaurant on the Upper East Side. "She should be here any minute. In the meantime, what's up with you?"

Caroline flipped her shoulder length straight blonde hair. "Absolutely nothing. Work is incredibly busy and it's all I really have time to do." She took a sip of her wine. "Happy to have a night off!" Caroline was vice president of a financial company. Although she shared the title with a slew of other people, her workload was all her own.

"Have you visited your dad lately?" I asked.

Caroline shook her head and frowned. "Nope. Been working weekends." Her face brightening, she said, "But I'm off tomorrow and heading upstate in the morning. I can't wait to see the little guy." Caroline's parents had divorced when she was younger and her dad had recently married a much younger woman who had gotten pregnant on their honeymoon.

"I can't even imagine having a four-month-old brother at my age!"

"Believe it or not, it's easier to cope with a brother who is thirty years younger than me than a stepmother who is only two years older." Caroline shook her head in bewilderment.

"Yeah, that must be awkward," I agreed. I silently prayed that my happily married parents would stay that way so I would never find myself in the same situation.

"So, read anything good lately? I saw your review of *Gladly Never After*. Already ordered a copy from Amazon."

"You'll like it. Reading Geffen's newest now."

Caroline's eyes opened wide. "No way! It's coming out this summer, right? I can't wait!" she squealed. Caroline loved chick lit as much as I did but she also read the occasional cozy mystery. We had met a few years earlier at a book club meeting and found out that we had more in common than similar taste in books. She was only a few years older, also had an annoying younger sister with a seemingly perfect life (in addition to the aforementioned half brother) and, like me, was currently boyfriendless. *Physically*, however, we had nothing in common. At 5'8", she literally towered over me.

"Not really loving it, to be honest." I had read almost half of it earlier that day and still wasn't thrilled. I was about to go into more detail when I saw Bridget enter the restaurant. I sucked in my breath. Although I barely remembered my life pre-Bridget, every once in a while it hit me how stunning she was, mostly when she substituted her usual attire of cargo pants and T-shirts she collected from various rock concerts for more trendy pieces. Tonight she was wearing dark blue skinny jeans, a form-fitting glittery grey top and matching high grey boots. Her long cherry red hair, normally up in a messy ponytail, cascaded down to her chest in curls and she had done her makeup to emphasize her emerald colored eyes.

When she saw us, she waved and hurried to the table. Out of breath, she said, "I'm so sorry I'm late. I missed every light from my apartment to here."

I narrowed my eyes. "You live around the corner."

Sitting down next to Caroline, she said, "It didn't help that I was already running late." Eyeing the bottle of wine chilling next to the table, she asked, "Is that what I think it is?"

Caroline said, "Yes! It's Ramona's wine from *Real Housewives of New York*. We couldn't resist."

The three of us watched that show religiously. Ramona was always drinking pinot grigio, so she launched her own line. She was a regular patron of Gina's, which I assumed was why they had it on the menu. I poured her a glass. "Try it. It's pretty good." I looked her up and down admiringly. "You look incredible by the way."

Bridget shrugged. "I haven't left my apartment much lately. I figured I'd go all out."

"Oh, to be able to work from home!" Caroline said, looking at Bridget with envy.

"Yeah, working in my pajamas is quite awesome. Only time I need to dress for work is when I meet with clients and we almost always do that with Skype anyway." Bridget blushed. "I usually change out of my pajamas before I Skype though."

"Usually huh?" I joked. "I seem to recall you wearing your pjs and sipping a martini when you designed *Pastel is the New Black*. I guess I didn't get the royal client treatment, huh?"

Bridget narrowed her eyes at me. "Well, clients who get the royal treatment actually pay me for my web design services." She smiled. "Speaking of which, I got another request from one of your author friends. Thanks for sending all of that business my way! I can pay my mortgage each month almost entirely because of your referrals."

"It's the least I can do to repay you for the freebie. As long as you don't make any of their websites as nice as mine," I said, only half joking. Bridget had done such a great job on the *Pastel is the New Black* website that many authors and bloggers had asked for the name of my designer.

Bridget winked at me. "No worries, sweetheart."

I smiled. "Cool. I'll say it again. You look gorgeous tonight."

"Thanks, K! You look adorable as always. And you look very pretty, Caroline."

Caroline beamed. "Thanks, Bridget!"

"Well, now that we've established our mutual admiration society, I've decided we're going to share the artichoke pizza and the artichoke and avocado salad. Does that work?" I asked.

Bridget nodded. "Don't even have to look at the menu." Glancing at Caroline with obvious concern, she said, "Probably not enough food for three though. What do you think?"

"No worries. I don't like artichokes. Going to order the penne vodka," Caroline said.

Bridget let out a sigh of relief and said, "We'll try not to judge you for your blatant disrespect of the artichoke."

About forty minutes later, the main courses had been served and we were each nearing the bottom of our second glass of wine. I had filled both girls in on Hannah's friend request. Bridget was adamant in her opinion that I should ignore it.

Bridget cringed. "Blow off that two-faced biatch!" she said, her fair skin now flushed from the wine.

Caroline laughed. "Geez. Did she torture you guys in high school or something?"

I wiped my mouth and placed my napkin back on my lap. "She tried."

Her chin held high, Bridget said, "But she didn't get very far. Kim and I had no interest in being in her clique and so her attempts to get us to bow down to her were in vain. Watching her try even harder was actually comical."

Even though it was true that we had no interest in hanging with her crowd, she seemed bent on making us look bad and it took a lot of effort to not let it get to me. Bridget always insisted that she didn't care how much Hannah toyed with her, but she drew the line when Hannah messed with her BFF. "But she did hurt our feelings," I admitted.

Bridget waved her hand in protest. "She hurt *your* feelings, which hurt *my* feelings. I couldn't care less whether her little sheep thought I was a lesbian."

Caroline opened her eyes wide. "Why would they think that?"

Playing with the remaining crust on her pizza, Bridget said, "Because Hannah's a lying bitch, that's why."

"What happened?" Caroline asked.

Bridget cocked her head in my direction. "You tell her, Kim."

As my stomach churned at the memory, I let out a breath. "Bridget had a meeting with the Guidance Counselor about college applications one morning and when she left his office, she saw one of our other classmates crying. The girl's grandmother had just died and she was waiting for her parents to pick her up. Bridget took the girl to the bathroom so she could cry in private and Hannah walked in on them hugging and told everyone how cool it was that Bridget was so open about being gay." I looked at Bridget and smiled softly. "I must say, you took it all in stride." Hannah had probably expected Bridget to fiercely deny that she was gay which would have added fuel to the fire, but Bridget refused to confirm her sexual orientation and speculation ceased in record time.

"Like I said, I couldn't care less what people thought," Bridget said. With a grin, she added, "I made a lot of new gay friends as a result of that rumor. One of them even talked me out of dying my hair brown."

I looked at Bridget's hair in envy. "Thank God for him. It should be a crime to mess with that color."

"His words exactly!" Bridget said.

"So...you think I should just accept the request being that I'll see her at the reunion?" I asked.

"No!" Bridget yelled at the same time Caroline said, "Yes!"

I looked at Caroline. "Plead your case."

Caroline put down her now empty glass of wine. "If you ignore the request, it will seem like you still care. On the flip side, if you say yes, it will look like you're completely over it."

"Or that you're dying to be her friend!" Bridget protested.

"I don't know what to do," I whined.

"It's only Facebook, girls," Caroline said. "Who cares?"

"I don't care about Facebook. I have nothing to hide and I'm sure Erin would gladly give her the scoop on my life anyway, but I don't want to hear about her stupid book."

"Knowing Hannah, she'll probably make a comment about the number of friends you have on Facebook and how *sad* it is that you aren't more popular," Bridget said, rolling her eyes.

I had to laugh at Bridget. She really had no patience for Hannah's phoniness.

"Okay. Time for a subject change. Anyone been on any good dates lately?" Caroline asked, sliding her chair closer to the table.

"No," I said.

"Nope. Although I haven't been on any bad dates either," said Bridget with a sheepish grin.

"That makes three of us," Caroline said. "So much for my attempted subject change."

"Kim got laid on Thursday night though," Bridget announced.

Caroline leaned over the table in interest and belted out an enthusiastic, "Woo Hoo! Why are holding out on me?"

"I'm not. He's old news," I said, yawning.

We remained silent until the waitress finished refilling our water glasses. When she left, Caroline said, "Jonathan?"

"You know about Jonathan?" Bridget asked.

"Only that Kim has sex with him from time to time," Caroline said.

"There's nothing else to know about him. He's not the one I want," I said.

"Ah, Nicholas," both girls said, again at the same time.

"Wow, we're all in sync tonight." I giggled.

"Anything new with that?" Caroline asked.

Casually, I said, "We had lunch together on Friday," but I couldn't contain my smile.

"Oh now we're making progress," Caroline said brightly.

I told the girls about our pseudo lunch date and Nicholas checking out my blog.

"Wow, he seems interested," Caroline said.

"Except that he hasn't asked me out! He's probably equally friendly to every other girl at the firm," I said. Of course, if I danced with the Rockettes or was up for a pediatric fellowship, he would have made a move already.

Shaking her head, Caroline said, "You guys work together. Better to take it slow. What do you know about him?"

"I obviously checked out his firm bio, but aside from the fact that he graduated college three years before me and published a few articles on copyright law, I don't know much. Oh, and he lives in the West Village."

"Maybe you should ask about him next time you talk," Caroline suggested.

Tipping my head to the side, I said, "You think? I don't want to come on too strong."

"It seems to me that Nicholas has made all of the attempts to get to know you so far. If you respond but never reciprocate, he might not get the hint that you're into him," Caroline said. I remembered Nicholas looking at his phone at Banc Café. From the smile plastered on his face, he was definitely texting a girl. But he did give up a working lunch to eat with me and that had to count for something.

"And seriously, what straight guy would read a blog about chick lit if he wasn't into a girl?" Bridget asked.

She has a point. "Okay. I'll try."

"You go girl!" Bridget said. "Where to next? Dancing?"

I shook my head.

"Karaoke?" she asked.

I laughed.

"Okay then. Where?" Bridget pouted.

Caroline said, "I'm sorry to be lame, but I'm gonna head back to Jersey. Exhausted and want to get on the road early tomorrow morning." Looking at Bridget, she said, "Seeing my baby brother tomorrow."

Bridget gave Caroline a wide smile and said, "Aw! Take some pictures of the cutie for us." Then she looked at me. "What about you, K?"

"Sorry, Bridge, but I think I need to call it in too. I am so behind on my reading and want to get up early tomorrow to catch up. You mad?" I asked.

Bridget continued to pout but shook her head. "Nah, that's fine. Next time I consider getting all gussied up, I'll reconsider."

Her pout won me over, and I relented. "Okay, how about we share a carafe of Watermelon Sangria at Vero next door?"

Bridget's face lit up and her frown turned into a wide grin. "Really?"

"Really! But a carafe means a carafe and not a pitcher, okay?"

Bridget extended her hand to me across the table. "Deal."

I gave her hand a firm shake and repeated, "Deal."

CHAPTER 6

Kimberly Long @pastelisnewblack

Check out my 4-star review of Beauty Meets
the Beast by @AliKatt tinyurl.com/1234 #chicklit

THE *PASTEL IS THE NEW BLACK* **TWITTER** and Facebook pages
now up-to-date with my most recent reviews, I took a sip of my
Monday morning coffee and hesitantly logged onto my personal
Facebook page. I took a deep breath and confirmed Hannah's friend
request. I decided that Caroline had a stronger and certainly more
objective case than Bridget. Besides, I had at least a hundred friends
on Facebook I never communicated with anyway. I would simply
add Hannah to that list.

By the time I finished performing the unusually long list of tasks
outlined for me in Rob's various emails, it was almost noon. I removed
a compact from my pocketbook, smiled into the mirror to confirm my
teeth were void of any unwanted food materials and replenished my lip
gloss. Then I got up and walked over to Rob's door. "Stepping away
for a few minutes. I'll bring my Blackberry in case you need me." Most
secretaries were not given firm Blackberries but Rob liked to consider
himself the exception to every rule and as his assistant, I became the
exception to that one. Thankfully, none of the other secretaries were
jealous since none of them had any desire to be accessible to their
partners 24/7. I didn't complain since Rob rarely took advantage.

Rob didn't answer except to brush me off with his hand.

I closed my eyes and took a calming breath. Then I straightened out my black pencil skirt and walked to the other side of the floor to Nicholas' office. Caroline was right. He had shown interest in my blog on two separate occasions and it was time to reciprocate by showing interest in *his* life. I stepped into the hallway and was about to turn left toward his office when I heard a high-pitched giggle followed by a deep masculine voice coming from the elevator bank to my right. I turned around and stopped in my tracks as I observed Nicholas talking to a blonde girl who looked to be about my age. Their voices trailed off as he placed his hand on the small of her back and followed her into the elevator. Although I didn't get a great look at her, I saw enough to confirm that I had never seen her before, she had the body of an Olympic beach volleyball player and she was pretty. My breath caught in my throat and my stomach plummeted into achiness as I headed back to my side of the floor.

Rob was hovering over my desk. "Can I help you?" I asked.

Looking up, he said, "Back so soon?"

I shrugged and squeezed in front of him to my chair. "It appears that way," I said flatly. At least I hadn't walked into Nicholas' office while he was in there with his leggy blonde lunch date. Based on their casual demeanor, I reluctantly ruled her out as a client.

"I was looking for your desk calendar. I couldn't remember if I had a lunch meeting today."

I shook my head. "Not that I am aware."

"Then I can safely assume I have nothing scheduled!" Rob grinned at me before heading back to his office and closing the door behind him.

I removed my phone from my bag and sent a text to Bridget and Caroline. "Nicholas is not interested in me. I accidentally spied him leaving for a lunch date with some blonde chick ☹" Hoping to stop thinking about Nicholas and "the girl", I chewed over what to do about lunch. I had brought a sandwich from home but as tempting as tuna fish, lettuce and tomato on a sesame seed bun had seemed when I prepared it the night before, I was no longer craving it, which is what always happened when I packed a lunch at home. I also wasn't thrilled about reading through lunch since I wasn't enjoying the Olivia Geffen novel nearly as much as I had expected. I sincerely hoped it would have a happy ending, but I was starting to think at

least one person was going to die an ugly death and those fortunate
to survive would wish they hadn't. The angel on my shoulder reminded
me that I spent way too much money lately going out to eat and so I
reluctantly stood up and started walking to the pantry where I had
left the sandwich in the refrigerator earlier that morning. As I
rounded the corner, my phone sounded the receipt of a text message
from Bridget. "Nicholas Strong rhymes with Long is just plain WRONG
if he's not interested in my BFF. Fuck him!" I could always count on
Bridget to make me giggle even in my moments of despair. Then I
received a text from Caroline. "First of all, it might not be a date. And if
it is a date, it doesn't mean he's with her exclusively. Don't make
assumptions." I bit my cheek pondering her words. Caroline was
always more level headed than Bridget who tended to jump to the
worst case scenario. They were like yin and yang. I hoped Caroline
was right but I sadly suspected she wasn't. After grabbing my brown
paper bag from the refrigerator, I began walking back to my desk as
I received another text from Caroline. "By the way, I walked past the
Shake Shack on my way back from American Apparel a second ago.
The line isn't long. I can get on it now if you want to meet for lunch."

In another indisputable win for the devil on my shoulder, I
tossed my lunch bag in the garbage can by my desk and texted her
back, "I'm on my way."

* * *

If the line at the famous Shake Shack burger joint in Madison
Square Park wasn't long when Caroline had sent her text, it certainly
was by the time I arrived. And to make matters worse, there were
two separate lines: one to place your order and one to pick up your
food when it was ready. It was not unusual for the process to take an
hour or more. I scanned the order line and thanks to her height and
shiny blonde hair, I quickly spotted Caroline smack in the middle.

I tapped her on the shoulder, clearly taking her by surprise as her
feet lifted slightly in the air. "Hey there," I said. I took in the smell of
juicy burgers radiating the air. "Great idea."

Smiling down at me, Caroline said, "So glad you were free." Scrunching her face in concern, she said, "Are you still upset about Nicholas?"

Trying to make light of it, I said, "I don't even really know the guy. I just think he's hot. I always assumed he had a girlfriend or was a player anyway." I knew my statement made sense logically, but no matter how hard I tried to convince myself, I kept playing back our lunch together in my head and the way my heart fluttered whenever he smiled at me and those slight crinkles appeared around his eyes. "It sucks though," I admitted.

"Well, like I wrote in my text, you don't know who that girl is. He might be single and he might be interested in you. Try to let things play out naturally."

I shrugged. "Okay. How was yesterday?"

"Seeing the little man was fun. I wish I could say the same about watching my dad slip Monica the tongue all day. Literally. All Day." Caroline stuck a finger in her mouth and made a gagging motion.

"Yikes. That sucks, I'm so sorry," I said, patting her on the arm.

Giving me a closed-mouth smile, Caroline said, "It is what it is. Let's change the subject, shall we? What are you getting?"

"Shack Burger and a strawberry shake," I said without hesitation.

"No fries?"

I shook my head. "Too much food. Either burger and fries or burger and shake. I can't do all three and expect to be productive this afternoon."

Caroline looked at me in envy. "Self control. That's why you're so skinny. I must have all three!"

I gave Caroline a once-over. Although I would not describe her as "skinny," she wasn't the slightest bit heavy either. I rolled my eyes and was about to tell her she was insane when I caught a glance of a familiar looking blonde walking over to the pick-up line. As it dawned on me why she looked familiar, the sight of Nicholas right behind her confirmed my suspicion. Although he was somewhat far away, I recognized the blue and white gingham shirt he was wearing when I spotted him in the elevator bank. I felt an ache in the back of my throat. "Oh God."

Her eyes wide as saucers, Caroline said, "What's wrong?"

I looked toward my feet, chewing on a fingernail. My stomach was rumbling with nervous energy.

Caroline placed her hand on my shoulder and in a soothing tone asked, "Kim? You okay?"

"Nicholas is here," I whispered as if he could hear me. "With the girl." I shook my head again. My appetite had completely left the vicinity.

"Where?" Caroline asked, looking frantically around the park.

I cocked my head toward the pick-up station. "Over there. Tan leather jacket over a blue and white gingham shirt . Please be slick. I don't want him to see me!" I placed the hood of my winter jacket over my head and stood behind Caroline hoping her tall frame would hide my short one.

"I can't see him well enough from here to tell if he's cute."

"He is. Trust me." I fought the urge to ask what he and the girl were doing. Were they holding hands? Sharing a French fry like *Lady and the Tramp?* I didn't want to know.

"Kim. Get a grip," she said with a weak smile.

"Easy for you to say."

Caroline looked me in the eyes and in a steady voice said, "You already knew he was going somewhere with that girl. Seeing him here doesn't tell you anything you didn't already know. And it doesn't change what you still *don't* know."

I nodded. "I know." *I don't know.* Before there was still a possibility she was a client. Now I knew for certain it was a lunch date. Delectable burgers notwithstanding, Nicholas would never take a client to the Shake Shack. "Just the same, I don't think I want to eat in the park. If you don't mind, I'm going to bring my food back to my desk. I really don't want to watch them. And I don't want to risk him seeing me. It's too cold anyway." I kicked at the dead grass beneath my feet.

Caroline smiled softly and gave me an understanding nod. "No worries. I don't blame you and I'm actually slammed at work. This line is taking longer than I thought. But at least we got to spend time together."

"True." *I should have eaten the damn tuna fish sandwich.*

*   *   *

Later that afternoon, I tried as hard as I could to concentrate on my work and not make a bigger deal out of the Nicholas situation than it warranted. Maybe he was a douche bag and I dodged a bullet. Maybe he was a horrible kisser. Maybe he had a tiny penis.

"Hey Kim. Good weekend?"

I looked up to see David standing at the side of my desk with a wide toothy grin. "Yes, it was decent." Looking at the smile still painted on his face that had reached his kind blue eyes, I said, "But why do I think yours was better?"

"Can I tell you a secret?" He leaned his stocky body in closer to me.

"You most certainly may," I said. I sat forward and angled my chair in his direction.

His eyes sparkling, David said, "I'm proposing to Amy this weekend."

"Oh My God, that's awesome, David! What's the plan?" I had met his girlfriend Amy at the firm's holiday party a couple of months earlier. She was a bit nondescript but as nice and wholesome as David. They seemed like a perfect couple.

"Well, I'm taking her out to dinner," he whispered as if he was afraid Amy would overhear.

As I leaned in closer to him to maintain the private nature of the conversation, I saw Nicholas approaching my desk out of the corner of my eye. Continuing to talk to David, I said, "So far so good. Where are you taking her?" I had assumed Nicholas was headed to Rob's office but he stopped right next to where David was standing and appeared to be in no hurry to move. My heart began beating at an accelerated pace but I tried to ignore it. *And him.*

"And then I'm going to propose over champagne and dessert," David said excitedly.

Unfortunately, I had been too distracted by Nicholas' appearance to hear most of David's story and I had no idea where this engagement dinner was taking place. Feeling too guilty to confess to my half-assed attention span, I cleared my throat and said, "Sounds like an awesome plan. So happy for you."

"Thanks, Kim!"

"Did you need to see Rob?" I had never seen David's posture so relaxed before and he radiated happiness. I hoped whatever Rob wanted wouldn't interfere with his elation.

He shook his head. "Nah. I came over to share the good news with you."

I stood up and gave him a hug. "I'm so glad you did."

When we separated from our embrace, David looked over at Nicholas and smiled. "I guess you heard too."

Nicholas smiled back and slapped David lightly on the back. "I did. Congratulations! Very happy for you."

"Thanks!" Glancing at his watch, David said, "Shit. I gotta get back to work. See you guys later."

After he walked away whistling to himself, I sat back down and started writing a fake email. Nicholas was still standing there and so I looked up and gave him a half smile. "Hi."

Grinning broadly, he said, "Hi yourself. I've been thinking about you."

Against my better judgment, his words warmed my heart. But I found it hard to believe he was thinking of me while having lunch with another girl. Skeptical, I arched an eyebrow at him. "Really?"

Leaning toward me, he said in his trademark deep whisper, "Yeah. Was curious whether you accepted that girl's friend request."

I jerked my head back in surprise that he had given that conversation any thought, but quickly nodded. "Yeah, I did."

"Was it a tough decision?"

Although he focused his attention on me like he truly cared, I couldn't get the image of his hand on the blonde girl's lower back out of my mind. He was simply being nice. It meant nothing. "Actually, it was. My left hand practically ripped my right hand from the socket as I clicked 'confirm.'" I shrugged. "But my friend Caroline convinced me it was the right choice."

Nicholas gave me a soft smile. "For what it's worth, I agree with your friend Caroline." As he opened his mouth to say something else, Rob's voice boomed out, "Nicholas!"

Nicholas glanced behind him to Rob's office. "The boss beckons."

I nodded. "Bosses do that sometimes."

"I better get in there," he said without moving.

"Strong!"

"Okay!" Nicholas rolled his eyes and smiled at me again. "See you."

"See you."

After Nicholas walked away, I decided to check my personal email account in order to avoid over analyzing what was simply a friendly conversation. Along with several emails from authors attaching Kindle compatible copies of their books for review, I had a new email from Candy Adams at Novel Inc. PR. I featured many of her clients' books on my blog and excitedly read the email to find out whose book she wanted me to review this time. Halfway through the third sentence, I felt my face go pale.

> *Dear Kimberly,*
>
> *I hope all is well. Great reviews lately on Pastel is the New Black! I am writing on behalf of a new client, Hannah Marshak. Her debut chick lit novel, Cut on the Bias, is being published by Three Monkeys Press this June. I'd like to provide you with the book for review, preferably shortly before it is released. You can read the synopsis on her website www.hannahmarshak.com*
>
> *Please confirm that this review will fit into your busy schedule. As always, I am excited to work with you.*
>
> *Best,*
>
> *Candace*

I leaned back in my chair, my jaw clenched. I should have known the timing of Hannah's friend request was not a coincidence. The Hannah I knew would never do anything unless there was something in it for her. How could I have been so clueless? I was the creator of a blog dedicated to the review of chick lit books and Hannah was the author of a chick lit book. Why wouldn't she try to use her connection to me to secure a positive review? I felt a pit in my stomach and was afraid I might purge the Shack Burger I'd just eaten for lunch. Before I could chicken out, I entered Hannah's website address into my browser. I had to read the synopsis to *Cut on the Bias*. What kind of dumb ass title was that anyway?

> *Jacqueline Milano graduated at the top of her class at the world famous Fashion Institute of Technology. Snagging the coveted position as an associate designer for the up and coming and seemingly impossible to please, Pierre Siciliano,*

Jacqueline leaves her family and fiancé in New York City to work in Paris, the city of blinding lights. She thinks her dreams are finally coming true until she is thrust headfirst into the cutthroat world of fashion. Jacqueline is unprepared for the insecure models, the backstabbing colleagues and, most of all, falling hard for Pierre. Will Jacqueline soar in the world of Paris fashion or will she book the first flight home to her parents and the love she left behind?

I took a long gulp of water and stared open-mouthed at my monitor. Much to my utter dismay, the plot actually sounded intriguing. And whoever had designed her website had done a really nice job. The background was the Paris skyline with the Eiffel Tower all lit up. Even Bridget would probably agree it was well done. I bit my fingernails as I read her bio. "Hannah Marshak's childhood dream of being a writer has finally come true with the launch of her debut novel, *Cut on the Bias*." *Childhood dream?* I had known Hannah since kindergarten and as far as I knew, the only dream she'd had since childhood was to have more devoted followers than Charles Manson.

Could my day have been any worse? It had to end. Immediately. I looked at my watch. It was almost 5. "I need to leave a bit early today," I said to Rob over the phone.

There was only one place I wanted to be. One place I *needed* to be. But since the neighborhood Barnes & Noble had sadly closed earlier that year, I walked south towards Union Square. I zipped my coat up to my neck and pulled my knit hat over my ears. When I finally arrived at The Strand, an independent bookstore, my hands and cheeks were numb from the cold but my heart was warm. I walked directly to the fiction section and began pulling books with pastel covers off the shelves. I quickly collected about ten books in my arms, sat in a corner and began reading the acknowledgement sections, where authors thanked the people who inspired and supported their writing journeys. I felt closer to the author when I recognized a name of an agent or promoter I knew from my blog. I grinned when I flipped to the back of *Heaven Can't Wait* and read, *"Thank you to blogger extraordinaire, Kimberly Long, for providing a pre-publication review with less than a week's notice and for organizing what I hope will be the best blog tour ever."*

I knew the mention was there since the author had also sent me an autographed hard copy of the book after it came out, but I never tired of reading my name within the covers of a book. Even more than the professional expressions of gratitude, I loved to read what writers said about their families and loved ones. Shaking myself out of my stupor, I stood up and began returning the books to the shelves until there was only one left. Although I had almost twenty unread books on my Kindle, I was incapable of leaving a bookstore empty handed and made my way to the cash register.

CHAPTER 7

THE NEXT COUPLE OF WEEKS went by fast and I counted the days until my high school reunion with the dread of an inmate on death row. I still hadn't decided what I was going to do about the review of *Cut on the Bias* and figured Hannah would ask me about it at the reunion. The plan was to maintain a distant eye on her and then *coincidentally* find myself on the opposite side of the room at all times. Bridget promised to play co-lookout. To buy time and maintain some semblance of professionalism, I had returned Candy's email indicating that I was extremely backlogged with book reviews (fact) but that I would try to move things around so I could read and review Hannah's novel prior to its publication date (fiction).

I was also doing my best to avoid face-to-face contact with Nicholas. If I had no chance with him, I really had no interest in being his friend. It would be too hard to pretend to be platonic when each time we made eye contact, my pulse quickened, my face warmed, I felt light-headed and my stomach flip-flopped. The only way to avoid it was to avoid *him*. When I felt him walk by my desk or heard Rob on the phone asking him to stop by, I either began typing on my computer at a frantic pace or feigned a very important telephone call with the dial tone until he was safely out of sight. If Rob called me into his office while he was meeting with Nicholas, I focused my attention solely on Rob even though I always felt Nicholas' eyes on me. I felt kind of bad for the guy considering he hadn't technically done anything wrong except not want to date me, but it was for self-preservation.

I had spent most of the morning waiting for a huge color copy job for one of Rob's cases. Ever since one of the copy guys misunderstood

Rob's instructions to collate the copies as making 100 copies of page one, 100 copies of page two, etc. rather than 100 copies of pages 1-20, Rob insisted I oversee his big jobs. So as to not be a distraction, I stood off to the side, reading *First Star I See Tonight*, a paranormal chick lit novel. Every so often I looked up from my Kindle to gauge their progress. I was on the last page and surprised by how much I had enjoyed the read since books where the characters had special powers like, in this case, the ability to travel through time, often fell short for me. Sensing someone watching me, I closed my Kindle, glanced up and saw 6'5" Tomas hovering over me with a stack of pages the length of his very long torso.

"Finished?"

Glancing at me and then lifting and lowering the papers in his arms, Tomas said, "All done. But you gonna be able to carry this yourself? I can help you. Or at least get you a box."

I hated when people associated my lack of height for my lack of strength. I was my family's resident jar opener despite being the smallest. I put out my hands palms up. "Try me."

Tomas chuckled. "Okay. If you insist," he said before transferring possession of the documents. He kept his hands beneath mine as if he thought the papers would slip right through my fingers.

The second the paper made contact with my skin, I felt my biceps burn and regretted my sense of independence. Pride kept me from reconsidering Tomas' offer for help and so I choked out, "Got it. But can you open the door for me and press the elevator button please?" There was no way I was taking the stairs from the 23rd to 24th floor while carrying the weight of a small country.

Holding the papers, I carefully followed Tomas to the elevator which had answered my prayers and arrived immediately. I smiled at Tomas as the door closed. "Thanks!"

By the time the elevator opened on the 24th floor, I was in serious pain and afraid I would lose all feeling in my arms, drop the papers and wind up spending the rest of the day on the floor putting them back in the correct order. I walked as fast as I could to Rob's office, quite the challenge since I could barely see over the documents and, out of breath, placed them on his desk. I momentarily kept a hand on either side of the stack in case the papers fell. Without looking up, I said, "Oh my fucking God. That was heavy."

I heard a cackle behind me, turned around and saw Nicholas sitting in Rob's guest chair looking at me beguilingly. *It figures.* At least this time my face was hot from sweating and not merely my body's reaction to being in the same room as him.

The moment it occurred to me that I was sweating and Nicholas was in the room, I brushed a damp hair away from my brow and turned back to Rob. "Sorry to interrupt."

Rob leaned back in his chair, his arms clasped behind his head. "Watch the language, Long. Good thing I don't have a client in here."

I began backing my way out of his office and said, "I'm going downstairs for lunch. And next time, we're hiring a body builder to carry your enormous copy jobs."

"Enjoy your lunch," Rob said. "And by the way, Tomas called and said you insisted on carrying them yourself. Dumb ass."

Defeated, I gave a half-hearted shrug and walked out.

Fifteen minutes later, the feeling had returned to my hands and I was happily eating my salad while writing a blog post.

* * *

I will never understand why the final three always act so surprised when they read the card from Chris Harrison inviting them to forego their individual rooms to spend the night as a couple in the Fantasy Suite. Are we really supposed to believe these girls haven't been watching the show for the past eleven years?

* * *

"Want company?"

I looked up from my note pad to see Nicholas staring down at me. I was mid-chew so I quickly swallowed and nodded. "Sure."

Nicholas sat down and while he removed his plates of food from the tray to make more room on the table, I drank him in. I knew I was supposed to avoid face-to-face contact but he was within touching distance and I couldn't help but stare.

When he was finished organizing the table, he frowned at me. "You mad at me or something?"

I absently scratched my head. "No. Why?"

Nicholas shrugged. "I feel like you're avoiding me. You practically run in the opposite direction whenever you see me."

"Not true!" Okay, so it was true but a) I couldn't exactly tell him that and b) he looked genuinely sad. "Sorry about that. Been really busy lately. Nothing personal. Promise." I crossed my fingers behind my back.

"Okay, good." He smiled and cut into his quarter roasted chicken. Glancing at my note pad, he said, "What are you working on?"

"A blog post. Just a silly recap of *The Bachelor*. I'm comparing the three hot messes who are still competing for the final rose. I take it you don't watch the show?"

A hint of pink painting Nicholas' cheeks, he said, "Don't laugh, but I've watched it. Only under severe pressure from the female persuasion though."

I felt my heart drop as I wondered if he was referring to the pretty blonde girl from the elevator. "Well, maybe you'll appreciate my blog then."

"I just might. How do you find the time to do all of this with a full time job?"

Tapping my hand lightly over his, I said, "I thought you read my blog post on juggling!" I mentally kicked myself for flirting. The plan was to get over him if I couldn't get *under* him.

Nicholas smiled. "I did. But refresh my memory."

"Rob knows that I won't let my job suffer as a result of the blog so as long as I'm caught up on stuff, he doesn't mind if I write during the day. He also knows I'm in a better mood after I've written a post. My mood is elevated after writing a blog post or even a review. I don't know what it is but I'd probably compare it to runner's high if I had ever actually experienced runner's high." I realized that Nicholas was staring at me and felt a rush of heat through my body. "Anyway, I make the time because I love doing it."

Studying me, Nicholas said, "I think it's very cool that you're so passionate about it. Ever thought about writing a book?"

I placed a piece of hair behind my ear. "Writing a book review and writing a book are two totally different animals."

"True. I figured after reading so many books, you might have some ideas of your own though. Especially since you're such a good writer."

I gave him a timid smile. "That's nice of you to say. But book writing is not for me."

Nodding, Nicholas said, "Duly noted. So, on to new topics. Been emailing your newest friend on Facebook?" Nicholas asked with a glint in his eye.

"Not exactly. And by the way, what makes you think she's my newest friend? You don't think I've had any friend requests since then?" I teased, silently cursing myself for flirting. *Again.*

Nicholas put down his knife and fork. "I know you have."

I looked at him curiously. "You know I have *what?*"

Holding my glance, he said, "I know you've had at least one friend request since then. Have you been on Facebook yet today?"

I stared at him a second before reaching into my handbag for my phone. When I clicked on Facebook, I saw that I had in fact received a new friend request. I looked at him again before opening the request.

He shrugged and raised his eyebrows.

I opened the request. *Nicholas Strong wants to be friends on Facebook.* From his profile picture, Nicholas' brown eyes peered at me and his sexy smile seemed to say, "Come hither." I looked back at him, my heart beating rapidly.

Laughing, he said, "I hope accepting my request won't be as difficult as your friend from high school."

"Hannah is *not* my friend," I argued. "But of course not." I secretly wished it wouldn't be rude to confirm the request later, after I had untagged myself from all unflattering pictures and brainstormed the decision with Bridget and Caroline.

"Cool," he said taking a bite of chicken.

"Speaking of which, I found out why Hannah friended me in the first place." If Nicholas insisted on being "friends," I figured there was no harm in giving him an update.

Nicholas dropped his fork and smiled. "So it wasn't to reminisce all your good times back in senior high?"

"Not so much," I said, shaking my head.

Nicholas leaned forward. "What happened?"

I took a deep breath as I prepared to tell the story again. "My friend Jonathan told me she's writing a book. A chick lit book." I gave Nicholas a knowing look. "You make the connection."

Understanding washed over Nicholas' face. "Oh. You think she's hoping for a great review, huh?"

Nodding, I said, "I *know* she is."

After downing the rest of his water and chewing a piece of ice, Nicholas said, "I agree. She's definitely trying to work you. Can you blame her though? I mean, she knows you, apparently you have some clout in the biz, why not?"

Despite being humored by his use of the word "biz," this was not what I wanted to hear.

"What'd she say when she asked you?" Nicholas asked.

"She didn't. She's way too slick for that. Or at least she thinks she is. But she friended me on Facebook the same week I received an email from her PR person asking me to review the book. Coincidence? I don't think so."

Nicholas smirked. "Doubtful. You must be at least a little curious about the book though, no?"

I threw my napkin on my plate. "Not even a little bit."

Nicholas laughed. "Okay, then." Glancing at his watch, he returned his empty plates to the tray and stood up. Smiling he said, "Once again, you have distracted me into taking way too long of a lunch break."

"Oops. Sorry."

"Don't be. I could use the distraction," he said with a wink before walking away.

As I watched him disappear into the crowd, I couldn't wipe the smile off of my face until, paranoid that people might be watching me, I looked around, cleared my throat and turned back to my blog post.

* * *

At home later, after I unwound with some television and read a few chapters of the newest book in my queue, I did what I had been willing myself not to do ever since I got back to my desk after lunch. I logged onto Facebook to check out Nicholas' profile.

I appreciated that Facebook could be a wonderful thing. I had reunited with old friends from senior high and college and gotten back in touch with colleagues from my days at the advertising agency and my first law firm. I was able to easily keep in touch with friends who resided too far away to actually see on any regular basis. And, of course, Facebook was great for promoting *Pastel is the New Black*. But in some ways, I truly believed Facebook was created by Satan as a way to turn completely sane people into obsessed stalkers. I had seen it happen to my friends and didn't want to join them in their insanity. What good could come out of seeing what other girls wrote on Nicholas' wall? I knew that I would start hypothesizing his relationships with these women and even though I'd have no way of really knowing what was real and what was invented by my overactive, not to mention paranoid, imagination, it wouldn't matter. If Facebook suggested he was dating or hooking up with someone, I would believe it. On the flip side, what I didn't know couldn't hurt me.

But I did it anyway.

Holding my breath, my eyes immediately went to the top of his profile page under relationship status. When I saw it said "single," I allowed myself a small exhale. So even if he was dating the girl from the Shake Shack it probably wasn't serious. *At least not yet.* I twirled some hair around my finger and put it in my mouth. Then I checked to see how many friends he had. 972. Almost three times the number of friends I had. I shook my head in disbelief and spit the hair out of my mouth. I held my hand steady on the mouse while I contemplated what to look at next. Pictures. The first was a picture of him asleep at his desk with a cute caption about sleeping in the office again. He looked so peaceful when he slept and I wished I could reach into the computer and plant a soft kiss on his forehead. I chewed on my cuticles as I wondered who had taken the picture. Was it another associate or had he brought someone with him to the office late at night? In the second picture, Nicholas sat in a rocking chair with a toddler on his lap. The adorable, chubby-faced toddler was wearing a Duke baseball cap. From the comments, all girls of course, I deduced that it was his nephew. The next few pictures were of him at a bar or a party with some friends making funny faces and clearly having a grand ole time and when he smiled, I felt like he was smiling at me. Not only was he beyond painfully cute to look at in person, he was photogenic too. Somehow I doubted that, like me, he only posted those pictures that made him look good. I had a feeling he always came out good in pictures. *The bastard.* I frowned at the screen until my eyes were drawn to one of the pictures of Nicholas with his friends, one friend in particular: a tanned blonde girl wearing white denim shorts and a red and white checkered sleeveless shirt knotted at the navel. I was positive she was the girl from the elevator and Shake Shack. I frantically scrolled through his list of friends until I found her thumbnail picture. Mary Jones. *Could she have a more generic name?* I clicked on her picture but her profile was private and I couldn't find anything that would tell me whether she was dating Nicholas, just his friend or his friend with benefits. I had one of those, why wouldn't he? Feeling a headache coming on, I pressed my fingers to my temples until I forced myself to snap out of it. The only way to know for sure what this girl meant to Nicholas was to straight out ask him. And I had no intention of doing any such thing. According to Facebook, Nicholas was single. That was all I needed to know for the time being.

Afraid that continuing to look at his albums would do more harm than good, I decided to do a brief perusal of his recent wall posts. I vowed to only check what was visible on the first screen and not under any circumstances, scroll farther down by clicking "older posts." It made me feel better to impose at least minimal conditions on my stalking experience.

It was interesting to note that he did not update his status too often. At least from what I could gauge from my limited investigation, there were no updates about what he ate for dinner, or a play-by-play of his daily activities. The last update was that he practically ran smack into Brett Michaels walking down Sullivan Street. I sort of hoped he'd show signs of being at least slightly dorky so I wouldn't feel immensely less cool but no, he had perfected subtlety to a science. But at least he hadn't tagged himself in any status updates with Mary Jones.

My stomach grumbled and I decided it was a sign that I should quit while I was ahead and make something for dinner before his status suddenly changed to "in a relationship." But as I stood up, I noticed a new notification at the top of my page that I'd received an email. When I opened the message and saw it was from Hannah, my mouth went dry. Opting not to put off the inevitable, I read it:

> Hi Kim,
> Long time, no see! Thanks for accepting my friend request. I hope all is well and look forward to catching up with you at the reunion. You're going right? Can't wait!
> Best,
> Hannah

My heart was pounding. She didn't even mention *Cut on the Bias*. Did she think I was stupid? Like I hadn't put two and two together as to why, after ten years, she would suddenly initiate a friendship with me? I shook my head in disbelief. If she had any respect for me at all, she would have come clean and at least mentioned our mutual interest in chick lit. It might have even made me question my reluctance to review her book. After all, it had been a decade since we shared the same hallways in high school. She might have matured from the girl who enthusiastically urged me to join the drama club the year they were performing *The Wizard of Oz* since I was *so* talented, but also because I wouldn't even need a costume to play one of the munchkins. Instead, her transparent phoniness convinced me that time had not changed her one bit.

I fucking hated Facebook.

CHAPTER 8

"I'LL BRING THE PROSECCO," Bridget said.

"Cool. I'll pick up cheese and crackers and some frozen hors d'oeuvres at Fairway." I was on the phone with Bridget discussing the pre-game party for the reunion.

"Sounds good, but don't bring anything too filling. I don't want to be so full from food that the booze has no effect. I must be pleasantly tipsy when we get to the main event! And I also don't want my dress to feel tight or show any gut from too much eating."

Picturing Bridget's size-4 body, I rolled my eyes, "What gut?"

"Everyone looks fat compared to you, K."

"Bridge, I might be about 15 pounds thinner than you but I'm also 4 inches shorter. That makes us equally thin and I'm actually bigger since my tits probably weigh about 5 pounds each."

"Oh, please rub that in while you're at it," Bridget said sarcastically. "You're still wearing the black wrap dress with the plunging neckline and long slit down the side, right?"

"That's the plan." Since I couldn't show off a husband and kids or brag about a high paying and exciting career, I wanted to at least look hot.

"Cool. I wanted to confirm before I aired out my racy number."

"I can't wait to see you in that dress! You're gonna look smokin'! Even Hannah will be left speechless."

"Speaking of Hannah, did you respond to her email?" Bridget asked with a catch in her voice.

"Nope! And I'm not going to." After mulling it over ad nauseam, I realized that for once, I had the power over Hannah. Although I had never needed her back in high school to propel me to popularity since I was quite happy with my social status, it would have been nice if she hadn't constantly found something to rag on about Bridget and me. And she always found a way to say things discreetly enough so as to not bring any negative attention to herself in the process. I remembered one instance in gym class when we were choosing teams for softball. Hannah was captain of one team and one of my friends was captain of the other. Our friend had already chosen me for her team and was probably going to select Bridget on her next turn. Even though some of Hannah's cronies were eager to be on her team, Hannah shocked almost everyone by picking Bridget. She loudly told her pouting groupies that Mrs. Dervish, our gym teacher, had asked her to pick some of the "less popular girls" first to make them feel important, but I always knew she had done it to purposely keep Bridget and I apart. Ten years later, I quite liked the thought of making her sweat over the book review.

"Atta girl! I'm high-fiving you through the phone," Bridget said happily.

I raised my left hand in a one sided high-five. "Back at you. By the way, I know you've got the Prosecco covered but I doubt Jonathan will drink it. Do you have any beer? Or vodka? Or anything that doesn't sparkle?"

As I heard the flick of a lighter, Bridget asked, "Jonathan's definitely pre-gaming with us?"

"Yeah. Pete and Andy had no desire to meet up first and Jonathan was too lazy to plan his own tailgate so I talked him into joining us. That way, we'll walk in a united front. You don't mind, do you?" I had forgotten to mention it to Bridget assuming she'd be okay with it, but since it was her apartment and not mine, I suddenly felt a twinge of guilt.

"No worries," Bridget said, exhaling deeply. "The more the merrier. And we'll be a united *drunk* front."

"True that." Relieved she wasn't annoyed I had invited Jonathan, I decided not to complain about her smoking again.

"Nothing that sparkles though, huh? I guess that leaves out 'Goldschlager?'"

Smiling, I said, "He'd probably drink it but I'll tell him to bring his own alcohol just in case, okay?"

"'K, K."

"Watch it. One more K and you'd be in trouble!"

* * *

"Stepping away," I said to Rob over speaker phone.

"I'll try to hold down the fort without you," he replied dryly.

"Not possible, boss man. That's why you pay me the big bucks."

Rob laughed. "Don't forget that the next time I need you to oversee a large copy job."

"Hardy har har." I hung up the phone and stood up, wincing when my toes pressed against the front of my new leopard printed flats. It was casual Friday and I decided to leave my heels at home, wrongly assuming that flats would be more comfortable. They weren't. Steve Madden shoes had historically disagreed with me but these were so cute and looked perfect with my skinny jeans.

After limping down the hallway, I stopped in front of Nicholas' office, tried to breathe easily despite the fluttering of my heart, and knocked lightly on his door.

He looked up and gave me a wide grin. "Come on in."

I sat down, my heart still thumping at an annoyingly fast rate. "So, it's Rob's 54th birthday next week."

Nicholas raised an eyebrow. "Is that so? Damn, I can't believe he's that old. Seems so much younger."

"Must be the trophy wife."

Nicholas offered a bemused smile. "That or the running with the bulls. Seriously. Who does that at his age?"

"Who does that at any age?" I giggled. "Anyway, I wanted to plan a lunch for him and figured you might have some suggestions as to where we should go." Looking at him, I swore he had gotten even cuter overnight. And his trademark scruff, always irresistible, was slightly thicker than usual giving him a sexy, "just rolled out of bed" look. I genuinely wanted his advice regarding the birthday lunch and didn't want to ask him over the phone in case Rob overheard. I probably could have emailed him instead of discussing it face-to-face, but his face was just so damn cute.

Nicholas looked pensive for a moment before responding. "Well, we should definitely go somewhere around here. Rob doesn't like to stray too far from the office. What about Primehouse? Or that new Lebanese place down the street? Or Duo? How many people are we including?"

"We? Who said you were invited? I asked for your input. Doesn't mean I want your company," I joked.

"Oh, so that's how it's gonna be? Exploiting me for my foody expertise?" Feigning hurt, he curled his lips into a frown.

I was momentarily mesmerized by the thought of nibbling on his pouty lips but forced myself to stop staring. "Yeah, I heard you were a walking Zagat guide."

"Nah. But I do write many reviews for Yelp. They even gave me Elite reviewer status." Nicholas smiled wide as if amused by what he'd said.

His grin was contagious and I smiled back. "Impressive! See I might be just a secretary, but I'm a very resourceful secretary."

Narrowing his eyes at me, he said, "You're not just a secretary, Kimmie."

My stomach flip-flopped at his use of a nickname. "Oh yeah, I'm also a stellar book reviewer."

Placing his elbows on the desk and leaning towards me, he said, "I bet you could also be a stellar book *writer* if you tried."

Raising my voice, I said, "I told you I wasn't interested in that!" I felt my face get warm and decided that emailing him would have been a much better idea.

Nicholas squinted at me. "Yes, you did. Sorry."

I slipped my feet out of my shoes for temporarily relief. "Anyway, what about you? Was it your lifelong dream to be an attorney?"

Nicholas shook his head. "Not quite."

Good. Time to turn the tables. "So how did you get here?"

His eyes twinkling, Nicholas said, "The condensed version or the truth?"

"The truth please," I said, rolling my eyes.

Nicholas chuckled and then lifted his shoulders in a shrug. "The truth is I always wanted to be like my dad when I was little. He's a doctor, though, and I get queasy at the sight of blood so that wasn't an option." Nicholas blushed and scratched his head. "Since I've always been a good liar, I figured law was a good match." He laughed again. "Anyway, it's a good fit for me and I honestly like what I do. The hours suck but at least the salary is good. Minus the loans I'll be paying off for the next thirty years."

I looked at Nicholas in admiration. I had never thought too much about being successful. Many teachers had told my parents my Bs could be As if I applied myself but I never wanted to prove them wrong and was more than happy to get by without killing myself or letting anyone down. I wasn't about to admit that to Nicholas. Pointing at the law school diploma hanging on his wall, I said, "And so here you are. Nicholas Strong, Esquire."

Nicholas nodded. "Yup."

"And you're happy. "

He smiled softly. "Mostly. Like I said, I think it's a good fit. But there are other things I'd rather get paid to do."

I leaned forward. "For instance?"

"Manage bands. Or a talent scout. Something like that. Unfortunately I didn't know what I wanted to be until I was already something else. Too late now."

"It's never too late," I said assuredly.

"I suppose not," Nicholas said, smiling.

I could have easily ended the conversation at that point and Rob was probably wondering where I was, but I didn't want to leave yet. "So, my high school reunion is tomorrow night."

Nicholas' face brightened. "You excited?"

"Yes and no," I answered truthfully.

"Hmm." He looked at me with interest. "Tell me more."

I shrugged. "There are some people I'm psyched to see after all of these years. People I liked. And don't judge, but I'm genuinely looking forward to seeing how many girls got fat."

Nicholas made a scratching motion with his fingers. "Meow!"

I giggled. "It is what it is."

Nicholas shook his head at me, but his eyes were smiling. "Girls will be girls. So, why *aren't* you looking forward to it?"

"One guess."

Nicholas tapped the tip of his nose and looked thoughtful. "Unrequited crush?"

I shook my head. "Nope."

Giving me a knowing look, he said, "Cuz all the guys liked you back, huh?"

Chuckling, I said, "Not exactly."

Nicholas stared me down in silence for a moment before lifting and lowering his shoulders. "I give up."

"Hannah 'queen bitch' Marshak!"

Looking confused, Nicholas said, "Who is Hannah Mar…" Then his eyes widened. "Oh wait. You mean Writer Chick? Seriously?"

I sighed. "Yes, seriously."

Furrowing his brow, he said, "That's ridiculous. She's only one person out of your entire graduating class."

I touched my hand to my forehead and closed my eyes. "I still can't believe she wrote a fucking book." I opened my eyes to find Nicholas studying me. "What?"

"So, she wrote a book. So what? Why do you care so much?"

"I really don't like her, Nicholas."

He kept his stare on me. "Clearly. But at least you're not in high school anymore. Once you review the book, you'll never have to see her again."

Until she writes another book. I looked down at the carpet in dread. "I actually haven't confirmed that I'm going to read it."

Nicholas gave me a stern look. "You're a book reviewer. Review it like you would anyone else's book. You're a professional." His face relaxing into a smile, he said, "Suck it up, Kimmie."

I felt my face burn. "You don't understand."

Nicholas shrugged. "Okay. Then don't even read the book and give it a shitty review."

"I can't do that." *Could I?*

"Where is this shindig anyway?"

Happy for a subject change, I said, "Soho Grand. Kind of cool that it's in the city. I guess so many alumni live here now."

"That's my hood," Nicholas said enthusiastically. He opened his mouth to say something else when his phone vibrated.

I glanced at his phone hoping to see who had texted him but it was too far away to do without being completely obvious. "You've got mail!" I said.

Not even glancing at the phone, Nicholas said, "I'm sure it can wait."

"Well now I'm curious."

Chuckling, he said, "Okay bossy pants, if you insist," and picked up his phone.

I watched him roll his eyes as he read the text, but rather than respond, he placed the phone back on his desk and looked back at me.

"Anyone interesting?" I inquired.

Nicholas shook his head. "Not really. A girl my friends and I met at The Noho Star last night."

"Oh." My stomach dropped and while I really wanted to say something more, I couldn't find the words. I much preferred picturing him burning the midnight oil at work than flirting with pretty girls at a trendy New York City restaurant.

"She was our waitress."

I nodded. "And you exchanged numbers?" On the plus side, this probably meant he wasn't exclusive with Mary Jones.

"She asked for mine." Nicholas smiled shyly as if this wasn't typical but I didn't buy it. I shuffled in my chair uncomfortably.

"*Blah blah blah blah.* Came on too strong."

I had missed the first half of his sentence visualizing a leggy blonde waitress handing Nicholas a plate of filet mignon while serving his less attractive buddies spam. "You came on too strong?"

"No. *She* did. But we left her a good tip." He shrugged. "So, um the reunion's at the Soho Grand?"

Still thinking about the aggressive, leggy blonde waitress, I absently nodded. "Yup."

Nicholas leaned slightly forward. "I live around the corner from there. Maybe we can get a post-reunion drink after if you're up for it?" He gazed at me questioningly.

My heart raced as I wondered if he was serious, but feigning nonchalance, I said, "Sure. Hopefully, I'll still be standing by then. We're having a little pre-party first."

Nicholas smiled. "Nice! Who's having the party?"

"Calling it a party might be a bit of an exaggeration. My best friend Bridget is just having me and our friend Jonathan over to her apartment for some pre-reunion liquid courage."

"Cool." His phone rang and he answered it while still looking at me. "Hi Rob. Yeah she's here." He hung up.

I slipped my feet back into my flats and stood up. "I'm being beckoned?" Last I checked there was no tracking device in my Blackberry and I wondered how Rob even knew I was with Nicholas.

Giving me a closed-mouth smile, he said, "It appears."

"Okay. So once I check Rob's schedule, I'll make a lunch reservation. Primehouse?"

Nicholas nodded. "Primehouse sounds good."

"Thanks for your expert opinion."

"Anytime. And have fun tomorrow night."

I stood at the edge of his office. "I'll try."

"I'll cross my fingers that all of the mean girls got fat."

Even though I knew from Facebook that at least one mean girl had not gotten fat, I grinned and started walking. Thinking better of it, I took a step backwards and stuck my head in his office. I bit my lip. "So, uh, should I still give you a call if I'm standing after the reunion and up for a drink?" My heart slammed against my chest. *Please say yes.*

Nicholas grinned. "Definitely."

I smiled shyly. "Cool." Then I limped back to my office vowing to never wear those shoes again.

CHAPTER 9

"SO, ERIN MENTIONED that your reunion was tonight. I think I knew about it but it must have slipped my mind. What are you wearing?" my mom asked.

"A sexy black dress and my new black patent leather peep toe Louboutins. I'll be at least 5'3" tonight!" I had just finished my yoga tape and was sitting with my legs stretched out on either side of me as we talked on the phone. I preferred my yoga class at the gym but there were no Saturday classes and I wanted to find my "zen" place before facing my former classmates, one in particular.

"I'm sure you and Bridget will be the best looking girls there!" My mom said with more than a hint of pride in her voice. "Wish I could be there to take pictures of you. I miss my girls." She sniffled in an overdramatized display of wistfulness. Although only in their early fifties, my parents had been fortunate enough to retire early after owning a very successful craft store and had relocated to sunny Florida a few years earlier.

"I miss you too, Mom. And if we take any pictures, I'll send them your way."

"Please do. And take some of Jonathan too. Erin said you still see him?"

"As friends, Mom." *Mostly.* I cleared my throat. "What else did Erin say?"

My mom sighed loudly. "She went on and on about Hannah Marshak. Honestly, what is her fascination with that girl after all of these years?"

"It beats me. I hate the bitch!"

Laughing, my mom said, "I remember. She was a bad egg. You'd think Erin would stick up for her sister rather than idolize her nemesis, but..."

I completed her sentence. "She's Erin."

Sighing again, my mom repeated, "Yes, she's Erin. Sorry sweetheart."

I switched my stretching position to downward facing dog and put my phone on speaker. "It's okay, Mom. Not your fault. Anyway, she's my sister and I love her." That was the truth. I didn't like her very much but I definitely loved her.

"She's my daughter and I love her too. I love both of you. But honestly her priorities are wack."

I laughed and returned to the seated position.

My mom continued, "Anyway, I heard the bitch wrote a book. I promise never to read it. And I won't recommend it to any of my friends. How do you like that?"

"I like it, Mom. Unfortunately, I might not have a choice in the matter." I felt an ache in the back of my throat as I thought about Candace's email and the fact that I still hadn't given her a straight answer about reading *Cut on the Bias*.

A catch in her voice, my mom said, "What do you mean?"

"My blog."

"Oh? What about it?"

I was determined not to lose the peaceful, easy feeling afforded by my yoga session. "Can we talk about it next time? I really need to get ready for tonight. Meeting Bridget in less than three hours and have some serious prepping ahead of me."

"Oh, I'll let you go then. And have a wonderful time tonight! And call me tomorrow if there's anything juicy to share."

After we hung up, I went directly into the shower, taking extra time to exfoliate my skin with the lavender scrub I'd picked up at Kiehl's. Then I leaned over my sink to carefully shave my legs from ankle to upper thigh. After blow-drying my hair, I applied six large hot curlers so that it would cascade down my shoulders in soft, loose curls.

While the curlers set, I read a few chapters of *Ain't Too Proud to Beg*, a romantic comedy I was reviewing for one of my favorite new indie authors. The writing was good but I had read almost 100 pages and nothing substantial had happened yet. The story definitely lacked conflict. Since the author was such a sweetie, I crossed my fingers that the book would get better.

Twenty minutes later, I was applying a second coat of mascara in an attempt to lengthen my eye lashes for a more dramatic effect when I felt my hands begin to shake. I placed the wand on the edge of the sink, sat down on my toilet with my head between my legs and breathed deeply, in and out. I hadn't even left my apartment and was already feeling symptoms of anxiety. I certainly wasn't stressed about hanging out with Jonathan and Bridget. And I wasn't nervous about the reunion itself, other than coming face-to-face with Hannah, but I had made a decision to let her drive the situation. I wasn't going to initiate conversation with her. If she approached me first, I would follow her lead and take it from there. The ball was in her court, not mine.

So why was my stomach tangled up in knots?

I walked into the living room and removed my phone from the coffee table. I scrolled down the length of my address book until I saw Nicholas' number. I flashed back to the day before when he'd told me to call him if I was up for a drink after the reunion. Closing my eyes, I gently massaged my temples with my fingers. I opened my eyes, put the phone back on the table and walked back into the bathroom to finish applying my makeup.

Less than an hour later, I stood in front of my opened freezer and removed the box of Cohen's assortment of pigs in a blanket, potato and spinach puffs and egg rolls. I threw them in my Trader Joe's bag along with a container of port wine cheese and a box of crackers and dropped the bag by the door of my apartment. Then I walked back to my full length mirror and took one last sober look at myself from all angles. The slit in my form fitting dress made my toned legs look long, the low neckline emphasized the line of my cleavage while still leaving something to the imagination and my four inch designer heels gave me some semblance of height. I looked fierce.

"Go ahead, Hannah Marshak. Make my day."

* * *

Bridget opened the door of her apartment and put her hand over her mouth. "Oh my God! You look a-may-zing!"

I twirled to give her the full effect. "Thank you!" I stopped to take her in. She was a vision in a Kelly green silk knee-length dress that made her matching green eyes pop against her long red hair which fell down to her chest in waves. I shook my head. "Bridget. You are *gorgeous*!

A film of pink blanketed her fair skin as Bridget laughed nervously. "For real?"

"Yes! For real! Now let me in and let's have a toast before Jonathan gets here." I had purposely arrived early so Bridget and I could have some girl time.

She moved to the side to let me in and I walked a few steps into the foyer of her studio apartment, taking a sideways glance at my reflection in her mirrored closet before turning left into her small kitchen. After Bridget poured us both a glass of Prosecco and we put the frozen appetizers in the oven, we made ourselves comfortable sitting side by side on her suede purple couch. Bridget took a sip of her drink, put her champagne flute on the glass coffee table and turned to me. "So, you ready?"

I nodded. "Ready! Who are you most excited to see?"

"Guess! It's probably not who you would expect."

I mentally pictured our graduating class. "I haven't a clue."

Bridget paused dramatically. "Denise Porter."

"Of course, Denise!" We had been best friends with Denise until sophomore year when she fell into a more "questionable" crowd. It was a gradual drifting apart with no animosity and she always smiled and waved when she saw us in the hallways. And while she and her friends were known for having nasty hair-pulling girl fights in the hallways, we instinctively knew that she'd never let any of her trouble-making friends lay a finger on us. "You know, I'd love to see her too." I smiled, remembering the vow the three of us made in seventh grade to give up our Barbie dolls for more age-appropriate activities like French kissing boys.

"You ready to face her?"

I didn't need to ask to whom "her" referred. I nodded. "I really hope I don't lose my lunch when she pours on the fake charm." I looked down towards my fabulous shoes, twisting my feet to better see the bright red soles.

"What are you thinking?"

I mumbled, "Besides how long it's going to take me to pay off these shoes?" I lifted my head and saw Bridget looking at me with her forehead scrunched in concern.

"Should I call him, Bridge?" While awaiting her response, I took a sip of my drink.

She took a gulp of hers and said, "Abso-fucking-lutely."

I pinched my bottom lip with my thumb and pointer finger. "You sure?"

"I'm positive. He brought it up twice!"

"Actually, he brought it up once," I said, rubbing my ear. "I brought it up the second time, although he did respond with an enthusiastic, 'definitely.' Either way, it doesn't mean he's interested. What if he's placed me squarely in the 'friend' zone and I'm making more of this than there is? What if he starts talking about Mary Jones, the beach bombshell? And even if he does make a move on me, meeting him after a high school reunion sounds a bit more 'booty call' than 'date' anyway." I had a million more "what ifs" occupying my brain space.

Bridget took a drag of her cigarette. "I'm not even going to bother to respond to the 'friend zone' comment. No guy would ask a 'friend' to meet for drinks late on a Saturday night."

I nodded in agreement. "Yeah, that would be kind of weird. But what about the other stuff?"

After putting out her cigarette, Bridget reached out and gently patted my leg. "First of all, if he was dating Mary Jones seriously, he probably would not be meeting another girl for drinks on a Saturday night. And second of all, meeting him for a drink doesn't mean you have to sleep with him."

I gave her a look. "Not sure I'd have the self-control to resist him!"

"I bet a bout of crabs would solve that problem," Bridget laughed. "But seriously, you're better off finding out what he's after sooner than later. You need to know for sure so you can get on with it or move on." Bridget paused. "Unless..."

I swallowed hard. "Unless what?" I asked as her buzzer rang.

Bridget stood up and walked into her foyer. Into the intercom on her wall, she said, "Yeah?" and released her finger.

"It's Jonathan."

"Come on up," she said. Then she looked at me with an eyebrow raised. "Unless you're planning to hook up with Jonathan."

"Not if I can have a drink with Nicholas!" I exclaimed.

Bridget started to respond but was interrupted by Jonathan announcing his arrival with three loud knocks. "Hold that thought," she said, lifting one finger at me as she turned towards the door. With one hand on the knob, she turned to face me. "Then yes, you should definitely text him later!"

She was right. If I didn't reach out tonight, who knew when or if I'd have another opportunity and I'd probably kick myself later wondering what might have happened. "Okay, I will. But no more talk about Nicholas in front of you-know-who," I said, pointing at her front door.

"My lips are sealed." She opened her door and said, "Hi, Jonathan."

As he leaned his tall frame down to give Bridget a kiss on the cheek, I stood up to greet him and refill my drink. Decked out in dark gray slacks and a button down light blue shirt, it was the first time I'd seen Jonathan wearing something besides ripped jeans, sweat pants, boxer shorts or nothing in a very long time. The curls in his black hair were still too unruly and needed to be cut in a bad way but all in all, he'd put himself together. "You clean up well," I said.

Jonathan, who I spotted checking out Bridget's ass while she hung up his coat, turned to face me and gave me a quick once over. "Looking pretty nice yourself, Long." He leaned down to kiss my cheek. Motioning to the paper bag in his arms, he said, "So, I brought over some beers and a bottle of Jameson whiskey." He walked into Bridget's kitchen and put the bag on the counter.

"Awesome! Let's do a shot now," Bridget suggested.

I crinkled my nose. "No shots for me. I'll be dead before we leave the apartment."

Removing two shot glasses from her cabinet, Bridget said, "More for us then," and smiled at Jonathan.

Jonathan smiled back. "I like your style, Bridge."

Her face radiating glee, Bridget exclaimed, "This is going to F.U.N. Fun!"

Twenty minutes later, we were sitting in Bridget's living room, Bridget and Jonathan next to each other on the couch and me on one of the matching chairs, reminiscing about our high school years over hot appetizers and port wine cheese. Bridget and Jonathan had already downed two shots of whiskey while I drank my Prosecco quickly enough to calm my nerves but slowly enough not to get me sloppy drunk. I also ate some cheese and crackers to coat my stomach.

Popping a spinach puff in his mouth, Jonathan asked, "Remember Mr. Swiggins?"

"The science teacher, right?" Bridget said.

Shaking his head furiously, Jonathan said, "No. The industrial arts guy. Always reeked of alcohol?"

"Oh yeah." Bridget said. "What about him?"

"I heard he got caught drinking with some kids after school in the parking lot and was fired."

"False," I said.

They both turned to look at me. "Why do you say that?" Jonathan said, taking a drag of his cigarette and flicking ashes in the ceramic ash tray in front of him.

Leaning over Jonathan, Bridget flicked her cigarette in the tray as well. "Yeah. Why do you say that?" I could tell she was already drunk and I hadn't seen her take a single bite of food.

"Sounds like a suburban high school teacher myth. What teacher would be dumb enough to drink with students in the school parking lot?"

At the same time, Bridget and Jonathan yelled, "Mr. Swiggins!" Then they looked at each other, high-fived and started laughing.

Nauseated from the smoke, I stood up. "Need some air. Be right back."

"You okay, Kim?"

I turned around to tell Bridget I was fine, but she was laughing hysterically at something Jonathan said and so I kept walking. After making sure the front door was unlocked, I let it close behind me and headed towards the fire escape. I only knew where it was because when Bridget first bought her apartment, she treated it with kid gloves. She only ate in the kitchen, kept all of her toiletries neatly tucked away in her mirrored bathroom cabinets and went outside to smoke. When we hung out in her apartment, she'd drag me with her to the fire escape when she wanted a cigarette. That phase didn't last very long and now she almost always ate in the living room in front of the television, left her makeup items and toothpaste on the bathroom countertop and smoked within the confines of her apartment. She still draped a blanket over her couch when she ate something particularly messy, though.

Shocked by the gust of wind that whipped across my body the second I stepped outside, I went back to get my jacket. As I grabbed it, I heard the sounds of Jonathan's deep voice and Bridget's alcohol-induced giggling. Before I had a chance to ask what was so funny, I saw that my phone was flashing, picked it up and checked my messages. Caroline had texted to tell me to have a great night. I responded, and when I saw that the other message was from Nicholas, I sucked in my breath.

"Knock'em dead tonight, Kimmie!"

I quickly typed back, "Thanks! Getting my pre-reunion drink-on now."

My heart racing, I dropped my coat on the floor and ran towards the living room to tell Bridget. I stopped in my tracks. Bridget and Jonathan were sitting obscenely close to each other on the couch. So close that Bridget was in danger of falling into his lap. Bridget's body was angled towards Jonathan while he appeared to be telling her a story. I couldn't understand the gist of it, probably walked in too late, but it must have been during a pivotal moment because Bridget's eyes were wide open with anticipation. She looked mesmerized. And I had never seen Jonathan gesticulate quite so much when engaging in conversation.

Interesting. Veeeerrry interesting.

Still clutching my phone, I said, "Ahem. Am I interrupting something?"

Bridget's head whipped around fast enough to get whiplash and, red-faced, she said, "Uh, no. Jonathan was in the midst of telling me a story about one of his particularly quirky clients." She quickly looked away from me as if I'd caught her looking through my underwear drawer.

Jonathan shrugged. "You probably wouldn't appreciate it, Long. Working at a big firm, I bet your clients aren't such cheapos."

"You'd be surprised." Rob had asked me to recalculate his billing many times because his billionaire clients had complained about the firm's high hourly rates. "But, yes, you and Bridget have more in common than I ever realized," I said, raising an eyebrow toward Bridget and trying not to laugh when she looked at me with a guilty look on her face. "Bridget, I have to tell you something. Can you come here a second?" I wanted to mock her obvious, if not surprising, connection with my ex-boyfriend and promise that I would never shag him again. I also wanted to tell her about Nicholas' text. He had called me Kimmie again!

And then my phone sounded another message from Nicholas. "Hooray for pre-reunion drinks! Don't forget me come time for post-reunion alcohol."

Bridget grabbed me by the elbow and dragged me to the kitchen. "Time for a refill."

I tried unsuccessfully to wipe the grin off of my face as Bridget refilled both of our glasses with the last of the Prosecco. "Down the hatch," she said swallowing the entire thing in one gulp. She removed her mouth from the glass and said, "Why are you smiling like that?"

I put my phone up to her face so she could see for herself.

Her face breaking out in a huge smile, she belted out a rowdy, "Woo hoo!"

"I know, right?" I jumped up and down until I decided Louboutins were meant to be seen in; not jumped in. "I *so* have to text him later."

Bridget nodded in agreement. "You *have* to!"

"And I think I'm done having sex with…" I looked behind me to make sure the coast was clear. "Jonathan."

Bridget casually said, "Might not want to put all your eggs in one bastard, K. You might change your mind later."

I grabbed her hand and squeezed. "This has nothing to do with what does or does not happen with Nicholas. I think it's time to move on, you know? Leave the past behind. I'm sure there is someone he's more compatible with anyway."

Bridget released my hand and looked into her now empty glass. "What shall I drink now?"

I glanced at my phone. "We should think about heading out soon. We have to go all the way downtown."

"I'd prefer to be fashionably late," Bridget said.

"I agree," Jonathan said, popping his head into the kitchen. "Is it safe to enter or are you chicks having a private conversation?"

"It's safe to enter," I said. Bridget was clearly not ready to admit she was digging Jonathan and after fifteen years of friendship I knew better than to push.

"So, I brought something else with me," Jonathan said. He opened his hand to reveal a nicely rolled joint. "Interested?"

"Yes!" Bridget answered eagerly.

I looked questionably at her. "Are you sure you want to mix Prosecco, whiskey and marijuana?"

With a curt nod, Bridget insisted, "I'm fine. I'll only take one or two hits."

I cocked my head to the side and raised my eyebrows. "Okay, but if you need your hair held back later while I'm having drinks with Nicholas, you're shit out of luck." I turned to Jonathan. "I'll pass."

"I'm not even gonna pretend to care who Nicholas is. Let's light this sucker up." Jonathan walked out of the kitchen motioning for us to join him.

"You act like smoking up is reserved for special occasions and not a daily ritual!" I said as we followed him into the living room.

Jonathan sat back on the couch and patted the cushion next to him for Bridget to join him. "Don't usually have company," he said with a wink. "Much more fun."

"Okay, smoke up and then let's get out of here." I checked my phone. It had been over ten minutes since Nicholas' last text—long enough for me to text him back. I typed, "I will definitely reach out later!" put down my phone and observed Bridget and Jonathan as they passed the joint between them. I knew Bridget was full of shit when she said she was only going to take one or two hits.

*   *   *

A half hour later, I'd finally convinced Jonathan and Bridget to leave and we hailed a cab on the corner of 85th and 2nd. Jonathan got in first and Bridget looked at me to see if I was going to slide in after him. I reached down, pretending to adjust the strap on my shoe and said, "You go. I hate the middle." I didn't really hate the middle and Bridget knew it, but she crawled into the cab after Jonathan without a word. "We're going to West Broadway and Grand," I said to the cab driver. If he hadn't nodded, I wouldn't have known he heard me since he continued talking into his mouth piece in a language that was clearly not English.

"You guys ready?" I asked.

"Ready for what?" Jonathan answered. "I'm only going cuz you begged me."

Reaching across Bridget to swat his leg, I said, "I didn't beg."

Jonathan said, "Whatever," and turned to look out his window.

"I'm ready," Bridget said.

Now that we were moments away from seeing people for the first time in ten years, I felt my stomach tighten with nerves and wished it wasn't too late to do a shot of whiskey. I had been so focused on having drinks with Nicholas that I forgot I first had to make it through the reunion. I whispered to Bridget, "You'll still have my back with Hannah, right?"

Turning to look at me, Bridget asked, "When have I ever not had your back with Hannah or anyone else for that matter?"

I smiled. "Never. Thanks."

"It's cash bar, right?" she asked.

"Unfortunately, yes. The reunion committee decided it wouldn't be fair to include alcohol in the cost of admission since not everyone drinks," I said.

"Bunch of losers on the reunion committee!" Bridget complained, causing Jonathan to laugh.

"Agreed." I said.

We drove in silence for the next few minutes, apparently lost in our own thoughts. My head was spinning between who I was excited to see, who I dreaded seeing (Hannah and her sheep) and what was going to happen later that night if I got together with Nicholas. I wondered if we'd hook up and if so, how it would happen. Before I got too far into my fantasy, the cab driver pulled over, stopped the car and turned around. "You wanted Soho Grand?"

"We're here folks!" I said. Handing him a twenty and a five, I said, "Keep the change." I carefully stepped out of the cab and onto the street. When the others joined me, I looked up at the hotel and said, "Here goes nothing."

Chapter 10

JONATHAN ENTERED THE HOTEL FIRST while Bridget and I, arms linked, trailed slightly behind.

Pointing to a display that was set off to the side, Jonathan said, "We're in the Club Room." According to the sign, the Mitchell Berman Bar Mitzvah was in the Harbor Room while our reunion was in the Club Room. Although at that moment I would have preferred joining Mitchell and his 13-year-old friends dancing to the Hora, we followed the signs to the Club Room, stopping outside of the banquet room to retrieve our name tags from the long table set off to the side. It seemed everyone else was already inside or hadn't arrived yet since no one else was looking for a name tag.

"Seriously? They spelled my name wrong," Bridget said, holding up her name tag.

I stopped searching for my own ID to laugh at the misspelling of "Bridget" as "Bridged."

"Bridged! Ha!" Jonathan laughed. "If it's any consolation, they got my name wrong too," he said, holding up his tag where his name was also spelled incorrectly as "Jonothan. "Let's see if they at least got Kim's name right."

"How difficult is it to spell Long?" I said. Spotting mine, I held it up proudly. "No mistakes!"

"Is that you, Kimberly?"

I turned around to face Plum Sheridan, one of Hannah's dim-witted cronies. We had shared the same study hall period senior year and temporarily bonded over prom dress talk. She looked the same, tall and slender with thin straight blonde hair and eyes so bright they seemed to defy the emptiness that lay beneath. So far I was zero for one with girls in my graduating class getting fat.

"Kim Short, right? You look adorable as ever!" She put a hand to her mouth and looked at me apologetically. "I meant Long!" Reaching down to hug me, she said, "I don't know why I can never get that right."

While I half-heartily hugged her back, knowing the reason she never got it right was because Hannah had "accidentally" called me Kim Short all through high school, I reached out my hand to punch a laughing Jonathan in the arm. When we separated, I said, "Hi, Plum. How've you been?" Gesturing toward my dates for the evening, I said, "You remember Bridget and Jonathan right?"

Plum nodded her head eagerly even though her face showed no recognition whatsoever.

"Dumb Sheridan! Been a while. So nice to see you!" Bridget said, with her hand extended.

Plum grimaced as she gave Bridget's hand a limp shake. "It's Plum."

Mirroring Plum's gesture from before, Bridget clamped a hand to her mouth. "Oh my God. So sorry about that *Plum*. My bad. I don't know why I can never get that right." She giggled innocently while Jonathan stood behind her laughing.

I glared at Bridget and then turned back to Plum. "Anyway, it was good to see you! Maybe we'll see you inside," I said, before grabbing Bridget by the hand and whispering, "C'mon," to Jonathan.

"Dumb Sheridan. Priceless, Bridged," Jonathan said, still laughing.

When we got to the entrance of the banquet room, I stopped for a second so we could get ourselves together. "Was that really necessary, Bridget? It's been ten years since high school. We should just let it go."

Bridget snorted. "Let it go, huh? Is that what Plum was doing? She called you Kim *Short*. Seems to me like she's still in high school."

I mumbled, "You're right." Finally appreciating the humor of the situation, I started giggling. "Although I'm not entirely sure Plum was being intentionally mean. It's possible Hannah's joke went right over her head."

"Hence, *Dumb* Sheridan. Betcha she didn't get *that* joke either," Bridget said, rolling her eyes.

"Probably not." I said.

I looked inside the banquet room where I estimated there to be about one hundred of my former classmates. I immediately spotted Gilbert Ames who had proudly donned our school mascot's uniform (tiger) at every football game. I had pictured the room set up with lots of tables for six or eight, like a wedding, but the Club Room was far more intimate. Almost everyone was either sitting on or standing around the many cozy looking couches that were spread around the room. There was even a roaring stone fireplace. There was a constant buzz in the room but it was too loud to make out any particular conversation. Beyonce's *Crazy in Love* was playing in the background. I guessed someone on the reunion committee had made a playlist featuring the most popular songs from 2003 since the class voted against spending money on a DJ.

"Nice," Jonathan said. "Very old school New York."

"Agreed," Bridget said.

Turning around to do a 360 of the room, I contemplated who to talk to first. "Should we stick together or go our separate ways?"

"I see Andy and Pete. I'm off," Jonathan said and without awaiting a response from us, walked away to meet up with his own best friends from high school.

"Okay, then. And then there were two." I looked at Bridget whose eyes watched Jonathan as he walked across the room. "Unless you want to follow him and say hi to Andy and Pete. Haven't seen them a while."

Bridget shrugged. "Nah. Let's go to the bar! I'm sure we'll see someone we want to say hi to there."

I didn't think Bridget needed another drink but since my own buzz was beginning to wear off, I took a quick look at my chest to make sure I wasn't exposing any boob and followed her toward the bar. We made it there without being stopped, possibly because I refrained from making eye contact with anyone in the hope that I would have a drink in my hand before being approached by another alum. I was pretty certain Bridget had done the same.

Bridget handed me a bottle of Amstel Light, I clinked it against hers and turned back around to face the crowd. Relieved I didn't see Hannah anywhere, I took a long gulp of my cold beer straight from the bottle. I contemplated asking for a glass since I doubted Christian Louboutin would have wanted his shoes worn by someone who drank beer straight from the bottle, but before I turned back around towards the bartender, I spotted Denise Porter approaching us. I recognized her immediately even though her naturally blonde hair had been dyed chocolate brown and her attire, a light blue knee-length wrap dress and simple black pumps, strayed dramatically from her old school wardrobe of obscenely short and tight-fitting mini-skirts. She had the legs for it back then and nothing had changed.

Bridget jabbed me in the side and excitedly yelped, "Denise!"

Smiling brightly, Denise said, "If it isn't the Two Musketeers! Not surprisingly together." As she reached down to hug us, it occurred to me that almost everyone in my graduating class towered over both Bridget and me. I was usually the shortest person in any room, with the exception of children, but at least in the real world, there were other height deprived people walking the streets.

"How have you guys been?" Denise asked. "I've thought about you two a lot over the past few years."

"We've thought about you too!" Bridget said nodding.

"Actually, you were the person we most looked forward to seeing tonight," I said.

Denise put her hand over her heart and looked at us with bright eyes. "That's so sweet. What are you guys up to? Do you both live in the city? I guess you guys have kept in touch all of this time?" She paused. "I'm sorry for all of the questions!"

"No worries," I said. "I work at a law firm as a legal secretary and I also run a book blog. I'll let Bridget tell you what she does. But, yes, we both live in the city and we've kept in touch all of this time." I turned to Bridget with a smile.

Bridget proceeded to tell Denise what she was doing and then we directed the same questions back at her.

"I'm actually a mommy of two." Denise said proudly. While Bridget and I tried not to look quite so shocked, Denise reached into her bag for her wallet and showed us her family holiday photo. I had to suppress a gasp of surprise when I saw Denise standing next to a very handsome man who, at least in the picture, looked almost nerdy with his short hair and glasses. He was a far cry from the burnouts she had dated in high school. Looking at the fair-haired little boy and girl toddlers in matching New York Mets T-shirts, I asked, "Are they twins?"

"Yes! Can you believe it? Me with twins. Who would have guessed?"

"Not in a million years," Bridget said a little too certainly and then let out a hiccup. "Damn hiccups. Happens every time!"

Denise laughed. "Do a shot of bitters and suck on a lemon. Trust me."

While Bridget asked the bartender to prepare Denise's hiccup cure, Denise looked at me fondly. "A book blogger, huh? You always loved to read!"

"I still do," I said.

"Word on the street is that Hannah Marshak, queen in her own mind, is publishing a book," Denise said with a frown. "I'm surprised it's not a memoir considering how self-absorbed she is."

My chest felt weighted and I took another glance around the room. "Is she here tonight?" Since I hadn't seen her yet, I held onto hope that she had decided to skip it. *Wishful thinking.*

Denise nodded. "How else do you think I know about her book? She told me."

My eyes bulging, I said, "She told you?" I didn't remember Denise and Hannah being friends in high school although I did recall that Hannah made sure to be friendly with anyone who could either help her or potentially hurt her. And if Hannah didn't play her cards right with Denise and her friends, they would not have hesitated to yank out every curly brown hair on Hannah's inflated head.

"She's making the rounds telling everyone. She's even talking to the little nerds from math club." Looking at me questionably, she added, "You weren't in the math club were you?"

Laughing, I said, "No. Did you think I was a little nerd?"

Denise shook her head. "I always thought you were cool as shit. Both of you guys. So, no, not nerdy but yes, little." Glancing at Bridget who had the bartender in hysterics, she said, "Both of you were little. Always made me feel like a fucking giant."

Before I could respond, I felt an arm on my shoulder, "Little Miss Long!"

I turned around to face Patrick Vaughn, quarterback of our school's football team. I took him in from his flawless brown skin, to his chestnut eyes to his bulging biceps. "Patrick! Still gorgeous after all of these years."

"And little Ms. Long. Still the perfect height for me," he said making a reference to his joke that my head was parallel to his groin, making me the perfect height to give him a blow job without even kneeling. "I can't believe I used to say that to you. I'm sorry. I swear, I've matured," he said crossing his heart.

Laughing, I said, "For some reason, I was never that offended when it came from you. I've heard it many times since then and wasn't quite as forgiving." In fact, I had started a few fights back in college when my guy friends insisted on defending me against some douche bag making inappropriate comments about my height.

"I guess I got lucky. For a tiny chick, you always were a tough cookie."

I stood taller and lifted my chin in the air. "Still am."

"Let me buy you guys another drink. Or shots?" Patrick said.

From behind us, Bridget called out, "Shots!"

After reminiscing with Denise from our days in middle school, doing shots with Patrick and talking to some other people I hadn't seen in forever, we were waxing nostalgic with Jonathan, Pete and Andy who had joined us at the bar, probably after smoking a doobie in the hotel's outdoor courtyard, "The Yard." Andy was refreshing my memory of him cheating off of me in Intro to Accounting junior year. Since Andy stood at 5'5" stretched out, people used to say that we'd make a perfect couple, but even though he was cute, our platonic feelings had always been mutual.

"I would have totally flunked if you hadn't let me look over your shoulder," Andy said.

"I honestly had no idea," I said.

"You must have known on some subconscious level," Jonathan said.

Ignoring Bridget who kept tapping me on the shoulder, I said, "Says the non-practicing Psych major." I turned to Bridget, "What?"

She gave me a sidelong glance and whispered, "Two o'clock."

I felt an ache in my chest as I realized it might be too late to meet up with Nicholas. "It's two o'clock already?"

Bridget said, "No. Han…"

"There you are. I've been looking for you all night!"

I immediately recognized Hannah's whiny voice and in what felt like slow motion, stood up a little straighter, planted on a smile and greeted her for the first time in ten years.

CHAPTER 11

HER NATURALLY CURLY DARK BROWN HAIR had been flat ironed within an inch of its life and fell past her shoulders and her thick bangs were meticulously cut right above her eyebrows emphasizing her topaz eyes and long black eyelashes. She had never been what I would describe as a "pretty" girl but she was "striking" and always knew how to play up her best features. That night she was wearing a strapless black bubble dress that was cinched at her narrow waist with a white belt and fell slightly above her knees to show off long, toned legs. Her black stiletto sandals probably gave her five inches of extra height and so even with my four-inch heels, she towered over me. I begrudgingly, although not surprisingly, concluded that she looked just as good if not better than she had in high school. Of course, I had no intention of telling her that.

I braced myself for the conversation I had been dreading for a month. I planted on a fake smile. "Hi, Hannah. Good to see you," I said, almost choking on the words. "But why would you be looking for me all night?" I already knew the answer but wanted to watch Hannah perspire. Maybe her pit stains would seep through the designer dress she was wearing and I could call her out on it the way she had done to one of her pitiful wannabes at our 8th grade prom. I shook my head in memory of the girl whose lavender dress turned dark purple from the sweat she excreted probably from trying so hard to stay off of Hannah's shit list. Of course, in typical Hannah fashion, it came across to others that she was merely concerned the girl was suffering from the flu, but I knew better.

Hannah smoothed out her bangs. "I figured you'd want to talk to me about my book, obviously." Then she gave me a smile that on anyone else's face might actually be described as "warm."

My mouth fell open, although it probably should not have shocked me that Hannah would assume I was anxious to speak to her and not the other way around. I quickly recovered on the outside while contemplating on the inside whether to play dumb or admit to knowing about her book. "Oh yeah, your book." I brushed an imaginary piece of lint off of my dress.

Beaming at me, Hannah said, "So exciting, right? Back in high school, I never imagined I would write a novel, much less publish one." She looked over my head and around the room. "Although I probably did have enough material. As the most popular girl in our class, I'm sure you can imagine the stories I could tell." Hannah sighed and looked at me thoughtfully. "Well, maybe not. You didn't really hang with my crowd." She placed a hand on her chest. "In any event, I still can't believe it."

I wondered if she was trying to sound humble. Since she had no actual experience being humble on which to base her performance, it wasn't working on me. *Maybe it worked on Dumb Sheridan though.* And so much for the proclamation on her website that her "childhood dream" was to be a writer. I knew that was bullshit. As she continued to beam at me in pride, I tried to hide my disgust and smiled again. "Yes. Candy at Novel Book PR asked me to review it for my blog." I reached for the phone in my bag. Pretending to type a note, I said, "Which reminds me, I have to get back to her."

Hannah looked at me expectantly. "Yes?"

I nodded. "Yes. I completely forgot to tell her I finished reviewing Jenna Weinberger's book and want her to do a guest post on *Pastel is the New Black*. Have you read any of Jenna's books? She's amazing!" I grinned widely at Hannah.

Hannah shook her head and proceeded to examine her perfectly manicured nails. "I actually haven't. But I was wondering if you…"

"Oh, you totally should. She is considered top notch in the genre. And her tweets are hilarious!"

Appearing at my side, Bridget handed me another beer. "I bought you another drink sweetie." Then she turned to Hannah with a sour expression. "Oh, hi."

Hannah smirked. "Well if it isn't the best friend. I should have guessed you wouldn't be far away." Giving Bridget the Manhattan once-over, she said, "Your hair looks the same as it did in high school."

Bridget nonchalantly ran a hand through her ruby locks. "I'll take that as a compliment. Thanks."

Hannah shrugged and turned back to me. "So, about my book?"

"What about it?" I asked sweetly.

"I spoke to Erin." Closing the distance between us as if to tell me a secret, she confided, "To be honest, I had no idea who she was when she friended me on Facebook but figured, what the hell. Not the first time that has happened. The more the merrier, right? Especially with the book coming out. After I accepted the request, she messaged me that her sister ran a chick lit blog but I didn't make the connection to you right away. She looks so tall in her pictures!" She paused while scanning me from head to toe. "Anyway, she thought my book would be perfect for your site. Sweet girl, by the way. So…" Hannah looked at me eagerly.

If she thought making nice with my little sister was the golden ticket to my website, she was as "wack" as Erin. Two could play at this game. Playing dumb, I said, "Oh! You want me to review *your* new book?" I twisted my ankles to get another look at my fabulous shoes. "Yes, Candy asked me and I told her I had to check my schedule. I have so many books on my TBR list," I said apologetically.

Hannah leaned in and whispered, "Maybe you can push mine to the top of the list? As a favor? I mean we've known each other since we were only yea big." Looking down at me, she covered her mouth with her hand. "I mean since we were children." Matter-of-factly, she continued, "And I'm sure your readers will want to hear your thoughts on the book. Great shoes by the way."

"Thank y…"

"Are they real?"

Responding for me, her nostrils flaring, Bridget snapped, "Everything about Kim is real. Which is more than I can say for some of your body parts!"

I put a hand to my mouth to cover the perfect combination of horror, amusement and gratitude I was feeling for my friend who had already made her way back to the bar. Holding back a laugh, I said, "I'm sorry. Bridget is a bit drunk." *I'm not really sorry at all.*

Smirking, Hannah said, "Evidently. I'm surprised you guys are still so close."

Feeling my muscles tense, I narrowed my eyes at her. "Oh? Why is that?"

Hannah shrugged. "I know you're just a secretary, but at least you have your blog. Doesn't Bridget work at home or something?"

I momentarily felt short of breath as if someone had cut off the supply of oxygen to my lungs. "Bridget runs her own web design company and has an office in the luxury doorman apartment that she owns, yes. And I'm *'just a secretary.'*"

Looking at me with pity, she said, "Not surprising you're a professional reader. Back in high school, you always had your nose behind a book. Although I probably shouldn't poke fun at readers since I need you all to buy my..." Hannah stopped mid-sentence and gawked at me. "Oh, my God. I just remembered something."

I took a gulp of beer and feigned boredom. "Yeah? What's that?"

"You wanted to be a writer too."

I felt my face drain of color. "What makes you say that?"

"That poetry contest sophomore year. The winner was going to have her poem published in *Self Magazine*." With a wry face, she said, "You showed so much promise. Too bad you didn't win. You came in second though, right?"

"No, I didn't." *Thanks for reminding me.*

Frowning, she said, "Sorry. I probably shouldn't have said anything. But your blog is great at least, right?"

I nodded. "Right." I decided this conversation had run its course. "Anyway, I'll let Candy know if I'll be able to review your book as soon as I can."

Her face noticeably brightening, Hannah said, "Great! *Cut on the Bias* is going to get a lot of publicity. I would hate for you to miss the boat."

Oh no she didn't! "Well, like I said, I'm pretty inundated right now with requests from editors, agents and the like. But I'll see if I can fit you in." I paused for a beat. "Since we've known each other since we were *yea big* and everything." Wanting to guarantee I got the last word, I said, "It was great seeing you, Hannah," quickly turned my back and walked over to Bridget.

Facing straight ahead, Bridget whispered, "Is she still behind you?"

I casually looked over my shoulder. "No sign of the Wicked Witch. Here's hoping she flies far, far away on her broomstick."

Turning to face me, Bridget flashed me a huge smile and held up her beer. Slurring, she said, "Karma's a bitch, init?"

"Yeah, I guess." Hannah had managed to get her passive/aggressive digs in but I had held my own. Studying Bridget, I said, "You okay?"

Shifting her body weight from one side to the other, Bridget said, "Yip. Why?"

"You're slurring and slightly off balance." I eyed the beer in her hand. "Maybe you should switch to water."

Bridget defiantly took a long gulp of beer and said, "Haven't had sex in a year!"

Guessing she probably had no idea how loud she'd said that, I looked around the room right in time to see Jonathan approaching us. "Okay then. Might not want to advertise that. And no one is forcing you to abstain! Let's talk about this later, okay?"

Gripping the bar for support, Bridget said, "Now's as good a time as an..." She stopped mid-sentence as Jonathan appeared in front of us. "Jonathan! What's up, Doc?"

Jonathan's brows crinkled together in concern. "You alright, Bridged?"

"Why wouldn't I be?" she said, slipping onto the bar stool next to her . "Shot?"

Jonathan's eyes met mine and he raised an eyebrow. "I don't know about you guys, but I need some water bad."

"Water schmater. Shot shot shot!" Bridget pounded her knuckles against the bar while Jonathan motioned to the bartender and made a slashing motion against his throat. "Official party is almost over, but the lobby bar is still open. Why don't we take a quick break and resume drinking there?"

Nodding in agreement, I said, "Sounds like a plan. Round of water all around and we'll pick up the drinking at the Grand Bar. Sound good, Bridge?"

"Whatever," she mumbled.

I glanced at Jonathan. "Can you keep her company a second? I've gotta use the bathroom."

"Can't she go with you?" Jonathan looked at me pleadingly.

I blurted out, "No!" but quickly composed myself. "I have to make a phone call and it's, er, kind of private. What's the big deal?"

"What if she throws up?" Jonathan looked horrified at the thought.

"She won't," I promised. Bridget had always been a next morning puker.

Jonathan made a gesturing motion towards the exit. "Fine. Go. Be fast!"

I hurried to the ladies' room to make sure my hair and makeup had held up, smiling at ex-classmates I passed along the way. When I faced my reflection in the mirror, I was pleased to note that the light spritz of Big Sexy Hairspray I borrowed from Bridget had kept every soft curl in place. And the primer I used on my eyelids had kept my smoky eye shadow smudge free. I looked great and felt even better remembering the defeated look on Hannah's face when I repeatedly refused to confirm or deny whether I'd review *Cut on the Bias*. I might always have my nose behind a book, but it wouldn't be *her* book. *"Miss the Boat"* my ass!

It was now or never. Locating Nicholas' last text on my phone, I wrote, "Having post-reunion drinks at the Grand Bar. Interested?" I didn't particularly like the idea of introducing Nicholas to my friends when I barely knew him myself, but I didn't know the neighborhood well enough to suggest another bar. I just hoped Jonathan would leave early and Bridget wouldn't say anything stupid.

To avoid staring at my phone waiting for a response, I popped a breath mint in my mouth and reapplied my lip gloss. By the time I put the gloss back in my bag, my phone beeped a text message from Nicholas. "Be there in a few." I took a deep inhale, let out a slow exhale and willed my heart to stop beating so damn fast. Apparently alcohol was not enough to dull my reactions to the very thought of spending time with Nicholas outside of the office.

The Club Room was almost cleared out by the time I got back, but Jonathan and Bridget were still standing at the bar. Although I wasn't sure what Bridget was doing would actually be considered "standing." She was slumped head-first over the wooden bar. Jonathan was gently rubbing her back but stopped when he saw me. "It's about time."

"It's been less than ten minutes since I left you. Relax." I glanced over at Bridget who had not uttered a sound. "Okay there, Bridge?"

From underneath her thick head of curls, I heard a muffled, "No."

"Maybe we should get you home," I said, gently patting the back of her head.

Still not looking up, she muttered, "Don't wanna go home yet. Wanna see Nicholas Strong Rhymes with Long."

Jonathan shook his head in confusion. "What the hell is she talking about?"

I felt my face get warm, removed my hand from Bridget's head and whispered, "Nothing. Gibberish. She's three sheets to the wind." I rolled my eyes for effect. Focusing on Bridget again, I said, "What do you want to do then?" I tried to discreetly check the time on my phone without Jonathan seeing me. I probably still had a few minutes before Nicholas arrived to get Bridget in better shape and at the very least, helping her would be a distraction from stressing over it.

Bridget sat up abruptly. "Need to pee."

"I'll take you," I offered.

"I'll meet you guys in the bar," Jonathan said before escaping the Club Room like it was Alcatraz.

* * *

I practiced patience while Bridget used the bathroom, checked herself out from every angle and splashed cold water on her cheeks, but I drew the line when she slapped herself across the face. "What the fuck are you doing?"

"Trying to sober up." Bridget said.

I chuckled. "Does that work?"

"Actually, it does. But it also hurts like a motherfucker!" Bridget giggled and I was pleased to see that some light had returned to her eyes.

Checking my hair in the mirror one last time, I said, "Good. Now that you're showing some semblance of returned sobriety, can we please make like a tree and get out of here?"

Cocking her head to the side, Bridget said, "You mean make like a tree and leave?"

I glanced at my watch. "Whatever it takes to get downstairs so I can meet up with Nicholas."

Bridget's eyes opened wide. "You called him?"

"Yes. Well, texted him. But he's on his way. He might be here already." I felt my stomach flutter and my pulse race at the thought.

"Then what the fuck are we still doing in the ladies' room? Let's go!"

* * *

When we got to the bar, I immediately spotted Jonathan, Pete and Andy perched at one of the many tables located around the edge of the room. They were drinking from bottles of Goose Island IPA and laughing as if ten years had not passed since they used to play poker every Friday night in high school. I walked Bridget over to their table and said, "I'm going to take a walk to see if Nicholas is here. I'll be back." I discreetly wiped my clammy hands on the table and willed my legs to stop quivering.

Bridget started to sit down but hesitated. Her eyes wide, she asked, "Do you want me to come with you?"

I debated. On the one hand, I would look less awkward circling the bar with Bridget than by myself. But then I would have to slickly lose her. Granted, she wasn't as sloppy as she'd been fifteen minutes earlier, but I was not all that confident she was capable of taking a "get lost" hint. "I appreciate the offer, but I think I'm good. I'll bring him to meet you at some point though." Hopefully after Jonathan had already left. That was an introduction I didn't really want to make.

Bridget extended her hand with her pinky pointed outward. "Swear?"

I entwined my pinky with hers. "Pinky swear."

Borrowing Nicholas' line from earlier that evening, she reached out to hug me and whispered, "Knock 'em dead, Kimmie" in my ear.

I returned her embrace and whispered back, "That's the plan."

I began walking clockwise around the bar. Suddenly infused with adrenaline, I didn't even try to remove the excited smile that was pasted on my face. I couldn't wait to see Nicholas!

Until I saw him.

CHAPTER 12

HE WAS STANDING BY THE BAR facing away from me, but since I had stared after him as he left a room on several occasions, I had his back memorized and recognized him at once. He was talking to *her*. Correction: He was laughing with her. And she was smiling at him, exposing a chemically whitened slightly too large mouthful of teeth. And her hand reached down to swipe his arm not once, but twice within a couple of seconds. He didn't try to brush it away.

My designer shoes felt glued to the floor. I was unable to move closer to them or head back in the other direction. And then she looked at me.

In a split second, her facial expression went from the evil stare she used to throw my way a decade earlier to a smile almost as bright as the one she had mere moments ago directed to Nicholas. It was as if she was temporarily lost in a time warp and then remembered that it was 2013 and I ran one of the most popular chick lit blogs on the Internet.

While still in an eye lock with Hannah, I saw Nicholas finally turn and see me standing there. In that moment, I didn't care that he looked me over appreciatively. I didn't care that unlike most straight guys, he actually knew how to wear a pair of jeans to show off his butt. At that moment, all I cared about was that he had come to the bar to have a drink with me and instead, was talking to *her*. Of course, he would talk to her. She was Hannah Marshak.

"There you are," Nicholas said, smiling brightly. "I was about to send you a text."

I wondered what the text would have said. *"I know I was supposed to have a drink with you, but I met another girl. She's confident and sexy.*

She wrote a novel! And she's tall." My legs felt weak. "Yeah, I was talking to an old friend and lost track of time," I lied.

In a soft voice, Hannah said, "You know each other?" before reaching out to graze his arm again.

Although Hannah was looking at Nicholas with glossy eyes and not me when she asked the question, I choked out, "Uh huh." Then I looked at Nicholas. "Can you excuse me a second? I need to, um, catch someone before she leaves. I'll be back." Before he could respond, I walked away as casually as I could and prayed that my knees wouldn't give out.

* * *

When I reached Jonathan's table, I removed Bridget's glass from in front of her and downed the remains in one sip. After a near escape from choking on the contents I said, "What the hell is this?"

"It's called a Blood and Sand. Scotch, Vermouth and some other stuff," Bridget said, patting my back as another choke escaped my throat.

After trying to discreetly wipe the leathery taste of scotch off of my tongue with a cocktail napkin, I said, "Might as well be dishwashing detergent. Nasty!"

"That's what you get for stealing someone else's drink." Looking at me through the bottom of the empty glass, Bridget asked, "Where's Nicholas?"

"Somewhere up the Wicked Witch's ass!" I consciously summoned up the self-control not to take Bridget's empty glass and knock it over Hannah's inflated head.

Bridget gave me a puzzled look. "What?"

"I went to find him and he was actually talking to Hannah." Loudly, I repeated, "Hannah!" as if Bridget might not have heard me the first time.

Bridget's eyes darted around the room. "Oh wow. Where are they?"

I kept my eyes on Bridget, afraid to spot Hannah and Nicholas making out in a corner somewhere. "Who cares? Fuck him. And fuck her. And let them fuck each other for all I care. I never should have bothered." I sat down, closed my eyes and pressed two fingers to my forehead. I was such a liar. I totally cared. "Maybe I'll just go home with Jonathan." I opened my eyes, wishing I could take back those last words. "Not really, of course."

Bridget stood up. "You should do what you want, Kim. He's your fuck buddy, not mine. I'm gonna head out anyway. Dying for a cigarette. Tell the guys I said goodnight, okay?" She grabbed her coat from behind the chair and started walking away.

I stood up and reached out my hand to grab her. "Wait."

Bridget quickly turned around, her face emotionless. "What?"

"Are you sure you're alright? Do you want me to take you home?"

Not blinking, Bridget said, "I'm fine, Kim."

"I'm not really gonna hook up with Jonathan, ya know?" I laughed hoping to break the tension.

Shrugging, Bridget said, "Do what you gotta do. It makes no difference to me," before turning back around and walking away.

I watched her disappear, muttered, "Nice job, Kim," and walked over to the bar. Having no patience for actually reading the list of cocktails, I ordered the first one on the menu—the Dirty Soho. As I nibbled on an olive, I wondered why I hadn't left with Bridget after all. At least she'd have known I wasn't serious about hooking up with Jonathan that night. She was right that he was mine first, but I wouldn't call dibs on a guy I no longer wanted, knowing that she did. I took another sip of my drink and tried to compose myself. I needed to find Nicholas and fake some semblance of coolness. It would hurt like hell if he chose Hannah over me but there was no way I would admit that to him. Or to Hannah.

I turned around to face the crowd and saw him approaching me. At least he wasn't with *her*. I took a deep breath.

Unsmiling, he said, "There you are. I thought you went to check on a friend."

"I did. She just left so I got a drink." I held up my Dirty Soho. I was too embarrassed about running away from him to make full-on eye contact so I took a sip of my drink and glanced both ways as if I was looking for someone.

Nicholas scratched his head, "Um, were you planning on finding me? You kind of abandoned me over there. I thought we were supposed to have a drink *together*."

I bit my lip and faced him head on. "Yeah, sorry about that. Seeing you with Hannah caught me off guard," I confessed. *So much for playing it cool.*

Nicholas' mouth dropped open. "That was Hannah?"

Nodding, I said, "Yeah. You didn't know?"

Nicholas shook his head. "We didn't get that far."

Recalling the visual of Hannah running her palm up and down his arm, I wondered how far it would have gone if I hadn't shown up. "What did you think of her?" I asked nervously.

Nicholas rubbed his stubbly chin. "I hadn't really given it any thought."

His scruff was definitely my Achilles heel. I had fantasized about his rough skin leaving my face red from passionate kissing, but now all I could think about was him kissing Hannah instead. "She seemed to like you," I whispered.

"Well, it doesn't really matter since I came here to have drinks..." His eyes firmly resting on mine, he touched his finger to my chin. "With you." He removed his finger.

I willed myself not to touch my chin even though I could still feel the warmth of his hand where his finger just was. I smiled softly, "Good." That was all the reassurance I needed. I opened my mouth to ask if he wanted to go someplace else, where we were less likely to be interrupted by more of my old classmates, just as Hannah appeared at Nicholas' side.

As if I wasn't standing there, she gleamed at Nicholas and said, "I turned away for one second to remind our class historian that the name of my book was *Cut on the Bias.* She wants to include it in the alumni newsletter." Hannah stopped talking and tapped a finger to her chin. "What was her name again?" She shook her head. "Anyhoo, when I turned back around, you were gone. I didn't even get your name."

Nicholas offered a polite smile and took a sidelong glance at me. "It's Nicholas. I went to see where Kim ran off to."

Finally acknowledging my presence, Hannah looked at me and in typical Hannah-speak said, "Oh yeah. You know our little friend Kim too, huh?"

Nicholas deadpanned, "Yeah, our little friend Kim is kind of cool."

Hannah smirked, "I suppose she's come a long way since high school." Motioning over my head, she said, "Although Jonathan certainly liked her well enough even back then. Didn't you, Jonathan?"

Ruh-roh. I quickly glanced up at Jonathan, who had just joined our little party, and back down towards my shoes. I figured failing to make eye contact with Jonathan was the best way to avoid having to introduce him to Nicholas. For someone who claimed that I "dragged him" to the reunion, Jonathan was certainly staying out late.

Running his hands through his hair, Jonathan looked at Hannah with a bored expression. "What are you babbling about Hannah?" Then he turned to me. "Andy and Pete just left."

I wanted to ask why he hadn't joined them but I just stood there mute.

Hannah smiled at Jonathan and said, "I was telling Nicholas here about you and Kim back in high school." Reaching out to touch Nicholas' arm *again*, she said, "They were such a cute couple."

I involuntarily snorted since back then Hannah used to insinuate almost daily that Jonathan was cheating on me. I would overhear her expressing to others in a very loud whisper how concerned she was for me that I was dating a cheater.

"Did you say something, Kim?" Hannah asked.

I muttered, "No" as my laughter turned into fear over where this conversation was headed. I snuck a peek at Nicholas, wondering what he was thinking. As if sensing my gaze, he turned to look at me but I couldn't read his expression. I realized I had to respond. "Jonathan and I used to go out," I confirmed.

Nicholas nodded. "I gathered that."

Jonathan chuckled, "Lucky me," and I fought the urge to kick him in the shin.

Hannah winked. "Rumor has it they're still knocking boots, if you know what I mean." Turning to me, she said, "Is it true that you guys are still fuck buddies after all of these years?"

As Jonathan's face turned strawberry red and Hannah's laughter boomed, I took a sharp intake of breath. I needed an escape route and fast. "Well, this has been fun," I said. I looked up at Nicholas, my heart beating fast. "But Nicholas and I are going to finish our drink somewhere else now." Taking his hand, I pleaded, "Is that okay?"

Nicholas said, "Yeah, let's..."

Interrupting, Hannah said, "Oh, I didn't realize you guys were *together*," Hannah said, the surprise in her voice a little more dramatic than necessary. Looking from me to Jonathan, she shrugged innocently, "I guess the whole 'fuck buddy' comment was a bit of a faux pas. My bad." She laughed.

Squeezing Nicholas' hand, I started dragging him away as Hannah called out, "Don't forget about my book." Then I heard her ask, "You know about my book, right?" I turned around as Hannah gripped Jonathan's arm, trapping him in place. He caught my eye and glared. I quickly mouthed, "I'm sorry" and continued walking with Nicholas.

Once in the lobby, Nicholas stopped in front of an unoccupied couch. He sat down and patted the seat next to him. I sat down and when I turned to face him, his eyes immediately locked with mine. I took a sip of my drink, "Okay, then. That was awkward."

Nicholas took a slow sip of his drink while keeping his stare on me. "So, your 'friend' Jonathan is actually your high school sweetheart, huh?"

"Yes, we dated back in high school." I added, "Ten years ago" as if he couldn't do the math.

"You've mentioned him before."

Since it wasn't a direct question, I wasn't sure how to respond. "I guess."

Nicholas looked at me quizzically. "How come you didn't mention that he was your ex-boyfriend?"

I felt my face get red. "Because it was irrelevant. It was ten years ago, Nicholas." I narrowed my eyes at him. "Don't you have a history with any girls?"

"Of course I do," Nicholas averted eye contact and looked down toward his toes. "But I'm not still 'knocking boots' with any of them and, according to Hannah, you are. Is that true? Is he your fuck buddy?"

I squirmed in my seat. "Yes, Jonathan and I still do it sometimes, but we don't..."

Interrupting, Nicholas said, "Do it?"

I giggled at my own childish euphemism for sex. "Yes, do *it*! If neither of us is dating someone, we sometimes do it." Not wanting Nicholas to misunderstand, I said, "But we don't have feelings for each other anymore and it's not like we hook up every weekend or anything. And we're not going to anymore." As the words left my mouth, I wondered why I was explaining myself to him. I still had no idea what he wanted from me and if it was nothing, my relationship with Jonathan, past or present, was none of his business. "Why do you care?" I held my breath, afraid of his answer.

"Because I like you and want to make sure we're on the same page," Nicholas said.

"We're on the same page. I like you too," I whispered. "Even though I caught you flirting with Hannah of all people. She's cute, right?" Cute like a rabid animal, but there was no accounting for male taste sometimes.

"I absolutely was not flirting with her, but I guess she's cute enough," he said, scratching his chin again.

I groaned. "For the love of God, why don't you just shave!"

Nicholas dropped his hand. "Do I need to shave that badly?"

"No," I said meekly.

"What then?"

"Have you looked at yourself recently?"

Nicholas shook his head softly.

"It's sexy," I whispered.

Nicholas gave me a closed-mouth smile. "Isn't that a good thing?"

I pinched my bottom lip. "It could be."

"Kim."

"What?"

He shook his head and said, "Yes, I guess Hannah is cute, but *you* are sexy."

I stared at him. "No. I'm cute."

He grinned. "Fine. You *are* cute. But you're also sexy. And I can't believe you'd think for a second I'd choose Hannah over you. I mean, she gives a good hand job but otherwise, no thanks," he said with a straight face.

I started laughing. "Really? You had to go there, didn't you?" Shaking my head, I added, "Although considering the way she was touching you, I wouldn't assume a hand job was out of the question," I joked.

Rolling his eyes, he said, "Yeah. She was touching me. Not the other way around. I guess I'm just that irresistible." He flashed me a cocky grin.

I poked him lightly in the arm. "You're such a player."

Nicholas' body froze in place. "You think I'm a player?"

I raised an eyebrow. "Aren't you?"

"I'm sorry if I've done anything to make you feel that way. But Kim..." He reached for my hand.

I looked at him eagerly, "Yeah?"

"Thanks for ditching me, Long."

I turned away from Nicholas and faced Jonathan. For the love of God. Why was he still here?

* * *

I reluctantly made the official introduction I had awkwardly avoided earlier. "Nicholas, this is Jonathan."

Nicholas stood up and shook Jonathan's hand. "Good to meet you."

"You didn't go to school with us, did you?" Jonathan asked.

Shaking his head, Nicholas said, "No. I work with Kim. I live a few blocks away."

Jonathan grinned at Nicholas. "Good. You didn't look at all familiar. Age has not been kind to my memory, but still..."

The banter between Nicholas and Jonathan flowed naturally and I wondered if I was the only one who felt the tension in the air. I raised an eyebrow at Jonathan. "Age? You're 28. I'd blame any memory loss on too much weed."

Jonathan looked at Nicholas and pointed at me. "And you went out of your way to hang out with this one? Hannah might be the better choice." Turning back to me, he said, "Speaking of which, thanks for leaving me alone with her before. She told me all about her book. You owe me one."

I gave him an apologetic frown. "Sorry." I said a silent prayer that he would drop the subject of Hannah entirely before the "fuck buddy" conversation was reborn.

"So you finally got Bridget to call it a night, huh? How did you manage that one?" Jonathan asked.

You don't want to know. "She finally had enough," I lied.

"Well, I'm right behind her. This was fun but I'm good for another ten years."

Recoiling, I said, "Let's not even discuss our twenty year yet." Jonathan glanced from me to Nicholas and then back to me. "You heading out?"

"I think I'm gonna stick around a little while longer," I said before turning to Nicholas. "Assuming you still want to hang out."

Nicholas said, "Definitely" and then looked at Jonathan. "Why don't you have a drink with us?"

I felt my heart drop to the floor. Was he serious?

Jonathan appeared to contemplate the offer, running his hands through his curly hair. "Thanks, but I'm gonna pass." Extending his hand to Nicholas, he said, "Good to meet you."

Nicholas shook Jonathan's hand firmly, smiled and said, "You too."

I stood and reached up to kiss Jonathan on the cheek. "Talk to you soon. Thanks for letting me drag you here."

Grinning, he said, "It wasn't as bad as I expected" and with a wave and another "Bye," he walked away.

I sat back down and turned to Nicholas. "Were you hoping for a three-way or something?"

Nicholas gave me an amused smile. "I was just being polite. But I'm sure I can catch him if you want."

I rolled my eyes. "No thanks."

With his eyes still on mine, he ran his hands along his jawline.

I laughed. "Seriously? I already told you I have a weakness for your lazy shaving habits. You're totally doing that on purpose!"

"You got me," Nicholas said, giving me a sly grin. "Like I said, I like you, Kimmie Long."

Hearing those words sent a jolt of electricity through my body and I took a sip of my drink to recover. Since the drink was pretty much all vodka, it was a tiny sip. "I do believe you like me, Nick."

With an eyebrow raised, Nicholas repeated, "Nick?"

"Doesn't anyone ever call you that?" I asked.

"Not if I can help it."

"Duly noted, Nicholas," I said, emphasizing the second two syllables. He smiled.

I shook my head and suppressed a smile. "Anyway, I do believe you like me. I've noticed you checking out my boobs on several occasions."

Leaning in towards me, he let his eyes drop down to my chest and back up to my eyes. "They're very nice boobs."

"I know," I laughed.

"Just like I know my five o'clock shadow is sexy. We're even."

I laughed again. "Okay so we've cleared the air. I like you and you like me. But exactly how many other girls do you like right now?" First and foremost on my mind was little Miss Mary Jones.

Without missing his beat, he said, "None as much as I like you."

"For real?"

Nicholas crossed his heart. "For real. What about you? Things really over with 'the ex'?"

"Absolutely," I said.

"For real?"

I nodded. "For real."

Nicholas wrinkled his nose. "You sure?"

"What part of 'for real' did you not understand?" I joked.

Nicholas' lips curled up. "Want another one?" He raised his empty glass.

"Do you?"

"I wouldn't mind another drink but they're kind of pricey here. On the other hand, my apartment is open bar."

Giggling, I said, "Do you admit to being a cheapskate or is this a not-so-smooth way to get me back to your place?"

Nicholas placed his hand on my knee. "It's definitely an extremely smooth way to get you to my place."

As my body officially took over my brain, I felt butterflies in my nether regions. If he was a player, he was really good at it. I placed my hand over his and stood up. "I hope you know how to make a dirty martini."

CHAPTER 13

I HAD NO RECOLLECTION of walking to his apartment on Broome Street from the hotel, but somehow I found myself standing in his living room where after I declined his offer for a drink (I didn't really want another dirty martini), he gently moved me against the wall and kissed me, softly but passionately. I was happy for the support of the wall because I lost all feeling in my legs as the blood moved its way up to the center of my body. As his hand found its way to the slit in my dress, I reached up and grabbed his face with my hands so I could kiss him hungrily while actually touching the roughness of his skin I had found so annoyingly irresistible over the past couple of months. As his lips and tongue met mine in perfect balance, I swooned. The boy could kiss. With his other hand, he gently tugged my shoulder strap so that it fell to my elbow and I grabbed the bottom of his T-shirt and pulled it over his head in one urgent motion. Then I giggled.

"What's so funny?" Nicholas asked, with a wounded look.

I clarified, "Well, I'm all gussied up in a fancy black dress and designer shoes and you're wearing an Elvis Costello T-shirt and jeans. We make an odd couple." Crap. One kiss, albeit a great kiss, hardly made us a "couple."

Seemingly unaffected by the "couple" comment, Nicholas said, "What? My Converse sneakers not fancy enough for you?" Laughing, he added, "No matter, we'll both be naked in a few minutes."

"What makes you think that?" I asked. I tugged my other strap from my shoulder and let the dress shimmy down to my ankles so I was wearing only a bra, panties and my Louboutins. The voice inside my head chastising me for being a slut was almost entirely drowned out by how badly I wanted to be naked and in bed with Nicholas.

Nicholas' eyes slowly grazed the length of my body. "I thought you might have been laughing at my lack of muscles." With a crooked smile, he said, "Am I one of those guys who looks better with his shirt on?"

Despite no bulging biceps or six-pack abs, Nicholas had a flat stomach and lean muscle tone and there was a smattering of hair across his chest, just enough to look manly. He definitely looked better with his shirt *off*. Touched by his insecurity, I reached out to run a finger from his belly button up to his throat. When he shivered in response, I said, "You look perfect to me." And then I second guessed my honesty, wondering if pretending to be insecure about his body was another way he worked his charm. "Of course, I haven't seen what's inside your pants," I said, giggling again.

Closing the distance between us, he said with confidence, "I can assure you it's bigger than what's inside yours!"

Moments later, well more like after 45 minutes of exquisitely torturous foreplay, we were having sex. Usually when I tried to predict what a guy would be like in bed, imagination did not match reality. This was not the case with Nicholas. I imagined he would be spectacular and he was. He wasn't one of those kiss for two minutes, cup my breasts for one and stick it in kind of guys. There was nothing mechanical about his love making skills, and I relished every second he was inside of me until I felt my body contract around him and I cried out. While I remained in a post-orgasmic daze, I was faintly aware of the squeaking of the bed and Nicholas' continued movements until his breathing quickened, his thrusts intensified and he collapsed on top of me. He stayed there unmoving for a beat before lifting his head from my chest.

I opened my eyes and saw him looking down at me with a huge grin on his face. "Wow."

Still breathing heavily, I ran a hand through his hair which was a bit damp from sweat. I echoed, "Wow" and smiled back at him. *What else am I supposed to say?*

When he reached over me to grab something from his desk drawer, I slid out from underneath him. "Please don't tell me you're a smoker."

Flipping onto his back, he said, "Definitely not," and swung a black and silver device in my face.

Peering closer at the small rectangular instrument, I saw that it was a harmonica. "I can't remember the last time I saw one of those."

Nicholas winked at me and said, "You're not the only writer in the house. I dabble in some music."

Snickering, I said, "Oh Jeez. This should be good. Play me something original."

Nicholas closed his eyes for a few seconds and I thought he was going to fall asleep, but then he opened them and sat up. "I'm just gonna wing it. Ready?"

I reached my arms behind my head, held onto his headboard for an extra stretch and yawned. "Ready."

Tickling my armpit, Nicholas said, "You look very sexy right now, by the way."

Squirming from his tickling, I pushed him away. "No stalling!"

"Okay!" He put his mouth to the harmonica, played a few notes and started singing to the tune of the chorus of *Penny Lane* by The Beatles. *"Kimmie Long was in my pants and it felt nice."*

Giving him a lighthearted slap on the arm, I said, "I've heard enough!"

He dropped the harmonica onto the bed and curled his lips into a frown. "Not impressed, huh?"

"That was horrible. And I've realized that my initial impression of you was way off. I thought you were Mr. Cool, not Mr. Dork!" I started laughing.

"Okay. Remind me not to ask you to post a review of my songs on your blog." Nicholas feigned a grieved look but returned the harmonica back to the drawer and leaned back against his pillow. "So, you never did tell me what happened with Writer Chick tonight."

Playfully poking him in the belly, I said, "Besides the fact that she hit on you?"

Looking at me innocently, Nicholas said, "Like I said, I can't help that I'm irresistible."

I rolled my eyes.

Nicholas laughed. "I have no interest in Hannah." Raising an eyebrow, he added, "Just like you have no interest in 'knocking boots' with Jonathan anymore, right?"

I pursed my lips. "Right. I thought we were over that."

"I'll move on if you do."

I gave him a closed-mouth smile and extended my hand. "Deal."

Nicholas returned my smile and gave my hand a firm shake. "Speaking of Ms. Hannah, did she mention her book as suspected?"

"Yeah. She pretended we were lifelong friends and actually insinuated she was doing me a favor by asking me to promote it on my website. And she managed to throw some back handed compliments my way in the process." I shook my head in disgust. "None of it surprised me."

Inching closer to me on the bed, Nicholas questioned, "So what did you say?"

Smiling, I said, "I made her suffer. Wouldn't give her an answer either way. Said I'd see if I could fit her book into my very busy review schedule. And then I walked away."

Nicholas high-fived me. "Yay, Kimmie!"

"Yup."

"So what are you gonna do?"

I lay on my side to face him. "Dunno. What do *you* think I should do?"

Without hesitation, he said, "I think you should read the book."

Not what I wanted to hear. "You do?"

Nicholas turned on his side and faced me. "Yes, I do. Aren't you curious whether it's any good?"

"I suppose," I mumbled. But ignorance was bliss.

Running his hand lightly up and down my arm, he smiled cheerfully and said, "Maybe it sucks and if that's the case, you get to write a crappy review."

I bit my lip. "But what if it's good?"

"You won't know until you read it. Why worry about it now?" Nicholas said, tousling my hair which I assumed was already in a state of disarray from the sex.

"Okay! I'll read it." I let out a long, low sigh. "I'm beat. Can I crash?" I had wanted to fool around with Nicholas some more, but the events of the night had caught up with me and I was too tired.

Nicholas shook his head. "Sorry, but I don't do overnights."

I punched him in the stomach. "It was rhetorical question, buster. If you want me to leave, you'll have to physically remove me from your bed! And I'm not as weak as I appear."

Nicholas gave me a bemused smile. "I will be sure to be mindful of your supernatural strength."

"Good," I giggled. "Night, Nicholas."

When he reached over and turned off his light, I closed my eyes again.

"Someone's gonna have to do the walk of shame in her dress and heels."

I opened my eyes. *Crap.*

*   *   *

I woke up and looked at the ceiling. I knew I wasn't in my bed since it wasn't a popcorn ceiling like the one in my studio. And then the events of the night before came back to me, ending with amazing sex with Nicholas. *Nicholas.* I turned to my side and he was fast asleep, curled up in the fetal position. He looked adorable. I softly ran my fingertips along his cheek.

Nicholas opened one eye and grabbed my finger. "Who goes there?"

"It's Kimmie. Who else were you expecting?" I paused for a beat. "Don't answer that."

Nicholas opened his other eye and drew me on top of him. "Can I have that encore performance now?"

I grabbed onto his shoulders. "May I," I corrected. "And, yes, you may."

*   *   *

Several hours later, after hailing a cab outside of Nicholas' place since there was no way I was taking the subway all the way uptown in my outfit from the night before, I took a long, hot shower, changed into a comfy T-shirt and yoga pants and called Bridget. My heart was beating wildly because of the way we had left things the night before.

"Hey!" she answered cheerily.

Relieved she didn't sound angry, I said, "Hi! How you feeling?" I cradled the phone with my neck while I opened my refrigerator. I was starving, not surprising after two rounds of sex on a pretty empty stomach.

"Like the cat's ass. What was I thinking last night?"

I grabbed a container of leftover Chinese food from earlier in the week and took a whiff to make sure it wasn't spoiled before heating it in the microwave. "Which part? Doing repeated rounds of shots on a practically empty stomach or mixing said shots with pot?"

"All of it," she mumbled. "Why didn't you stop me?"

"I tried!" *Repeatedly.*

"Ugh. So, how was the rest of your night? What time did you get home?"

"A couple of hours ago," I said as if it was no big deal.

After a brief hesitation, Bridget said, "Oh? What happened?"

Unable to contain my excitement any longer, I shouted, "I went home with Nicholas!"

"Way to go, Kimmie! But I thought you said he was flirting with Hannah."

Shaking my head as if she could see me, I said, "No. He wasn't flirting with her. But she did almost ruin everything by blurting out that Jonathan and I used to date. It was so awkward." I bit down on my lip. Now that I knew Bridget liked Jonathan, I wondered if it would be awkward every time I mentioned his name. "But I told Nicholas we were just friends now and he dropped it."

"Good. So, what happened?"

I removed the container of chicken and broccoli from the microwave, grabbed a fork and sat down on my couch. "I was seriously slutty, Bridge. But I couldn't help myself."

She giggled. "Was it as good as you imagined?"

"Yeah, it was. Both times." I took a tiny bite of broccoli, realized it was entirely too hot and placed the container on my coffee table to cool down.

"What happened with Jonathan?"

"He went home. After I introduced him to Nicholas. More awkwardness ensued."

Bridget let out a weak laugh.

"Bridge?" I said as I chewed on a fingernail.

"Yeah?"

"Are you going to be a born-again virgin for the rest of your life?"

"No!"

"Just checking." I paused. "Bridge?"

"Yeah?"

"Do you like Jonathan?"

Silence.

"You can tell me. I won't be mad! There was some serious flirting at your place last night and it didn't involve me. That's all I'm sayin'." I picked up the container of food for a second attempt and cautiously took another miniscule bite. Satisfied that it was sufficiently cooled down, I dared an even bigger piece.

"Aargh!"

I swallowed the nugget of chicken in my mouth. "What?"

"This is so embarrassing. And awkward. Aarrgh! Let's not do this now, okay? I need to take another nap."

"Okay." At least she was admitting there was something to talk about.

"So, are you and Nicholas dating now?"

"When I left his place he gave me a hug and said, 'See you tomorrow, Kimmie' not 'Want to go to the movies this week?' I don't even know if Nicholas dates. He probably doesn't have to if girls like me make it so easy for him to get laid." Even as the words left my mouth, I was positive if I had a chance to go back in time, I would have slept with him all over again. I might have been a slut but I wasn't delusional.

"You really like him though?"

I would have been more comfortable with the question if I could truthfully answer that I only liked him because he was hot and the sex was fantastic. I'd never lied to Bridget before and I wasn't about to start now, so with a mixture of excitement and dread, I confessed, "Yeah, I really like him." His dorky harmonica performance, the boxer shorts emblazoned with designs of record albums I had spied on the top of his laundry hamper, and even the collection of old MAD magazines he'd collected since he was a little boy made him real to me. The "real" Nicholas was even hotter, if that was even possible, than the Nicholas I had imagined in my head. I repeated, "Yeah, I like him, Bridge. God help me, but I like him."

After we hung up, I finished my chicken and broccoli and logged onto *Pastel is the New Black*. When I saw how many books I had listed as "reviews coming soon," I snuggled into my favorite reclining chair with my Kindle. Then I remembered the decision I had made the night before, closed my Kindle and emailed Candy at Novel Inc. PR. Before I changed my mind again, I told her to send me Hannah's book. I crossed my fingers that *Cut on the Bias* would suck so that I could write a shitty review that was based on fact and not my own personal feelings for the author. But I wasn't holding my breath.

CHAPTER 14

THE NEXT MORNING, I sat at my desk drinking from my second cup of coffee of the day. I hadn't slept very well the night before. Part of me was still basking in the afterglow of having sex with Nicholas. The other part of me was afraid it was the beginning of the end. Maybe Nicholas had been curious about me and now that his curiosity was satisfied, he would move on to someone else. He also knew that I wasn't necessarily opposed to having a fuck buddy since Hannah had so kindly blurted out my relationship with Jonathan. Maybe that was all he thought I wanted. Or worse, maybe that was all *he* wanted. We hadn't talked since I left his apartment the previous morning and he hadn't come by Rob's office yet. I wanted to get our first post-hook-up communication over with but there was no way I was going to him first.

My phone alerted a text message from Caroline. I had texted her the night before to tell her what had gone down. "I told you he liked you! We have to get drinks soon so you can give me the details!" I was about to text her back when my office phone rang. The caller ID told me it was Erin. I reluctantly picked up the phone, "Hey."

"Hey. How was the reunion?" Before I had a chance to respond, she kept talking. "I saw pictures on Facebook. You weren't in any of them."

"Whose pictures were they?" I knew the answer before I asked.

"Hannah's, of course. Her dress was stunning!"

I rolled my eyes. Bridget's dress was much nicer and so was mine! "I would hope her dress would be nice considering she works in fashion."

"Work*ed* in fashion. She's a writer now."

I sighed heavily before responding. "Her book hasn't even been released yet. I seriously doubt she's quitting her day job anytime soon."

"Soon enough, I'm sure. Did you talk to her?"

"Talk to who?"

Sounding annoyed, Erin said, "Hannah! She said she talked to you."

It was way too early for this conversation I thought, as I took a gulp of my now lukewarm coffee. "If you knew we talked, why are you asking me?" I lay my head on my desk.

"I wanted to get your side of the story."

I lifted my head. "Side of the story? What story?"

"She said you agreed to read her book."

"She did, did she?" What a presumptuous bitch! "I never actually said that but, yes, I will be reading her book." Was it too late to recall my message to Candace?

"Awesome!"

"Yay!" I said sarcastically, reaching for my coffee again.

"So, who's Nicholas?"

Almost spilling my coffee across the desk, I said, "Wha...What? Why?"

"Hannah said she met this cute guy and that he was a friend of yours."

Why wasn't I surprised that Hannah referred to Nicholas as my "friend" as if she couldn't believe he'd actually be interested in me? "What else did she say about Nicholas?"

"Did I hear my name?"

I looked up from my phone and felt my get face got hot as I made eye contact with Nicholas. "I'll talk to you later, Erin." I hung up before she could say anything else. "Hi there," I said with a casual smile.

Smiling back, he said, "Hi. Did I hear my name?"

I quickly debated making up a lie but decided it wasn't worth it. "Apparently, Hannah asked my sister about you."

"Really? What did she want to know?" Nicholas asked, his eyes twinkling in amusement.

Scowling at him, I said, "I didn't get that far, but I can connect you two on Facebook if you're interested."

Nicholas' close-lipped smile trembled slightly. "Here," he said, handing me a light pink silk-screened journal. "I bought it for you."

I held up the journal and looked at Nicholas. "What's this for?"

Giving me a devilish grin, he said, "Consider it payment for services rendered."

Feeling myself flush, I said, "I'm not a prostitute, Nicholas!" I knew being a slut would work against me. Why couldn't I have stopped at kissing?

Laughing, Nicholas put two fingers to his lips. "Shh. I went to dinner with my sister last night and she dragged me to some stationary store that was having a major sale. I saw it and thought of you."

When Rob called out "Nicholas!" he said, "Gotta go," and walked away, waving behind him.

I stared at the journal gobsmacked. Why would Nicholas give me a journal? On the one hand, it was kind of sweet, not to mention surprising, that he bought me anything, but a journal? If he bought me flowers or chocolate, I would take it to mean he was interested in me and would be half giddy and half creeped out that he liked me a bit too much too soon. *Not that I would ever refuse chocolate, of course.* But a journal was neither an obvious sign of romantic interest nor creepy. Unless he wrote in it first. If he wrote a love letter or something otherwise cheesy, I'd die. I quickly opened the journal and flipped through the pages. I let out a sigh of relief when I saw it was completely blank. I scratched my forehead. What did this mean? Did it mean *anything*? It was times like this I wished I had a brother instead of a sister. I'd actually wished Erin was a boy more times than I could count, but that was neither here nor there.

When Rob's phone rang twice without him answering, I picked it up. "Rob Forrester's office." I was in the process of taking a message since the guy didn't want to go into voicemail when Nicholas walked out of Rob's office. He winked and I gave him a closed-mouth smile in response. I hadn't had a chance to thank him for the journal and so after I hung up and handed Rob the message, I grabbed the journal from my desk and walked to his office.

"Knock, knock," I said.

Looking up from typing furiously on his computer, Nicholas smiled. "Who's there?"

"Thanks."

"Thanks who?"

"No, thanks *you!*" I said giggling. Sometimes I impressed myself with my quick wit.

Nicholas smiled softly. "Nice one."

"Actually, I'm here to thank you for the journal. Very thoughtful of you. I could probably use it to take notes while reading for my blog."

"Or you can document our X-rated activities," he said, lifting and lowering his eyebrows.

"Will we be partaking in more X-rated activities?"

"I certainly hope so."

I took it upon myself to sit down on his guest chair. "Listen, Nicholas."

Nicholas placed his elbows on his desk and looked at me intently. "I'm all ears."

I took a deep breath in and out hoping to slow my pulse. "I had a lot of fun with you on Saturday night."

"And Sunday morning," Nicholas interrupted.

"And Sunday morning." My face contorted into a small smile against my will. "But you should know I'm not looking for a fuck buddy or friends with benefits situation." Something I probably should have mentioned *before* I spread my legs.

Nicholas nodded and rubbed his chin. I rolled my eyes and he grinned. "Good. Because I hate when chicks use me for sex. It's so humiliating."

I had a feeling this conversation was going nowhere fast and so I stood up. Waving the journal at him, I said, "Thanks again."

"You're very welcome. And Kimmie?"

I had one foot out of his office but turned around. "Yeah?"

"I hope the journal inspires you to write great things."

My stomach lurching, I said, "I'll do my best."

Nicholas leaned back in his chair with his feet against his desk. "Good girl."

I returned to my desk, logged onto Facebook and immediately wished I hadn't.

> *Hi Kim,*
> *So great to see you at the reunion. I wish I had more time to talk to you about "Cut on the Bias" though. As you've no doubt*

heard, it takes place in Paris. You've probably never been there but it's the most romantic city in the world and the perfect setting for a novel. I wanted to make sure you were on the short list of reviewers because I'm positive it will make your 2013 favorites list. You can thank me later.

Salut à bientôt.

Hannah

PS: Nice touch with the Louboutins. They actually gave you a little height ☺.

After checking a French to English translation site, I shook my head in repulsion. Why couldn't she just say "*Au Revoir*" or better yet "*Bye*" like a normal person?

* * *

I had a pit in my stomach that lasted the entire afternoon and into the evening. I tried to work on blog maintenance but each time I tweeted a new review, I thought about having to do that for Hannah at some point. The thought of helping Hannah promote her book on any level made my skin run cold, especially since I wasn't paid for my services. Although, receiving compensation for reviewing her book would only be mildly less nausea inducing. I thought about what Nicholas had said while we were in bed. "*Maybe it sucks. And if that's the case, you get to write a crappy review.*" It was easy for him to be so calm. He didn't have to help the mean girl from his high school with her burgeoning writing career. I should ask him how he would feel representing a bully who repeatedly stole his lunch at recess in the 3rd grade.

Suddenly, I was no longer thinking about Hannah. I was thinking about being in bed with Nicholas. Had I shot myself in the foot by telling him I didn't want to be his fuck buddy? I *really* wanted to sleep with him again! Now that I made my feelings clear, he would either continue to pursue me or cut his losses. And if it was the latter, I couldn't retract my statement and bed him anyway. He'd lose all respect for me and I'd lose all respect for myself. I was screwed. Or rather, time would tell if I'd be screwed. I removed the journal he bought me from my coffee table and ran my hands up and down the silk bound cover waiting for inspiration to hit. I wondered how long it would take Hannah to fill the journal with notes for her next novel.

And just like that, I was back to thinking about Hannah. I looked up towards my ceiling, threw my hands in the air and exclaimed, "Oy vey!"

CHAPTER 15

I EYED THE LAST BITE of my rib eye steak sandwich. I was seriously tempted to clean my plate, but already felt the need to pull my gray pencil skirt down past my hips so I could breathe again.

"Just do it, Kim," David said.

I looked over at him and he smiled. "You know you want to finish it."

I rubbed my belly. "I do. But I'm so full!" I glanced at Rob's plate. He left half a tuna steak uneaten. "Seriously, Rob. You're making the rest of us look like pigs!"

Rob tossed his napkin on the plate. "I've lost ten pounds over the past six months. Don't want to gain it back over the course of one lunch."

Rob had always been fit, but ever since he married his second and significantly younger wife, he had become obsessed. Considering his lunches usually consisted of yogurt, an apple and maybe half a turkey sandwich, I was happy he hadn't ordered the Farmers Market Salad with balsamic vinegar. "Well, as long as you saved some room for dessert."

"I always save room for dessert," Rob said assuredly.

"No sorbet either!" Standing up, I said, "Excuse me. I need to use the ladies' room." At both firms where I had worked with Rob, whenever our group took someone in the department out for his or her birthday, one of us (usually me) had to slickly tell the waiter. And then the birthday boy or girl had to pretend to be surprised when the waiter brought over a piece of birthday cake and we all started singing "Happy Birthday."

After I tracked down our waiter, I went to the bathroom, ran a brush through my hair and reapplied my lip gloss. When I returned to the table, all of the plates had been removed.

Rob cleared his throat. "Now that my right hand is back, I'd like to make an announcement."

Another one of Rob's famous announcements. I chuckled and glanced at David. He gave me a knowing look and flashed me a wide grin. I covered my mouth with my hand in an effort not to laugh.

"What's so funny, Long?" Rob asked accusingly.

I bit my lip and looked at Rob with wide eyes. "Absolutely nothing. Unless you're gonna tell us about the time the electricity went out during your trial and even the backup generators didn't work. And how the lights went back on just as someone from the other side was about to abscond with your exhibits, and your junior associate was held in contempt of court for wrestling him to the ground. That's a funny story." I paused dramatically. "No matter how many times you tell it."

Rob calmly nodded at me with his lips pursed. "Okay then. Well, I was *going* to thank my lovely assistant for organizing a wonderful 29th birthday lunch for me. But since my assistant isn't lovely and it's my 54th birthday, I think I'll skip the thank you and announce that I've hired a lateral associate who will be starting next week."

I jerked my head back in surprise. I was generally kept in the loop on these things, especially since I was usually responsible for scheduling interviews, yet this was the first I'd heard of a new hire. "What's his name?"

"*Her* name is Daneen. She's a third year coming to us from Cravath. Solid background in trademark litigation. She'll be working closely with Nicholas on the Soap case."

I looked over at Nicholas to see his reaction to this new information but he was nodding at Rob and didn't look at all surprised. Then he looked my way and winked.

When our eyes locked, I felt my body flood with warmth and forced myself to look away. I still had no idea what the previous weekend had meant to him and I was trying to pretend I didn't care either way. *Even though I did. Of course.* I turned to David. "How are the wedding plans coming along?"

His cheeks glowing, David said, "Amy is already looking into venues. I wanted us to enjoy being engaged for a while before getting too caught up in wedding plans, but she's so excited that I'm just letting her run with it."

"That's so cool! We should get drinks or something to celebrate one night." Although I was genuinely happy for David and his upcoming nuptials, I couldn't shake off a feeling of discomfort about Rob hiring Daneen without even telling me. In all of the years we'd worked together, Rob had made me feel like an important member of his team, telling me all the big news before almost anyone else, but suddenly I felt like an outsider, a measly secretary.

Rob had moved across the table to sit next to Nicholas. Their heads were bent towards each other and they were talking in hushed voices until the waiter brought over our coffees and cappuccinos. After we sang, "Happy Birthday," Rob returned to his own seat and I whispered, "How come this is the first I've heard about Daneen?"

Rob widened his eyes. "I didn't tell you?"

I shook my head and frowned. I was surprised and embarrassed by how upset I was about this. I pushed the remains of my chocolate cake around my plate.

"I'm sorry, Kim. We didn't go through regular channels with this one. In fact, we weren't even looking for anyone but she's a major coup. Comes highly recommended with trial experience beyond her three years." Looking genuinely apologetic, he said, "Didn't mean to keep it from you."

"Well, that's great then." Trying to shrug off the insecurity that had caught me off guard, I enthusiastically added, "Congrats!"

"Thanks, Long. It's good for the squad. And stealing an associate from Cravath is certainly an added benefit." He gave me a cocky smile.

"Who's her secretary?" So far, Rob had avoided sharing me with anyone else but I was the only secretary at the firm with only one assignment and I knew it wouldn't last forever.

"We're still working out the details." Rob looked at his watch. "Time to get back. Time is money, folks!"

The best part of "taking" Rob out for his birthday was that he expensed it and after he signed the bill, he put his credit card back in his wallet and stood up.

Everyone quickly followed suit and began gathering up their things to head back to work.

As we waited to cross Park Avenue to our building across the street, Nicholas came up behind me. "Nice job on the lunch, Kim."

I turned to face him with a knowing grin. "Thanks! I'm the preeminent reservation maker."

Nicholas winked. "And don't you forget it! What are you doing tonight?"

"Don't know yet. Laundry?"

When the light changed to green, we walked side by side to the opposite side of the street. I was dying to know why Nicholas asked about my plans for the evening. In hindsight, I could have said something much cooler in response than "doing laundry", but at least it was honest. We stopped walking when we reached the sidewalk and trailed behind the others who went directly inside the building.

"Well, I don't know if I could top laundry, but if you have enough underwear to last an extra day, want to get a bite after work?"

I narrowed my eyes at him and joked, "Is 'bite' a euphemism for something?"

Nicholas gave me a lazy smile. "No, it's not."

"Well then count me in. Assuming I ever get my appetite back."

"Excellent." He held the door open for me and as I walked through it ahead of him, I tried to wipe the giant smile off of my face.

* * *

As I sat next to Nicholas at the bar at the South Pacific themed The Hurricane Club later that evening, I felt overdressed. Not only because I was wearing a buttoned up long sleeve white silk blouse in the presence of scantily clad, cleavage-bearing women, but because I was overheating. The upscale bar was crowded and so our stools were right on top of each other, and I hoped I wouldn't break out in a sweat simply from being in such close quarters with him. The last time we had been so close was in his bed. I pushed a hair behind my ear and angled my body toward him.

Nicholas pointed at the plate of fish tacos. "Do you want the last one?" As with all trendy restaurants in New York City, appetizers and small plates always came in odd numbers.

"You can have it. I'm still digesting my steak sandwich from lunch."

Nicholas smiled and shoved the taco in his mouth in one bite.

Laughing, I said, "What would you have done if I wanted the last one?"

"I would have let you have it, of course."

I nodded. "Good to know."

"And then I would have ordered another plate." When Nicholas looked down at an incoming message on his phone, I took the opportunity to unbutton my top button. I'd have dressed less corporate and more sexy had I known we'd be going out after work, especially to a restaurant packed with fabulous looking women.

"Sorry about that," Nicholas said pushing his phone away. "The Soap case is killing me." Squinting his eyes, Nicholas said, "Did you do something different?"

I took a sip of rum from my hollowed out coconut. "What do you mean?"

"You look different."

Shrugging, I took another sip.

"I got it."

"You got what?"

"You unbuttoned your blouse, didn't you?"

My face burning, I said, "Oh, that. Yeah, it's hot in here. Right?"

Nicholas shook his head at me and smiled. "*Riiight.*"

"Knock it off!" I laughed, knowing I was busted.

"I love how the girl who doesn't want a strictly sexual relationship is undressing in the bar."

"I'm not undressing!" I whipped my head around hoping no one was listening to our conversation. "I just feel a bit overdressed in here compared to some of the other girls."

"What other girls?"

I cocked my head to the side. "*Please.*"

Nicholas laughed. Then his phone went off and I watched his brow furrow as he read the text and typed a response.

Looking up at me, he frowned and said, "Kim, I'm sorry, but I'm gonna have to go back to the office after these drinks."

I felt my stomach drop in disappointment but adopted a poker face. "No worries. Glamorous life of an associate, right?"

Nicholas ran a hand through his hair and shook his head. "We're so understaffed for this case, Kimmie. I'm doing junior associate work because there's no one else available."

"That new attorney is starting next week though, right?"

His face brightening, Nicholas said, "Yeah, Daneen. Thank God. Should take a load off my back."

"Have you met her?" I still felt a lump in my throat about being the last to know about her.

"Yeah. Rob wanted me involved in the interview process since we'll be working so closely." Giving me a wry smile, he said, "Although I have a feeling he would have hired her regardless of what I thought."

"What do you think of her?" *Is she pretty? Nice body?*

Nicholas took a final swig of his drink. "She seems nice." Shrugging he said, "She's supposedly a good lawyer. That's really all I care about."

I had a feeling that meant she wasn't pretty and she didn't have a nice body and I felt a rush of relief flow through my body. "Good then. Rob said she's highly recommended." I removed my coconut from the bar and took one last sip before putting it down and looking back at Nicholas. "I'm ready when you are."

Eyeing my cup, he said, "We can stay until you're finished. No reason you should be cheated out of a full drink."

"No worries. I'm finished."

Nicholas motioned for the bartender and asked him to close out our tab. After he signed the bill, we got up and silently walked out of the bar. When we got outside, we stood on the sidewalk before parting ways since I would be taking the subway in one direction and he needed to walk in the other to get back to the office.

Fiddling with my necklace, I said, "Thanks for the drink and apps."

Nicholas smiled and took a step closer to me. "My pleasure. I'm sorry it got cut short. I promise to make it up to you."

"No worries." I consciously forced myself to stop tapping my heel on the sidewalk as I realized I had now uttered the phrase "no worries" three times that night. I assumed he probably picked up on it too. I felt incredibly awkward standing there wondering if I was supposed to just say, "Bye" and leave like this was nothing more than a drink between colleagues or if I was supposed to wait for him to kiss me like this was the end of a date.

As if reading my mind, Nicholas leaned down and lightly brushed his lips against mine.

Before I had a chance to react, he had stepped back. "See you bright and early tomorrow." With a crooked smile, he added, "Although depending on how late I work tonight, I might not feel too bright and it won't be that early."

Still tasting his lips on mine, I smiled back. "Don't work too hard."

With a final wave, I turned and walked away. And I wondered when and if he'd really make it up to me.

CHAPTER 16

IT TURNED OUT I didn't have to wait long for Nicholas to make things up to me. Although the only time I saw him the day after our half-assed date was when I brought his and Rob's lunch order from Seamless Web into the conference room and he smiled at me from behind very tired looking eyes, he came by my desk as I was getting my stuff together to leave for the weekend. When he asked if I was around on Saturday night, I quickly dismissed the option of playing "The Rules" and told him I was free.

We planned to meet at Uva, an Italian restaurant near my apartment, for dinner at 8, and so at 8:05, wearing dark blue skinny jeans, a green one shoulder rayon top that gathered on the side, and knee-high black boots, I walked through the front door, opened the red velvet curtain and peered to the bar on my right hoping Nicholas had arrived before me. The lighting was dark and romantic and the place was packed with couples but I didn't see Nicholas. I was contemplating pushing my way to the bar to order a glass of wine when I felt a tap on my shoulder. Before I had a chance to turn around, a breath of warm air caressed the back of my neck.

"You beat me," Nicholas whispered.

When I turned around, he was looking down at me with his warm brown eyes. I joked, "I tried to be fashionably late but I guess you're more fashionable than me."

When he moved to the side to let two girls walk in front of us, we were pushed closer together and I felt my arm brush against the hair on his. "Go easy. Isn't this your neighborhood? I had to commute all the way from the village," he said.

"All the way, huh? Wow, I'm flattered," I said with a giggle.

"I had to take the local!"

"Well, I'm honored you deem me worthy of the long trek uptown," I swatted him playfully on the arm.

Nicholas winked. "Absolutely." Glancing at the bar, he leaned in towards my ear and murmured, "Our reservation isn't until 9. I thought we'd get a drink first. Is that cool?"

His low but soft voice always made me feel like he was confiding a secret and my knees wobbled. "It's cool," I said.

Nicholas grabbed my hand and led me to the bar where two spots had conveniently opened up.

A few minutes later, we sat side by side, each with a glass of Montepulciano in front of us. I angled my body toward his. "So besides writing diddies like 'Kimmie Long was in my pants', tell me more about your love of music."

His face turning red, Nicholas started laughing.

"What's so funny?"

Still laughing, Nicholas covered his mouth with one hand and held two fingers of his other hand up to me.

"What the…" I started laughing along with him even though I wasn't in on the joke.

Finally, Nicholas stopped laughing and wiped a tear from his eye. "I'm sorry about that." He started laughing again.

"C'mon!"

"Okay. It's really stupid." Nicholas clamped his lips together.

"What's really stupid?" I took a sip of my wine.

"Diddies," he said without embellishment.

"What about them?"

His lips trembling again, he said, "I assume you mean 'ditties', as in the plural of 'ditty' or short song. But it sounded like you said diddies, which is different."

I rolled my eyes. "Thanks for the grammar lesson, counselor."

Nicholas scooted closer to me and gently moved a hair away from my face. Smiling softly, he said, "I'm sorry. It's just that 'diddies' is slang for titties and, well, hearing it come out of your mouth made me…" he started cracking up again.

I threw me head back and laughed out loud. "*That's* why you broke out in uncontrollable laughter? Because you thought I said 'titties'?" Shaking my head at him in disbelief, I said, "How old are you?"

Nodding, he said, "I know. I'm totally embarrassed that I lost it." He started laughing again.

"I can see that!" We laughed together for a second until we both stopped at the same time and smiled at each other, neither of us saying anything.

Breaking the silence, Nicholas raised his shoulders in a shrug. "I've always loved music. Started listening to punk and new wave as a baby and saw my first concert as a toddler – The B-52s."

I pictured a young Nicholas clapping his hands and dancing along to the music. "So even as a young'un, you enjoyed diddies, huh?" I flashed him a devilish grin.

Nicholas winked. "Yeah. And I thought music was pretty cool too."

About two hours later, we finished our Moscata while Nicholas paid the check. We had shared artichoke salad and ricotta cheese and black truffle honey bruschetta to start and then I had eaten almost an entire plate of gnocchi. If anyone besides Nicholas had been my dining partner, I would probably have been in a food coma, but he kept me alert and on my toes. Enjoying the brisk air that met us when we left the restaurant, I led Nicholas in the direction of my apartment. When we stood in front of the entrance, I said, "This is me."

Nicholas looked up at the white seven-story building and back at me. "Seems like a nice place to live."

I nodded. "It is."

We stood facing each other in silence until Nicholas gave me a sheepish grin. "I feel like we did this sort of backwards."

I tilted my head to the side. "How's that?"

Nicholas rubbed his lips. "Isn't it supposed to be first comes date, then comes sex? We had sex before the date."

"I think the correct words to that *ditty* are 'first comes love then comes marriage.' But lots of people get that order wrong too."

Nicholas smiled and before I knew what was happening, he drew me to him and kissed me with force, one hand grabbing my hair. When he released me a few moments later, I stared at him, breathless. "What was that for?" *Not that I'm complaining.*

"I don't know. I couldn't help myself." He gave me another sheepish grin.

"Good answer. So…" I motioned toward my front door as my nerve endings stirred. "You coming in or not?"

Nicholas raised his eyebrows. "I'm right behind you."

CHAPTER 17

ROB HAD BEATEN ME TO WORK for a change and was behind closed doors when I arrived on Monday and so I printed out his emails and posted some updates on my blog while I waited for him to come out. I was still riding the high from my night with Nicholas and while I completed my morning tasks, I replayed the events of the date in my mind, from the glass of wine at the bar, to sitting across from each other at our cozy table in the corner where we talked about everything from my favorite books to his favorite music. And last but certainly not least were the hours spent rolling around in my bed after dinner and the next morning where we collaborated on his *Penny Lane* remix. Then he showered at my place before heading into work on Sunday.

At about 10:30, Rob's office door finally opened and I heard a female laughing before Rob walked out with a tall, pretty girl who looked to be about my age with straight auburn hair that fell past her shoulders.

Rob smiled and approached my desk. "And this is Kimberly, my loyal assistant. Kimberly, meet Daneen, the newest member of the squad."

I smiled into her amber eyes. "Hi there. Welcome to the group!"

She gave me a tight smile, her upper lip disappearing into her gums. "Nice to meet you."

"Kim was my assistant at T & F before I came here," Rob said.

"Feels like forever," I joked.

Looking at Rob, Daneen said, "I'm sure."

Giving me a crisp nod, Rob said, "Well, Kim's invaluable. No one else can multi-task like her."

I knew he was making a jab about my blog and shook my head at him. "Rob's a great boss. You'll see."

Daneen glanced at me dismissively and turned back to Rob. "Should we go find Nicholas?"

Rob nodded. "Yeah. He should be here by now. Kim, can you make a reservation for five at A Voce? 12:30?"

"Sure," I said, reaching for the Zagat guide on my desk.

"Thanks. We'll be in Nicholas' office," Rob said.

"Okay. See you guys later," I said.

With a toss of her hair, Daneen said, "Thanks" before walking away with Rob.

After I made the reservation at A Voce, I chewed on my pen, accessing my initial impression of Daneen. I had a sour taste in my mouth I couldn't swallow down. I scratched my head and let out a deep exhale. I didn't like her.

After I finished printing and filing Rob's emails, I went to make copies of some letters. When I got back to my desk, there were sounds coming from Rob's office, most notably an irritating female laugh. Imitating it, I muttered, "*ahahahahaha*" and snorted. And then I heard the muffled sounds of Nicholas' deep voice. I stood up and walked to Rob's door. "Sorry to interrupt."

"No worries," Rob said.

"You're all set for A Voce at 12:30." I could have called Rob with the information, but I was dying to see Nicholas. I looked over at him and smiled. He smiled back and gave me a slight wave.

"Great," Rob said. "Can you email Lucy and David and tell them to meet Nicholas, Daneen and me outside my office at about 12:25?"

I tore my eyes from Nicholas and caught Daneen watching our exchange with intense concentration. I met her eyes and she quickly flashed me a smile. "No problem," I said. As I walked back to my desk, I gave an extra shake of my hips since I knew Nicholas was watching.

I emailed David and Lucy and then switched my focus from work to my blog.

"Terminally Single" by Emily Anderson
*Twenty-nine-year-old Tamara Woodland hasn't had a boyfriend since senior year of college and does not predict a wedding in her foreseeable future. Correction: she doesn't see a **marriage** in her future. Although Tamara's love life leaves*

much to be desired, she has been a bridesmaid six times in the past two years. When her closest friend's boyfriend asks Tamara to help him choose an engagement ring, she's positive she'll be a lady-in-waiting again very soon.

I stopped typing and looked up from my computer for at least the tenth time since I started writing the review. I concentrated on the sounds coming from Rob's office, trying to hear what Rob, Nicholas and Daneen were talking about. From what I could make out, it seemed to be work-related, but then Nicholas or Rob would say something and Daneen would cackle in response. I gave up drafting the review and was trying to distract myself with thoughts of what I would eat for lunch when David and Lucy came by.

"You coming to lunch with us?" David asked.

Rob hadn't said anything to me about joining them but since almost everyone else in the group was going, I momentarily thought maybe I was invited and Rob assumed I was a mind reader. It wouldn't be the first time. But then I remembered that the reservation was for five people and I would make six. I shook my head. "I guess not."

"Too bad," Lucy said. "I love when you and Rob bicker."

"Kim and I bicker? Never!" Rob said with a laugh as he walked out of his office with Nicholas and Daneen. Looking from David to Lucy, he said, "You guys ready?"

In unison, they said, "Ready."

"Alright then, let's go." Turning to me, he said, "If anyone calls, tell them I'll be back in about an hour."

"Oh, should I bring my legal pad?" Lucy asked.

"Not necessary," Daneen said. "This is actually a fun lunch for me to meet the crew, although I have a feeling this will be my only non-working lunch for the next several months." Daneen smiled sweetly at Lucy and I watched her upper lip disappear into her gums again.

I would have understood being left behind if they planned to discuss a case or something, but at the realization that I wasn't considered part of "the crew" for the purposes of a friendly lunch, I felt like a door had been slammed in my face. I forced out a smile. "Have fun guys."

As they walked out, I felt Nicholas' eyes on me. I reluctantly met his glance and gave him a closed-mouth smile before turning back to my keyboard. I was afraid to make prolonged eye contact at the risk of tearing up.

Squeezing my shoulder on his way out, he whispered, "Talk to you later."

I nodded and absently tapped my keyboard until "the crew" had left the vicinity.

*   *   *

Thanks to a really good book I was reading, written entirely in emails, I felt better about being left out of lunch. I was sure Rob hadn't intentionally left me out and I knew the topic of conversation at the restaurant was probably work, work and more work, a topic I found endlessly boring. The only upside to attending a work event was to stare at Nicholas, but since office functions were no longer my only outlet for that, I was more than happy to be left out of department lunches, working or not. This change of heart, however, did not affect my impression of Daneen. I still didn't like her. I wondered what Nicholas really thought of her but didn't want to come out and ask, especially since his ability to delegate a big portion of his work to her gave him the freedom to leave work early enough to take me out to dinner later that week.

After sushi at Haru, we went back to my apartment, had mind-blowing sex and then like an old married couple, he caught up on the hundreds of work emails he'd received in the last two hours while I checked my personal email. My inbox was full of messages from authors and publicists, including Candace Adams. I had almost forgotten about my agreement to review Hannah's book and wondered if maybe Candace was writing on behalf of a different client. I bit my nails and opened the email which, of course, was about *Cut on the Bias*. Candace had sent me an ARC of the manuscript and wanted to confirm I had received it. I moved my laptop to the side, got out of bed and walked to my kitchen table where I had dropped the package I had received in the mail that day but was too busy kissing Nicholas to open. Inside was a book with a mannequin draped in silk on a pale blue cover and the words "Cut on the Bias, a novel by Hannah Marshak." With the book in my hand, I walked back to my bed, sat on the edge and stared at it.

From behind me, I felt Nicholas' breath in my ear as he said, "What's the matter, Kimmie?"

I sighed loudly, turned around and lifting and raising the book, said, "The bitch's book."

Grabbing it from me, Nicholas opened it to the first page and I watched his eyes move across the page. "It sucks."

I laughed. "You're basing that on the ten or so words you've read?"

Nicholas put the book down, stood up and pushed me down on the bed, sliding me farther towards the headboard. Propped on his elbows, he hovered over me and said, "No, I'm basing it on the fact that you want it to suck and I want you to get what you want."

I recalled his hand on Mary's lower back in the elevator and the waitress who came on too strong. He could have anyone he wanted and I couldn't help but wonder what exactly he wanted from me. "Who are you?" I asked, tracing my fingers through his hair.

Nicholas reached for my hand and held it in his. Laughing, he said, "That's a pretty leading question. Who are *you*?"

I bit the inside of my cheek and shrugged. "I can't figure you out, that's all."

Nicholas didn't respond. He just released my hand and flipped over on his back. I hovered over him and with my head buried in the crook of his neck mumbled, "Hellooo?"

Behind closed eyes, Nicholas asked, "What's there to figure out?"

I lifted my head and looked into his now opened eyes. How could I possibly ask if he was serious about me or just killing time? I wasn't even comfortable asking how many other girls he was sleeping with and *that*, I had a right to know.

Nicholas ran his fingers gently up and down my arm, the heat of his hands warming my skin. "Now it's my turn to say 'hello.'" Knocking lightly on my head, he said, "Anyone in there?"

"I'm here," I said meekly.

Pulling me on top of him, he said, "Okay Missie, I think we've officially concluded the talking part of this meeting."

Remembering Hannah's perfectly manicured nails grazing Nicholas' arm at the reunion, I tossed Hannah's book on the floor. I didn't want Nicholas' bodily fluids anywhere near Hannah Marshak or her stupid book.

* * *

Later that night, as Nicholas slept silently beside me, I reached over and removed *Cut on the Bias* from the floor by his side of the bed. I figured if I read the first paragraph and was unimpressed, I would sleep a lot easier. After I read the first page, I skimmed to the chapter break. Since chapter one was only six pages, I read it in its entirety.

Nicholas lied. It didn't suck.

CHAPTER 18

I SAT NEXT TO BRIDGET on her purple couch drinking Skinny Girl Margaritas and watching a marathon of *The Real Housewives of Orange Country*. It wasn't our favorite, but there were currently no new episodes of *The Real Housewives of New York* and at least the OC was better than Beverly Hills.

I got up during a commercial to use the bathroom and when I returned to the couch, Bridget was wearing feety pajamas and had her legs stretched out on her coffee table.

Eyeing her pig-printed one-piece jumper, I laughed. "I see you've made yourself comfortable."

Bridget wiggled a fuzzy pink foot at me. "Don't you love them?"

"They're adorbs. So long as you only bring them out for special houseguests, like me, and keep them away from those with male genitalia."

Bridget stretched her arms above her head and yawned, not bothering to cover her mouth. "Speaking of male genitalia, how's Nicholas Strong-rhymes-with-Long?"

"He's good." I hesitated before adding, "Although he works all of the time."

"He's an attorney. You've worked with them before and should know they have crazy hours. I even seem to recall you telling me you never wanted to date a lawyer."

Sitting down next to her on the couch, I said, "That was before I started at this firm and fell in lust with Nicholas."

Bridget smiled. "Then you have to take the good with the bad. But things are good when you're together?"

"Definitely. We have great sex and interesting conversations." I ran a hand through my hair. "But we definitely do more of the former than the latter."

Bridget removed her feet from the table and bent her body toward mine. "(a) You're in the honeymoon stage when sex should take precedence and (b) you have limited time together because he works all of the time, so sex should take precedence. I wouldn't be too concerned."

I knew Nicholas liked me but still had no idea if I was a temporary distraction or someone he took seriously. What if he didn't think we were any different than me and Jonathan, i.e. "fuck buddies"? "I kind of wonder what he's doing with me sometimes," I admitted.

Bridget frowned. "What do you mean?"

"He's a catch," I said, looking down.

"And you're not?"

"I don't know. Nicholas is so ambitious. He'll probably make partner in a few years. And he's seriously cute. I catch girls checking him out all of the time." I raised my head and looked over at Bridget who was studying me with her lips pursed.

"Yeah. And he's with you." Placing her hand over mine, she said, "Where did this inferiority complex come from all of a sudden?"

I shrugged.

Jabbing me lightly in the arm with her pointer finger, she said, "Well get over it! It's very unbecoming."

I laughed. "Okay boss!" Bridget was right. I hated feeling "less than" or not good enough for Nicholas. It was bullshit and so not me. I vowed to snap out of it and fast. It was time for a subject change. "What about you?"

Shifting in her seat, Bridget lit up a cigarette and said, "What about me?"

"Are we going to talk about the Jonathan issue in this lifetime?"

"Not if I can help it," Bridget mumbled before taking a drag of her cigarette.

I muted the television set. It wasn't like we were watching anyway. "You like him though?"

A film of red cloaked Bridget's face. "I swear I didn't like him when he was your boyfriend."

I knew every single one of Bridget's crushes in high school and never suspected Jonathan was one of them. I still didn't. "I believe you. But when did it start?"

Bridget looked down towards her dark wooden floor and appeared to contemplate. After a few moments, she lifted her face, put out her cigarette and cast her eyes back on me. "I think it was that day we all went to the Beer Garden in Queens. Jonathan and I got so drunk and started dancing the Polka with the Polish band. I had so much fun with him, but when we took the subway back into Manhattan and arrived at your apartment, he went inside with you and I walked home alone."

I remembered that day. I hadn't thought much of Jonathan and Bridget dancing together because Bridget always had a way of bringing out the playfulness in people. I also didn't have strong enough romantic feelings for Jonathan to care whether he danced with another girl, certainly not Bridget who I trusted implicitly and never imagined had a crush on my ex- boyfriend/fuck buddy. "Why didn't you say anything?"

Bridget opened her eyes wide. "Because he was your boyfriend! It's part of the unspoken girlfriend pact that you don't covet a best friend's old boyfriend."

"Yeah, there's that," I nodded.

"And besides, he doesn't like me." Bridget grabbed the copy of *Real Simple Magazine* from her coffee table and started flipping through the pages.

I flashed back to our reunion pre-party when I caught Bridget and Jonathan in heated conversation on the very couch I was sitting on. "I don't know about that, Bridge."

Looking up from the magazine, Bridget said, "What do you mean?"

I could tell she was trying to be nonchalant but the glint in her eyes gave her away. "Jonathan's different around you. Animated. Usually he moves at a snail's pace but with you, he laughs. A lot! Maybe he doesn't realize he likes you, but there's something there. I saw it that night. Plain as I'm seeing pigs on your pajamas."

Bridget shot me a guilty look. "Yeah, I got carried away and then realized I was flirting shamelessly with your fuck buddy and you busted me big time."

"I admit I was a bit taken off guard. You were practically sitting on his lap."

Her face draining of color, Bridget said, "I'm sorry. I'm such a slut."

Almost choking on my margarita, I started laughing. "I wish you were more of a slut these days. You make me feel like a Kardashian!"

Bridget started laughing too but then took on a serious expression. "So there it is. I have feelings for Jonathan."

I lifted my hands in the air and dropped them to my sides. "Finally. So what are you going to do about it?"

"Should I do something about it?"

"Yes!"

Bridget looked at me skeptically. "Really? What about you?"

I exhaled deeply and took a moment since I knew I would not be able to retract my next words once they came out. If things didn't work out with Nicholas (or the next guy), I would no longer have a backup plan in Jonathan. "I'm not gonna lie, the idea of you and me having sex with the same person is kind of *Gossip Girl* for my taste, but the fact that we've made it all these years without so much as kissing the same guy is kind of cool, right? I don't love Jonathan. That way. And I don't want to stand in your way if you do."

Bridget looked at me horrified and started singing, "*Love! Lord Above. Now you're trying to trick me in love!*"

"Ha ha," I said standing up. "I should get going."

Standing up with me, Bridget said, "That's okay, I have an appointment with two new potential clients tomorrow, including RomComs Plus. Another one I owe to you! I should get some sleep so I can wake up early and prepare. Don't want to make you look bad by being off my game."

"You could never be off your game! Very cool about the new clients. It must be going around. Caroline told me that her company picked up a huge new client too. My friends are so important."

Walking me to the door, Bridget gave me a hug and said, "You're important too."

I shrugged. "Whatever you say. Anyway, Daneen 'Ms. Phony Queen' has been giving me assignments lately even though I'm not officially her secretary. It leaves me less time to read for the blog so I'll read tonight in bed until my eyes close."

"*Cut on the Bias*?"

I nodded. "I want to get it over with but don't want to give Hannah the satisfaction of knowing it was an easy-breezy fast read."

In a quiet voice, Bridget asked, "But it is? An easy-breezy fast read?"

"It could be," I admitted. "If the reader didn't hate the author's guts."

Bridget frowned. "Sorry, chickie. I guess I shouldn't mention that I saw a review, huh?"

I bit the inside of my cheek. "Where would you see a review?" I stammered.

Bridget lowered her gaze. "Plum Sheridan shared it on Facebook."

"Plum Sheridan?" I yelped. "You're friends with her on Facebook? How the hell did *that* happen?"

"She friended me after the reunion. I guess my Dumb comment didn't offend her." Bridget gave me a sheepish grin.

I shook my head in disbelief. "Wow. So...uh, the review was good?" If I hadn't taken Nicholas' advice and hidden Hannah's newsfeeds the day I accepted her friend request, I would have seen it too. I wondered what other bloggers had been asked to provide advance reviews. Lucky for me, the answer would be revealed in good time.

Bridget pursed her lips and shrugged. "I barely read it. Just like I'm gonna barely read the book. More like not at all."

"That makes one of us," I said glumly.

*   *   *

Torrential downpours put a nix on my plan to meet Caroline at the Shake Shack for lunch the next day. Although the weather meant a shorter line, no burger was good enough to risk being struck by lightning, not even a Shack Burger, and so I decided to treat myself to a grilled cheese sandwich in the cafeteria as a consolation prize. The rain had clearly derailed other people's lunch plans too since nearly every table was occupied. I had almost walked through the entire lunch room when I spotted Nicholas sitting with Daneen. They were hunched over stacks of documents. I stopped in my tracks, hating the idea of them eating together, but quickly remembered that they were spending countless hours working on the case and this was likely not the first or last meal they'd share. Daneen looked up, met my eye and quickly looked away without acknowledging me. I muttered "bitch" to myself just as Nicholas lifted his eyes from the table, stretched his arms over his head and looked my way. His lips curled into a wide grin and he motioned for me to join them.

I nodded, walked to their table and placed my tray in front of an empty chair. "Hi guys!"

Daneen looked up at me with a blank stare. "Oh, hello."

Pretending not to notice her usual cold shoulder where I was concerned, I said, "There are absolutely no empty tables left. I should have known to come down either before 12:30 or after 2:00 in this weather to beat the crowds."

Nicholas patted the seat next to him. "Sit with us."

Daneen looked at me like I was a rescued stray cat she wished would get lost again. "Yes, join us if you'd like. Although, it will probably be super boring for you. We're working." She pointed towards the pile of papers like I wouldn't have noticed them otherwise.

"A little break won't kill us," Nicholas said winking at me.

I smiled at him and took a bite of my sandwich. When no one said anything, I took another bite and decided to feign interest in what they were working on just to break the awkward silence. "So…"

"So, how long have you been a legal secretary?" Daneen interrupted.

"Almost three years," I answered. I was too taken aback that Daneen had actually initiated a conversation with me to go into more details.

"Have you taken the LSAT yet?" Daneen asked.

Surprised by the randomness of the question, I stuttered, "Huh? Um, no."

"You *are* going to law school, right?" She probed.

"Why do you ask?" Nicholas questioned.

Daneen looked at Nicholas like he had an eyeball in the middle of his forehead. "I just can't imagine anyone graduating college and working as a legal secretary unless she hoped to get good recommendations from attorneys for law school." Turning her attention to me, she said, "You went to college, right?"

I shredded my napkin wishing it was her face. "Yes."

Daneen nodded. "Where'd you go?"

"Syracuse," I said.

Momentarily looking at me with envy, Daneen said, "I wished my parents would have let me go to a party school!"

"Syracuse had a great communications program and it might seem shocking to you, but I've never had any desire to go to law school," I said assuredly.

"It's not shocking to me," Nicholas said, squeezing my knee under the table. "And Syracuse did a great job. Kimmie is a super communicator. You should check out her blog."

Daneen looked at me with renewed interest. "What kind of blog?"

"It's a chick lit blog where I post about chick lit novels. I write reviews, interview authors. That sort of thing," I said.

With a furrowed brow, Daneen said, "I thought chick lit was declared dead ages ago. I read *Bridget Jones's Diary* in college but don't know anyone who reads it now. Except my sixteen year old niece. She has that Shopaholic series, but I assume she'll grow out of it soon."

"No one writes chick lit like Sophie Kinsella," I said.

Daneen looked at me blankly. "Well, that's great, Kimmie! Your blog sounds cute."

I tried not to lose my lunch over *her* use of *his* nickname for me, especially since it might have been the first time she had ever directed me by name.

Daneen turned to Nicholas and said, "I think we should get back to work now, don't you?"

Taking that as my cue, I stood up and placed a hand on each side of my tray.

"We probably *should* get back to work but you can stay as long as you want," Nicholas said looking up at me.

I glanced at my watch pretending to care what time it was. "Thanks, but I should get back. I have a ton of work to do as well." Even if it wasn't up to the intellectual standards of Daneen. "See you guys later."

"Later, Kimmie," Nicholas said with a soft smile.

Daneen gave me a quick glance and said, "Bye," before turning her attention back to the papers on the table.

I walked away deciding I would much rather get struck by lightning than sit through another lunch with Condescending Daneen.

When I returned to my desk, there was a note from Rob that he would be out of the office for the rest of the afternoon. I finished the 'ton of work' I had waiting for me in record time and went on the *Pastel is the New Black* Facebook page. An author had posted a 5-star review she'd received from another blogger and tagged me. I assumed it was because I had given the same book 3 stars and she wanted me to know that another blogger loved it. When were authors going to understand that not everyone was going to enjoy the same book equally? In the almost two years I had been running the blog, most of the authors whose books I had reviewed were extremely professional. They always thanked me for my honest review even when it included some constructive criticism. It was those authors whose second books I accepted for review without hesitation. But there were a few who couldn't handle being told that I didn't consider their books among my favorites. I *wanted* to comment on the Facebook post that everyone was entitled to her opinion but decided to take the high road and simply "like" the status. I was sure it took most authors a long time to acquire the thick skin required to shrug off the critics. I wanted that for this author and was happy that another blogger had enjoyed her book more than I did. I didn't wish bad reviews on anyone. *Well, almost anyone…*

When an email popped up on my screen that all attorney billable time for the previous month had to be released by the following Monday, I realized I still had a few days to release for Rob. Just as I was about to exit Facebook, I saw it and my heart stopped for a beat. *Chick Lit Flavor* had posted about an upcoming blog tour for *Cut on the Bias*. Ten people had "liked" the status and three people had already left comments: "I can't wait to read this one!", "This one sounds good!" and "Totally excited for this book!" I buried my head in my keyboard, wishing I could magically bleep myself to an island in the Caribbean where there was no Internet access.

Thinking of a bright side, I lifted my head. At least all of the enthusiasm for *Cut on the Bias* disproved Daneen's statement that no one read chick lit anymore.

I bent my head back down. It wasn't much of a bright side.

CHAPTER 19

"YEAH, IT SHOULD BE FUN," I said to Caroline on the phone as I stared at my reflection in the bathroom mirror. I brushed a bit of bronzer on the apples of my cheeks and forehead to create a "natural" glow to my face. "I'm really nervous about meeting his friends though. What if they hate me?" Nicholas had invited me to his buddy George's birthday dinner at Anthony &Vic's Steak House that night after work.

"I'm sure they'll love you. Just be yourself. Enjoy."

"I'll try." I glanced at my watch. "Crap, I told Nicholas I'd meet him in the elevator bank at 7:30 and it's 7:36. Reservation isn't till 8 but we're having drinks first. Gotta run! I'll call you tomorrow." After I hung up the phone, I tossed it in my bag and ran out the bathroom door. I hoped Nicholas was running late too but he was already in the hallway by the elevators, tapping away on his phone. "Sorry! Got distracted."

Nicholas looked up from his phone and smiled. "No biggie. I don't want to be the first ones there anyway."

"Too cool for that, huh?" I teased.

"Way too cool." He glanced at his watch. "I think we're pretty safe at this point."

"We're good then."

Nicholas pressed the elevator button and walked over to me, closing the space between us. After scoping out the hallway for onlookers, he leaned down and kissed me tenderly leaving me weak in the knees. "We're very good."

I planted my high-heeled black suede boots firmly on the ground to recover my stability and touched his scruffy cheek. We quickly pulled away from each other when the elevator doors opened and Rob walked out.

When he saw me, his blue eyes widened in surprise. "What are you still doing here? It's almost 8 on a Friday night."

I stole a quick glance at Nicholas. We hadn't discussed whether to make it public that we were seeing each other. I blurted out, "Finishing up some blog stuff."

"I dropped some documents in your in-box, saw she was still here and asked if she wanted to get a drink," Nicholas said.

Rob nodded. "Where you going? Maybe I'll meet you guys in a few minutes."

I bit my lip and looked toward the carpet, deferring responsibility for responding to Nicholas. He was the trial attorney and was paid generously to be quick on his feet.

"We're actually meeting..."

Before Nicholas could finish, Rob interrupted, "Never mind, I promised the Wife I'd actually be home at a reasonable hour tonight."

Nicholas nodded. "Too bad. Next time."

"Yeah, definitely next time, boss man!" I said.

Walking away, Rob said, "Later guys," and waved behind him.

When he disappeared through the entrance to our offices down the hallway, Nicholas and I looked at each other and burst out laughing. "Too bad," I mimicked in a deep voice.

In a high pitched voice, Nicholas mocked, "Next time, boss man!"

Swatting him playfully on the arm, I said, "Let's get out of here. I think we've segued from fashionably late to officially tardy!"

When we walked into Anthony & Vic's a few minutes later, we circled the bar area first to see if Nicholas' friends were still there. "They must have sat down already," he said.

I followed him with shaky legs to the maître d' and a minute later, a hostess ushered us to his friend's table in the back of the bustling restaurant. As the smell of steak cooking in its own juices tickled my nose, I knew I'd never be able to stick to my plan to be heart conscious and order fish.

A fair skinned guy with curly black hair stood up from the round table. His dark blue business suit did nothing to disguise his broad shoulders and bulging biceps. Smiling broadly at Nicholas, he said, "It's about time. I was beginning to think you were ditching!"

Nicholas gave him a bro-hug while I felt the eyes of the others on me and tried to look cool and collected.

"Sorry. We got delayed by the boss," Nicholas said reaching for my hand. "This is Kim, guys."

As I smiled and waved a hello, the table greeted me with a collective, "Hi, Kim!"

Nicholas nodded his head towards the curly haired guy. "This is George, the birthday boy. And his girlfriend, Sarah," he said, pointing at a girl with a dark pixie-cut hairstyle sitting next to him. "And Brian, Alison, Peter, Paul and Mary." Looking at me with a twinkle in his eyes, he said, "Be prepared for the trio to break out into *Puff the Magic Dragon* at any time."

I willed my head not to whip around at the name "Mary." Trying to remain calm even as my heart was beating like crazy, I said, "Ha! Nice to meet you guys. And happy birthday, George." I snuck a glance at Mary through the corner of my eye to see if she was sizing me up, but she looked to be in deep conversation with Paul. Or it might have been Peter.

"Thanks, Kim!" George motioned toward the two empty chairs next to each other at the table. "You plan on sitting? We already ordered a few bottles of wine but if we don't get some apps on the table soon, Sarah is gonna turn into Aretha Franklin." He laughed while everyone at the table gave him a blank stare.

"The Snickers commercial. 'You're not yourself when you're hungry,'" I said, giggling with him. I stole another look at Mary. Although her hair was in a ponytail in her pictures on Facebook and when I saw her with Nicholas that day by the elevator, it was currently loose and hung past her shoulders in long layers. She still looked tan which I suspected was actually her natural bronzed complexion. She looked up, caught my eye and smiled softly. I felt my face flush at getting caught staring, smiled back and quickly looked away.

"Seriously, people. Doesn't anyone here besides my new friend Kim watch television?" George said, grinning at me.

"Some of us have DVRs and can skip the commercials," Nicholas said, pouring a glass of wine. Turning to me, he said, "Red or white?"

"Red." I watched him pour me a tall glass. "Thanks."

Squeezing my thigh under the table, he whispered, "Anytime."

"So when's your next marathon?" Nicholas asked George.

"Next week. Vegas!" George said with a devilish grin as Sarah rolled her eyes.

"You're running a marathon?" I asked. I was impressed since the longest I'd ever run was a 5k.

"How many will it be now?" Nicholas asked.

"Lucky 13," George said.

"Holy crap!" I blurted out. "That's awesome."

"He's insane. He ran the last one with a partially torn meniscus. And don't even get me started on his black toenails." Scrunching up her face, Sarah said, "Gross."

Kissing her cheek, George said, "You know you think it's sexy that I'm manly enough to run in pain."

"Whatever you say, sweetheart." Sarah looked at me, shook her head and mouthed, "Not really."

I gave her a knowing look, smiled and turned back towards George. "What do you think of barefoot running? My boss swears by it."

"We think our boss might be a masochist," Nicholas said laughing.

George put down his glass of wine. "Your boss is right. The best runners leave no tracks. I've run a few half marathons with the toe shoes but not a full. If you read…"

"*Born to Run*," the table said in unison and started cracking up.

Clearly the only one not in on the joke, I asked, "Did I miss something?"

Brian said, "The book *Born to Run* is the guy's bible."

"Gotcha," I said, even though I still had no idea what they were talking about.

"Anyway, I'm trying to get my company involved in the Long Island Triathlon," George said proudly.

"George is Vice President and Assistant General Counsel of Alston Financial Corp," Nicholas said for my benefit.

George nodded. "Yeah, the average weight of my company is increasing by the second."

"So shallow," Sarah said, laughing.

"What do you do, Sarah?" I asked.

"I'm in culinary school. I guess I'm partially responsible for my boyfriend's obsession with running." She gave George a guilty look. "My homework means fattening dinners a few times a week."

"Cool. And what about you guys?" I asked of Brian, Peter, Paul and Mary.

Speaking up first, Mary said, "I'm finishing my second year of law school."

"I tried to talk her out of it," Nicholas laughed. "But she wouldn't listen to me. I figured I could at least help her get a summer associate spot at our firm."

Lifting her chin in Nicholas' direction, Mary said, "Yes, Nicholas was very helpful. But I like to think my grades had something to do with it!"

"Think what you want," Nicholas said dryly.

Mary shook her head and stuck her tongue out at Nicholas.

As I observed Mary's comfortable banter with Nicholas, it struck me that she was going to be working at my firm over the summer and I took a gulp of wine. Interrupting what I hoped was just friendly banter among the two and not flirting, Brian, a chubby baby-faced guy with freckles, said, "I'm in medical school."

After hearing Peter and Paul were a CPA and actuary respectively, I felt pretty lame and wished I had not brought up the topic of career. I knew what was coming.

"What about you, Kim? You an associate too?" Sarah asked.

Sitting up straighter in my chair, I said as proudly as I could muster, "No, I'm a legal secretary."

"Kim is being modest. She pretty much runs our group," Nicholas said assuredly.

I gave him a quizzical look. "Um, I don't know about that."

"Sure you do." Looking around the table, he said, "Kim's the anchor of our team."

He was practically beaming at me, but I wasn't sure if he was trying to make me feel better or convince himself I was more important than I was. As the others focused their attention on me, I felt a flush creep across my cheeks. I wished he'd let it go.

Brian looked at Nicholas with interest and asked, "How so?"

Matter-of-factly, Nicholas responded, "She's more organized than anyone I know. Schedules all of our meetings, maintains our docket of deadlines since our paralegal is challenged. And most…"

Feeling the need to defend the only other person in my department without an advanced degree, I interrupted, "Hey! Don't make fun of David. I like him."

Nicholas gave me a close-mouthed smile. "I like him too, but unlike me, you don't have to rely on him to get things done." Turning to the rest of the table, he said, "Not the most reliable kid on the block unlike Kim. But her most important role?" He paused dramatically while his friends looked at him expectantly.

This should be good, I thought to myself praying it was not some ridiculously exaggerated compliment regarding my contribution to the team. *Me thinks Nicholas doth protest too much.*

"Keeps the boss in line." Squeezing my knee under the table again, he smiled at me and said, "Seriously. I love the way you boldly put Rob in his place."

The group looked at me in admiration, but I got the sneaky suspicion they assumed the only reason Nicholas was dating a secretary was because I had big boobs and probably gave phenomenal head. "Someone's gotta do it," I joked.

Nicholas looked at me proudly, "And she does it all while maintaining an enormously popular blog."

I impulsively kicked Nicholas' leg under the table.

He stopped mid-sentence and looked at me with a furrowed brow. "You alright?"

I cleared my throat, "Yeah, I'm okay." Defending myself for daring to support and actually enjoy the "dead" genre of chick lit was not how I wanted to spend my Friday night, especially after my identical conversation with Daneen the day before. I was pretty certain Nicholas' over-achieving friends were more likely to read Jonathan Franzen and Kurt Vonnegut than Helen Fielding and Candace Bushnell. Desperate to change the subject, I said, "This skirt steak is amazing!"

"What do you think, Sarah?" George asked. "Gotta see what the expert says."

"I agree wholeheartedly with Kim's assessment!" Sarah said brightly.

"More wine, Kimmie?" Nicholas asked.

Happy that the topic of my blog had successfully been dropped, I lifted my glass and I said, "Sure."

*   *   *

"Oh God!" I screamed, grabbing the headboard as I came.

"You feel so good," Nicholas whispered into my ear as his strokes intensified and he fell on top of me.

We remained still for a few minutes breathing heavily until Nicholas flipped over on his back. "You're amazing, Kim."

"You're not so bad yourself," I said.

"We make a good team."

"I'm the anchor!"

Leaning on his elbow facing me, he gave me an amused smile, "The anchor?"

"Didn't you say I'm the anchor of our team?"

Nicholas grinned. "Oh! Yes, I did say that."

"Did you mean it?" I wanted to add, "because I would have slept with you anyway" but refrained.

"Of course. Although I wasn't talking about the 'work' team just now."

I nodded. "I know. But are all of your friends so... I don't know... motivated?"

"Of course! I only hang out with the cream of the crop," Nicholas said with a laugh.

"And me," I mumbled.

"Don't be silly." He kissed me on the nose and stood up. "Including you, miss big-time blogger. I gotta use the bathroom. Don't go anywhere."

I wished he didn't have to mention the blogging as if it made up for the fact that I didn't have a law degree or even a masters. "I won't." I turned to my side and when Nicholas got back in the bed and spooned me, I pretended to be asleep. But then I turned around so our heads were practically touching. "So you don't like David, huh?"

"I do like the guy. It's just his lack of the 'hustle' gene made us late for court earlier this week. It's difficult enough keeping up with my own workload. Constantly following up with David is draining. But I didn't mean to come across so harsh before. I'm sorry." Nicholas kissed my forehead and then closed his eyes.

"At least he's pleasant. Which is more than I can say for Daneen," I muttered.

Nicholas opened his eyes again. "Yeah, she's a bit of a snob. But she's harmless."

"If you say so," I said, turning around again.

His arms encircling me, Nicholas said, "I say so."

"Uh-huh," I mumbled.

Nicholas chuckled and gave me a light squeeze. "Just try to shrug her off. It's because of her that I'm not working right now."

"That's what I keep telling myself." I refrained from mentioning my certainty that Daneen wished it was her in the bed with him and not me.

CHAPTER 20

I FLIPPED ANOTHER PAGE and muttered, "Fuck." My biggest fear had been realized. Despite myself, *Cut on the Bias* had me hooked. It read like a Lauren Weisberger novel: fast-paced, sophisticated and much to my displeasure, well-written. I hoped her editor was responsible for that part. Or better yet, maybe a secret ghost writer would come out of the woodwork demanding the credit. And the main character, Jacqueline, was actually relatable. I had no idea how a completely unlikeable author could create such a sympathetic and believable main character. "Unless she's a good writer," I said out loud to myself as my phone rang. I put the book on my night table and picked up my phone. "Hey Bridge. What's up?"

"You sound sad. Should I be asking you that question?"

"No, I'm fine." Better to get my mind on something else than continue to bash Hannah's writing skills when the worst thing I could say about *Cut on the Bias* so far was that her supporting characters could have been fleshed out a bit more. I probably would have given them more distinctive personalities and maybe included additional information about their lives. "How are you?"

Bridget let out a deep exhale. "I made an appointment with Jonathan."

"An appointment?"

"I thought about what you said and decided I wanted to be alone with him and see what happened. But I didn't want to ask him on a date. That would be too weird." Bridget giggled, sounding a bit embarrassed. "So I asked if he had some time to talk to me about expanding my business. He's an entrepreneur too, but he's been at it a few years longer than me. I thought it was a good and believable excuse."

"And what did he say?" I held my breath.

"He said 'absolutely' in that laid-back stoned voice of his," Bridget said with a giggle. "Anyway we're going to meet at Two Little Red Hens Bakery tomorrow afternoon."

I smiled to myself. "Great!" It was nice to see Bridget excited about a guy for a change, even if the guy *was* my first boyfriend and backup shag. It sounded like a plot line of a chick lit novel. Although we'd probably get in a big fight over Jonathan if this was a book. "So what's the plan?"

"There is no plan. I figured I'd play it by ear and see if we have chemistry first." Bridget stopped talking for a beat. "Why? Should I have a plan?" She sounded nervous.

"No, I was just wondering if you did, that's all."

"Nope. No plan."

"Well, no plan sounds like a good plan to me."

"Good," Bridget said, sounding relieved.

"Let me know how it goes, okay?"

"Of course. I'm nervous. Do you get nervous around Nicholas?"

I sat back against my headrest and closed my eyes, thinking about Nicholas. "I used to big time, but not anymore. Sometimes, when we're talking and I watch his face muscles move, I feel like all of the air has been sucked out of the room and I want to kiss him so badly, it hurts."

"Aw. That's precious, K."

"Yeah…" I heard a beep and looked at my phone as a text message popped up from Nicholas. "Working late with Daneen and the slow paralegal who shall remain nameless. Could really use some secretarial support here."

"Speak of the devil. He's working late with *Daneen* tonight."

"Sorry Kim. It's just work."

"I know. And David the paralegal is with them so there is no danger of unkosher behavior."

"I hate to break it to you, but it's called a three-way," Bridget said, laughing.

Cringing at the thought, I said, "That's a visual I didn't need. Thanks, Bridge."

"Ha ha. Sorry. Besides, you said Nicholas doesn't even like David."

"Which means he'd spend more time on Daneen. At that unpleasant thought, I'm out of here."

"Bye!"

I texted Nicholas back. "What kind of support were you thinking? Need assistance inserting documents into the scanner?"

Less than ten seconds later, he responded, "Oh, I've got a document to insert in your scanner if you know what I mean ;)"

Giggling, I responded, "Only if it's a large document."

"Oh, it's very large, babe. Getting larger by the second."

I shook my head and started laughing. I only hoped Daneen was looking over his shoulder as he was texting me. I bet she wished Nicholas would insert his document in *her* scanner.

* * *

The following morning, I was reading *Cut on the Bias* at my desk. I was waiting impatiently for the book to jump the shark so I could write a genuinely unfavorable review. I still thought Hannah could have better distinguished the secondary characters and if I was her editor, I probably would have cut out a few unnecessary scenes, but as it stood, the book was at least 4 flutes-worthy. I was relieved it wasn't flawless but it was pretty darn good, especially for a debut novel.

"Ahem."

I lifted my head from the book and into the tired eyes of Daneen. It looked like she had tried to compensate a lack of sleep with extra makeup, but I could still see dark circles. Adopting an annoyed tone to match hers, I said, "Yes?"

"Rob wanted me to ask if you were busy."

"Um…" I tried to stall while I figured out what she wanted.

Daneen cocked an eyebrow. "He said if you were doing something for your book hobby…"

Interrupting, I said, "You mean my blog?"

Brushing me off, Daneen said, "Whatever. Yeah, I guess. Anyway, he said if you had time, you should go to Starbucks and pick up coffees for us."

My face burning, I narrowed my eyes at her. "There's free coffee in the pantry." And Rob had never, in close to three years, asked me to fetch coffee for him.

Daneen shrugged. "We were hoping for something better than the firm's crappy coffee. And stronger. I was here practically all night with Nicholas." She stopped talking and looked me dead in the eyes as if inviting a reaction.

I was dying to tell her I knew David had been with them too, as well as mention the string of dirty text messages Nicholas and I had exchanged while they were supposedly working so hard. Instead, I stood up and walked into Rob's office. I felt Daneen follow but gently shut the door behind me before she could enter.

"Really, Rob?"

Rob raised his head from the stack of documents he was reviewing. "Wha—"

"You want me to fetch you guys coffee from Starbucks? What's next? Picking up your laundry? Or worse, *doing* your laundry?"

Rob's lips curled up in amusement.

I felt my fingernails biting into my palms as I clenched my fists. "It's not funny. First you leave me out of a friendly group lunch and now you're having me run errands for you I never had to run before."

Rob raised his hand. "May I speak?"

I placed a hand on my hip. "If you must."

"If you wanted to join us for lunch, you should have. I just assumed you wouldn't be interested. You know you're always welcome."

I *used to* know that, but my recent inferiority complex made me question everything, even Rob. Although his explanation made me feel better about being left out of lunch, it didn't explain why I was suddenly being asked to fetch coffee. "Whose idea was it for me to go to Starbucks?"

Rob pursed his lips. "I thought you wouldn't mind an excuse to leave the office. You could read while in line."

"That's not what I asked." I crossed my arms across my chest. I felt like a petulant child for droning on about this but I couldn't help myself.

Rob leaned forward with his elbows on the desk. "Neither of us wanted to drink the firm's coffee but we're too busy to take a break. Daneen suggested I ask if you had time. I thought you'd be happy for an excuse to get out of the office."

The truth was I *didn't* mind taking a walk if it meant leaving the building, even if was to pick up coffee. But I hated the fact that the request came from Daneen. And I knew it was a power-play on her part. But if I said that to Rob, he'd think I was crazy. Or maybe he'd take me seriously, but the last thing I wanted to do was add more stress to his day. He was working his tail off and had more important things to do than play mediator between Daneen and me. "Fine," I grunted. "I'll pick up the damn coffee." I held up my hand. "Money?"

Rob smiled, reached into his wallet and pulled out a fifty. Handing it to me, he said, "Buy yourself something too. And maybe a rice krispy treat to get you out of your funk."

"Okay, but I draw the line at taking actual drink orders. No Vanilla Lattes or White Chocolate Mochas. You're both getting Venti coffees and you can add cream and sugar here."

Saluting me, Rob said, "Aye Aye, Captain."

When I walked out of his office, Daneen was outside talking to Nicholas. She glanced at the bill in my hand and gave me a satisfied smile. "I'll have a …"

Pulling a "Daneen", I swung my hand in her face dismissively. "Rob already told me to get everyone a Venti coffee. Black. Cream and sugar is in the pantry." I turned to Nicholas and tried to ignore his furrowed brow, "Do you want me to pick you up anything?"

He shook his head. "No, I'm good. You going to Starbucks?"

Avoiding eye contact with Daneen, I said, "It appears that way." I walked over to my chair and put on my jacket before facing them again. Nicholas was looking at me with a confused expression.

"Will you be able to carry them yourself? Want company?" he asked.

Daneen and I both looked at Nicholas. She appeared equally startled by his offer to join me. He probably didn't like the idea of dating the office gopher.

Recovering quicker than me, Daneen said, "That would defeat the purpose, Nicholas. We asked her to go so we could work." She grabbed him by the elbow and started leading him into Rob's office.

"Thanks for the offer," I said to their backs.

As I walked the three blocks to the closest Starbucks, I clenched my teeth and let my high heeled pumps roughly hit the pavement with each brisk step. I fantasized about punching Daneen in her non-existent gut and tripping her so that she fell and her pointy chin hit the floor and bled all over the carpet.

By the time I walked into Starbucks and took my place in line, I was out of breath and my feet hurt. I let the air out of my cheeks and, one at a time, slipped my feet out of my pumps for relief. I instinctively reached into my bag for *Cut on the Bias* since reading always had a calming effect, but put it back since that particular book was unlikely to do the trick. I was unaccustomed to waiting in line without the distraction of a book and so I counted how many girls ahead of me were taller. *All of them.* I ordered two Venti coffees for Rob and Daneen and a skinny vanilla latte with whip for me. I had my hand outstretched to pay the barista when I asked for a blueberry scone at the last minute. Careful not to spill the coffees, I walked back slowly and enjoyed the spring air.

I placed the cardboard tray on Rob's desk and handed him the change. I removed my latte and the scone and said, "Here you go."

"Thanks Kim. You're the best," Rob said.

I rolled my eyes.

Daneen took a sip of her coffee and snarled. Batting her eyelashes at me innocently, she said, "Is there any milk or sugar?"

Don't say anything you'll regret. Don't say anything you'll regret. I silently counted to five.

"I'll get it," Nicholas said. He stood up. "I have to use the bathroom anyway."

I followed him out into the hallway. Once outside, I said, "Do you really have to use the bathroom?"

Nicholas nodded. "Yeah."

"Cuz I can get the stupid milk and sugar." I didn't need him to come to my rescue.

"It's not a problem." He smiled. "I need to stretch my legs and give my eyes a rest anyway. Been looking at those documents for too long."

"Just go to the bathroom. I can handle it." I turned on my heel and began walking to the pantry.

"Kim!" Nicholas said, catching up to me.

I stopped walking. "What?" My heart was beating quickly for no apparent reason.

Frowning, he said, "Are you okay?"

I sighed. "I'm fine."

"You don't have to wait on us you know."

I shrugged. "You do your job and I'll do mine."

Narrowing his eyes, he said, "C'mon now."

"You're right," I whispered. It wasn't his fault I'd been relegated to coffee girl.

Placing his hand on my shoulder, he said, "You sure you're alright?"

"I'm fine." I smiled. "Stop by my desk on your way back, I have something for you."

He eyed me suspiciously. "What is it?"

"You'll see when you stop by. Now go pee before you have an accident."

Laughing, he said, "I'm going!"

I grabbed a few individual containers of milk and half and half and a few packets of sugar, Equal, Sweet 'n Low and Splenda from the pantry and tossed them on Rob's desk without making eye contact with Rob or Daneen and walked back to my desk where Nicholas was waiting.

I handed him the blueberry scone. "I know you said you didn't want anything but it felt wrong to get something for everyone but you."

"I was actually thinking I could use something sweet. You're the best." He touched his finger to my chin and smiled. "Thank you."

I loved and hated in equal measure that despite seeing him in the throes of passion in the double digits, he still made me blush shamelessly. "You're welcome. Enjoy." Motioning towards Rob's office, I said, "And get back in there before Daneen comes looking for you. I've had about enough of her for one day."

Nicholas shook his head and gave me an amused smile. "She's not that…"

I could not bear the idea of him defending her. *Again*. So, holding my hand up, I said, "Shh…Go!" I flashed a wide grin to signify I was joking. *Even though I wasn't.*

CHAPTER 21

THE THREE OF THEM SPENT the next few hours in Rob's office, only leaving to go to the bathroom. I kept busy attaching backup to Rob's client's bills, but that only took me a little over an hour. I used the rest of the time to organize my review schedule. Only three books were in the queue before *Cut on the Bias*. I was dying to know how Jacqueline and Pierre were going to hook up. I knew they would eventually – *hello, it was chick lit* – but I could not predict *how* it would happen.

Since I figured Nicholas would be tied up with work into the wee hours and I hadn't made any other plans, I decided it was a good night to go to the gym and run a few errands. When I glanced at the clock and saw it was past five, I thought about asking Rob if I could head out early since I didn't have anything to do. He'd always been cool with it in the past unless he was expecting something to come in that would require my assistance. Under normal circumstances, it would be a no-brainer, but I was reluctant to ask while Daneen was in there because she'd probably come up with some brilliant assignment for me to do, like cook a five course meal so *the lawyers* could work without being interrupted for dinner. And then maybe she'd comment to Nicholas later about how I led such a charmed life, what with having no real career to speak of. I decided the measly thirty extra minutes of freedom were not worth the bother. Twitter was a great time-sucker and so I began scrolling through my updates, stopping when one caught my eye from *We Love Books* calling for bloggers for a future blog tour of *Cut on the Bias*. Although I could liken my desire to organize Hannah's blog tour with my desire to stick my head in a toilet bowl, I couldn't help feeling slighted since Candy coordinated almost all of her client's chick lit blog tours through *Pastel is the New Black*. Considering it had taken me so long to agree to even read the book, I couldn't really blame her. I only hoped that some of the participating bloggers would find more fault with *Cut on the Bias* than I had so far. I glanced at my watch and groaned when I saw that I had barely managed to kill ten minutes.

I checked my phone when I remembered that Bridget's "appointment" with Jonathan was that day, but there were no text messages. I wondered if maybe they were still together. *Only one way to find out!*

I sent her a text. "How'd it go?" and stood up to go to the bathroom. I didn't actually have to go but figured it was another good way to waste some time and I still had twenty-three minutes before the day was officially over. (Twenty-seven minutes if I wanted to avoid the clock-watchers' rush to the elevator at exactly 5:30.) Before I could put one foot in front of the other to walk around the corner, my phone rang. I kept walking and, smiling into the phone, said, "Hey! How was your *appointment*?"

"It was good! Jonathan was really helpful."

Entering the bathroom, I repeated, "Really helpful, huh?" I bent down and checked the stalls for feet. "How so?"

"He gave me lots of advice for expanding my business. I told him I've been inundated with clients, which is great but I'm having trouble keeping up, and he suggested I consider hiring an assistant to help manage the administrative side of things. He also mentioned something about branding myself as a designer for the creative types, like authors and photographers since they already take up much of my portfolio. He thought if I focused on a particular industry, it might help me control my workload until I can afford to hire an assistant." Bridget took a loud breath. "I'm babbling, I know."

Laughing, I said, "You're just excited. That's a good thing."

"He's so smart, Kim!"

I placed the phone in the crook of my neck and checked out my outfit from all angles in the mirror. "Yeah, I know. It's a shame the way he fries his brain with all that pot. And his lungs with all that nicotine."

"Commandment number seven, 'thou shalt not judge!'"

"Um, that would be 'thou shalt not commit adultery.'"

"Whatever. Thou shalt not throw one's superior knowledge of the commandments in her best friend's face."

Laughing, I said, "Okay! Thou shalt stop post haste." We both knew I didn't call to discuss Jonathan's high intelligence quotient anyway. "So?"

"So?"

Groaning, I said, "C'mon Bridge! What happened?"

When Bridget didn't say anything, I felt my stomach drop. What if I was wrong? What if I'd set her up for failure? Jonathan was the first guy Bridget had been excited about in more than a year and if I was responsible for getting her hopes up only to have them crushed, I'd never forgive my...

Interrupting my worries, Bridget finally said, "I think you were right." Her voice was calm and steady.

Tired of standing, I walked into one of the stalls, threw some toilet paper on the toilet seat and sat down.

"Sparks were flying, Kim," she continued.

"Yeah? Did something happen?" I suddenly had a vision of them going at it doggie style in Jonathan's black and white tiled bathroom and shuddered.

"No. Nothing happened. But I felt it. We were laughing constantly and every so often, we'd lock eyes and there would be this awkward silence until one of us looked away. And I felt this warmth in my belly whenever that happened." She paused. "I don't know Kim. I think he likes me too."

"I told you so!" The two of them as a couple felt a bit incestuous to me but she sounded so happy that I'd learn to live with it.

"Anyway, we set up another appointment for Friday because he said he has more to show me."

"If he brings out the Astroglide, run in the opposite direction. Been there, done that. Just sayin…"

"Kim!"

Chuckling, I said, "Sorry. Keep me posted okay?"

"Of course."

After we hung up, I headed back to my desk to close up shop since it was almost 5:30. I exited out of all of the applications on my computer and was about to log off when my phone rang. I glanced at the face of my phone to see who was calling. *Interesting.* "Hey."

"What's up?"

"Not much. What's up with you?" It could not be a coincidence that Jonathan happened to call me the very same day he had an appointment with Bridget where sparks were apparently flying.

"Not much. I haven't spoken to you since the reunion and wanted to see how you were. How's purple is the new green?" He laughed in acknowledgement that he butchered the name of my blog again.

Not bothering to correct him this time, I said, "It's fine." I saw *Cut on the Bias* peeking out of my pocketbook. "It's great."

Jonathan coughed. "So, um, how's that guy from the reunion? Nick?"

"Nicholas," I corrected, remembering Nicholas' aversion to being called Nick. "He's good. Why?"

Jonathan coughed again. "Nothing. He seemed like a decent guy. You guys dating?"

"Yeah." Dating seemed like a reasonable description for what we were doing. "We've been spending a lot of time together."

"Cool."

"Why? Wondering why I haven't called you in a while?" I teased.

When Jonathan choked out another cough, I remembered Bridget and instantly felt my face heat up. I realized my rapport with Jonathan would have to change drastically if a romance developed between him and my best friend. Recovering, I said, "Joking!"

Quickly changing the subject, Jonathan said, "I hung out with Bridget today."

Playing dumb, I said, "Yeah? How'd that go?"

"Fine. Good."

An awkward silence filled the air. Was I supposed to offer my permission for him to date her? Was he asking for my permission? Was he even interested in dating Bridget or was his brain too fried up on marijuana to even recognize her interest?

"Does she date?" When he coughed again, it became clear that it was a nervous tick and not a result of too much nicotine in his lungs.

I wasn't sure how to answer. The truthful answer at least with respect to the last 400 or so days was that "no, she didn't date," but that might suggest she wasn't interested in dating *him*. "She's not dating anyone right now," I said. Then I added, "No one special at least," so as to not paint her as a desperate hermit. Somewhat enjoying his obvious discomfort with the topic of conversation, I said, "Why do you ask?" I resisted the urge to laugh out loud.

"Curious, that's all. I've never heard her talk about guys. She's not a lesbian, is she?"

Unable to restrain myself any longer, I chuckled into the phone. "Most definitely not. Bridget is definitely straight, despite Hannah's attempt to convince our classmates of the contrary."

"Okay," Jonathan said, letting out a sigh that sounded a lot like relief.

There was no way I was going to blatantly offer him my blessing to date her, nor was I going to out her interest in him without her permission. The conversation was becoming painfully awkward, though, so I searched my brain for a way to slickly give Jonathan the heads up. I recalled my conversation with Bridget from earlier and a bell rang in my brain. "When Bridget likes a guy, she tends to giggle a lot. And she has trouble maintaining eye contact for too long before looking away. Oh and when she really likes a guy, she's not always upfront about it. Sometimes she comes up with excuses to spend time with him hoping he'll get the hint." *Please get the hint Jonathan.*

"Great!" Jonathan said brightly.

"I would love to see her happy."

"Yeah, she's a great girl," Jonathan agreed.

Trying to convey my approval without being specific, I said, "I would love to see her happy with the right guy." I paused for an extra beat. "No matter who he is."

"Got it," Jonathan said. "And, Kim?"

"Yeah?"

"Thanks."

I smiled. I could have had a career in politics.

By the time we got off of the phone, it was 5:45. Wanting to leave before yet another person called me, I dialed Rob's extension.

Picking up after one ring, he said, "Hey." I could tell he had me on speaker phone.

"Calling to let you know I'm leaving for the night." I began logging out of my computer.

"Okay. Have a good one."

"You too," I said. I placed the phone back on the receiver and stood up to grab my jacket as Nicholas walked out of Rob's office.

"Glad I caught you," he said with a lazy grin.

I looked at him longingly. "I'm glad too. Don't work too hard tonight." I looked down at my toes and back at him. "Not sure why I always say that. Of course, you'll work too hard!"

Nicholas leaned over my desk so he was closer to where I was still standing on the other side. "What are you doing later?" he asked in a soft voice.

"The plan is to go to the gym and run some errands." I glanced at my watch. "Was hoping to get out of here early so I'd have more time."

"I won't keep you. Just wondered if you might want some company later. I can come by after work. It will be too late for an actual date, but I'd like to see you anyway."

Laughing at him, I said, "You mean for a booty call?"

Nicholas brushed his hand gently across my cheek and nodded. "If you're good, I'll throw in a little conversation too. Tell you all about my day in the office."

I raised an eyebrow. "Is that supposed to be incentive to be 'good'? And besides, I thought I was always good."

Winking at me, he said, "You are."

"Okay, but it depends on how late you work. I'm not waiting up for you to come by at 2 a.m."

Nicholas shook his head. "It should be closer to 11. Midnight at the latest. Otherwise, I'll go straight home."

"That should work." After a quick check to my left and right to make sure no one was watching, I gave Nicholas a soft peck on the lips, smiled and said, "See you later."

On my way home, I stopped at Fairway to restock my refrigerator and then to the gym for a combination spin and Pilates class. After my shower, I luxuriated in the bathtub with a glass of wine. And then I put on the new pink teddy I had picked up at Victoria's Secret and a long fuzzy pale blue robe. I lost myself in the second half of *Cut on the Bias* without interruption until I received a text from Nicholas shortly before 11. "Finished for the night! Still up for company?"

I put the book down on my coffee table and texted back, "Who did you have in mind?"

"It's a bit early in the relationship to resort to fantasy, but I can be anyone you want. Spider Man, maybe?"

"Superheroes are super sexy. Come on over!"

When my bell rang about twenty minutes later, I wrapped my robe tightly around my waist and buzzed him in.

When I opened the door, he gave me a huge smile and then eyed me from head to toe. "You look comfy."

"You think?" I stuck my head into the hallway and looked both ways. After I made sure no one was there, I untied my robe and opened it very slowly. Nicholas didn't say anything as he stared down the length of my body. I stood on my tippy toes and nuzzled his neck while his hands found their way inside my robe and began caressing my lower back. I pulled away and never removing my eyes from his, reached up to let the robe fall over my shoulders and to the ground at my feet.

He smiled and without a word grabbed my hand and walked inside my apartment, kicking the door behind him. "I must have you now."

And he did. We didn't even make it to my bed less than ten feet away.

Later that night, I couldn't sleep. I looked over at Nicholas who was sleeping soundly with his head on the edge of my over-sized pillow. I had to know how it ended.

I slid out of the bed, grabbed the book from my coffee table and stretched the length of my couch. By the time I reached the bio section at the end and tossed the book on the floor, I could see the sun starting to rise. I wiped the tears from the corners of my eyes and crawled back into bed. Nicholas was still sleeping and I wrapped my body around his. He shuddered and abruptly sat up. "What's wrong?" He looked around the room as if trying to orient himself with his surroundings. "What happened?"

I mumbled, "Nothing" and pushed him back on the bed, burying my face in his chest. I let my fingers rest on the soft dark hair on his flat stomach.

"Did you have a bad dream?"

I shook my head. "I wish it was a dream. It's certainly a nightmare."

Nicholas lifted me off of him and placed his hands on my shoulders forcing me to look at him. "What's going on? Why are you crying?"

"I'm crying over Hannah's book! Partly because the ending gave me the warm and fuzzies and I always cry over happy endings. But also because…"

Nicholas looked at me with concern and urged me to continue. "Because of what?" he said, wiping a tear from my eye.

"But also because..." I lowered my chin to my chest. "Because it was really good. The book. It was really, really good, Nicholas."

Nicholas frowned. "I'm sorry, Kimmie. I know you were hoping the book would suck so you wouldn't have to write a positive review."

I nodded, feeling my lips tremble.

"But it's not the worst thing in the world," he said matter-of-factly.

"Easy for you to say," I muttered.

Nicholas let out a deep exhale. "No. It's not 'easy for me to say.' I know how hard this has been for you. I know you really don't like the chick. And, yeah, it sucks that the bitch from high school, who you hate, is a good writer. But maybe you should acknowledge the real reason it upsets you so much."

I cocked my head to the side. "What do you mean by that?"

Nicholas looked me directly in the eyes. "I don't think you're this upset simply because Hannah the Bitch wrote a good book." He paused for a beat. "I think you're upset because Hannah wrote a book and you didn't. Period."

I gasped. "What?"

"I'm sorry Kimmie, but I think it's time you admitted to yourself that you want to be a writer. Like Hannah."

Feeling my eyes water, I asked, "Why would you say something like that?"

Frowning at me, Nicholas said. "Because it's true, Kimmie. Maybe you have your friends fooled but you can't fool me. I've seen the way you react when the subject of Hannah's book comes up. It's way too strong a reaction for someone who just didn't like the chick in high school. You're jealous."

I took a sharp intake of breath. It was true I had strong feelings for Hannah but jealousy was *not* one of them. My heart pounding, I asked, "I can't believe you would say that to me."

Nicholas shrugged. "Someone had to."

I recalled with annoyance the numerous times Nicholas had asked me about writing a book. "Why do you care so much if I write?"

Nicholas' eyebrows squished together. "What do you mean?"

"You even bought me a stupid journal!"

Nicholas jerked his head back. "It was a gift, Kim. I was trying to be supportive."

"Like you were being supportive at dinner with your friends when you totally inflated my role as a secretary? I hate to break it to you, but I'm a secretary. I'm not the anchor of any team."

"I meant it as a compliment," Nicholas said softly.

"It was condescending. I don't know who is worse, you or Daneen. At least she's blatant about it, but you seem embarrassed by it. Embarrassed by me."

Nicholas' eyes opened wide. "What?"

"Because I'm just a secretary. At least my popular blog makes me a little bit more important, right?"

Nicholas buried his head in his hands.

My pulse speeding, I continued, "That's why you care so much, isn't it? If I was an actual writer, maybe I'd be good enough for you. Someone you would take seriously."

"Whoa! Who said I didn't take you seriously?" Nicholas said, pushing the blankets away and standing up.

I shrugged. "You're a big-time lawyer. I'm sure you'd prefer to date someone at your professional level. Like Mary!"

Nicholas looked at me with his eyes bugging out. "Mary? What are you talking about?" He stepped into his pants, which had been tossed at the side of my bed. "Let me ask you something. Why would you want to be with someone you think so little of?"

The tears stung my eyes but I refused to brush them away. "What?"

His face now flushed with anger, he said, "If you think I'm such a fucking snob, why am I here?" He walked over to my doorway, grabbed the briefcase he had dropped next to my robe and turned around to face me. "Kim. The truth is it makes no difference to me what you do for a living as long as you're passionate about it. I wouldn't care if you were a garbage collector if you loved the job or if it made you happy. But for you to say you're passionate about being a legal secretary is a joke. I've watched you at work, Kim. It's a good job and you do it well, but you're bored out of your mind! You put more enthusiasm into tweeting about your blog than anything you do for Rob and you have zero motivation to change it."

Unwilling to relent my position, I followed him to the door. "All the compliments about my communication skills and my being the anchor of the team? Bunch of bullshit to make you feel better about dating a measly secretary, right? In fact, you barely spoke to me until Rob told you about my blog."

Nicholas shook his head at me in disbelief. "If anyone in this room is embarrassed about what you do for a living, it's you, not me. I had a crush on you since your very first day, before I knew anything about your stupid blog. The blog just gave me a good opening." Nicholas' hand was on the doorknob but he turned to face me one last time. His facial expression had turned from angry to sad. "Truth is I did take you seriously, Kim. I wanted you to be happy and was trying to give you a push in the right direction. I actually thought I might be falling for you. But now I see that you're complacent and that's not what I'm looking for." Shaking his head, he said, "I would say that maybe I'd give Hannah a call after all since, unlike you, she's not afraid to take risks. But that would just be cruel, wouldn't it?" With that, he turned the doorknob and walked out, letting the door slam behind him.

After he left, I stared at my front door as if waiting for him to walk back in. Too stunned to react to what had just happened, I crawled into bed and cried myself to sleep.

CHAPTER 22

WHEN I WOKE UP FOR WORK, over a half hour late, my eyes felt swollen as if I'd bathed in a tub of pollen. I showered, replaying in horror the events of the night before, from crying over the ending of Hannah's book, to confiding my devastation to Nicholas, to accusing him of being ashamed of me. I recoiled at the memory and turned up the temperature of the water, hoping to burn the memory to ashes. But when I opened my eyes, I could still see the astonished look in Nicholas' eyes. *And the anger.* There was a part of me that wanted to apologize. Nicholas had looked sincerely shocked by my accusations and maybe I *had* gotten carried away as a result of finishing Hannah's book. But I couldn't erase the way Nicholas' claim that I was jealous of Hannah made me feel. And he had definitely gone too far by threatening to give her a call.

When I got to work, I walked directly over to Rob's office. "Sorry I'm late."

Rob looked up from his computer with a furrowed brow, "Not a problem. Everything okay?"

I wanted so badly to tell him the truth, that no, everything was not okay. He'd probably tell me to shut his door, sit down and confide in him. And if Nicholas had been some random guy I was dating, I might have been tempted. But Nicholas was Rob's star associate and in Rob's world, work always trumped romance and so I responded, "Everything's fine. Thanks." and returned to my desk.

I tried to concentrate on work but each time I heard someone walk by, I wondered if it was Nicholas and looked up frantically. I picked up the phone, dialed the first two numbers of his extension and hung up. *Twice.* I buried my face in my hands, contemplating my options and finally stood up and walked over to his office even though I had no idea what I was going to say. As I raised my hand to knock on his closed door, I heard him laugh. I figured he was on the phone and started to walk away when I heard a female voice coming from his office. I bent my ear towards the door and tried to make out who he was with when suddenly I heard the scuffling of feet. I backed away from his door as quickly as I could and ducked into the empty office next to his. I held my breath as Nicholas and Daneen walked down the hallway, still laughing. I had expected Nicholas to share my anxiety over our fight but he walked lightly on his feet next to Daneen as if entirely unfettered. I waited until they turned the corner, followed them back in the direction of Rob's office and sat down at my desk.

I pretended to do some work, absently responded to comments on my blog and scanned the same paragraph from a new book on my review schedule at least three times. All the while, I tried to keep one ear on the conversation taking place in Rob's office. I couldn't get my heart rate to slow down knowing that Nicholas would have to walk past me at some point. I went through the different scenarios in my head. Maybe he would approach my desk, look at me with concern, and ask if I was okay. Or maybe he would give me a stern look and say we needed to talk. Or maybe, before he had the chance to say anything, I would catch his eye, give him a sheepish glance and ask if we could just let it go.

As it stood, I heard a shuffle of feet and looked up as a shadow passed my desk so quickly and without any acknowledgement of my presence in the room that it took several seconds of gaping with my mouth opened to reconcile that the shadow and Nicholas were one and the same.

I swallowed hard and turned to face Daneen, who was now standing in front of me. "Hey."

"I need you to reserve a car for tonight," Daneen said.

So much for the friendly chitchat. "Can you be more specific?"

Waving a skinny finger at me, Daneen sighed impatiently. "I need a car to pick us up here at 7. We're going to Caviar Russe on 55th Street and Madison."

"You and Rob?"

Daneen gave me a closed-mouth smile and gently shook her head. "No. Nicholas *and I*," she said, with an emphasis on "and I" as if encouraging me to use proper grammar. The joke was on her, since "Nicholas and *me*" was grammatically correct, not "Nicholas and I." Although the joke was also on me since she was spending the evening with Nicholas and I wasn't. "Got it. I need a client number."

Already walking away, she called out, "Bill it to business development."

The phone in my hand, I mumbled "You're welcome," under my breath. *Bitch.*

I was tempted to reserve an ugly stretch hummer or a party bus like the one driven by the Partridge Family. But I didn't like the idea of Nicholas and Daneen alone together in the back of a limo and I liked the idea of them alone on a bus, where there might be a bed, even less. I was dying to know what this fancy dinner was about. Billing the car to business development could mean they were meeting with a client or a potential client, but it could also be a convenient way to charge the firm to reserve a car for personal use.

After I reserved the car, a simple dark four-door sedan, I tossed aside my concerns about Nicholas and Daneen doing the nasty. They had hung out after hours numerous times over the past few weeks and yet he had always chosen to be with me. He was clearly upset, but he couldn't ignore me forever.

* * *

A week later, Nicholas was still ignoring me. Actually, he had moved beyond simply ignoring me. Now he managed to acknowledge my existence, but from the way he looked right through me, I might as well have been a ghost. One person who wasn't ignoring me was Hannah Marshak. Earlier that week, she had sent me an email with the subject line "Gentle reminder" asking when I would be posting my review of *Cut on the Bias*. I wanted to respond that my review would be posted when fruit stopped growing on trees but I ignored her instead. If Nicholas could play that game, so could I.

He was in Rob's office with Daneen and David. Daneen's obnoxious cackle ran at regular intervals of every ten seconds and I sat on my hands to restrain myself from going in there and using them to strangle her to silence.

It was excruciating watching Nicholas walk in and out of Rob's office without so much as a glance in my direction. Although Daneen was trying to turn me into her indentured servant, Nicholas hadn't asked for my assistance in anything work-related since our fight. It was as if I no longer existed in his world and it was killing me. That morning, I had stood before my closet determined to wear something that even Nicholas could not ignore. It was casual Friday and I was wearing my most flattering tight blue skinny jeans, a v-neck form-fitting white T-shirt and my Louboutins. Simple but hot. If his eyes didn't roam the length of my body while I was wearing that outfit, I might as well be dead to him.

I took a deep breath and walked over to Rob's desk, carrying three pieces of note paper. Knocking gently on his opened door, I said, quietly, "Rob?" My heart was pounding against my chest. *Please turn around and look at me. Please.*

Giving me his attention, Rob said, "Yup?"

Through my peripheral vision, I saw that David and Daneen had turned around to look at me but Nicholas was still facing Rob and casually typing on his phone. *Damn him.* Walking over to Rob, my legs a bit shaky, I choked out, "A couple people called while you were away from your desk this morning. I forgot to give you the messages." I handed him the notes and prayed that Nicholas was at least looking at my ass. My face felt feverish and I mentally kicked myself for being so flustered.

"Thanks, Kim," Rob said, taking the messages from me.

I cleared my throat. "Okay then. Bye."

I started to walk out with my head down but instinctively looked over at Nicholas, assuming his head was still down as well. My mouth opened involuntarily when our eyes met for a flash but Nicholas lackadaisically turned back towards his phone without any indication that he had even seen me, much less noticed my attire.

I went back to my desk, my stomach all a flutter and tears threatening to escape my eyes as a result of both sadness and frustration. Sure, Nicholas was angry at me but I was pissed at him too!

The difference was, I wanted to reconcile and apparently he did not. I was dead to him.

CHAPTER 23

STARTLED BY THE RINGING of my phone, I lifted my head from the thick pile of documents on which it was resting. I wiped the corners of my eyes and picked up the phone. "Hey, Bridge."

"Whatcha doin?" Bridget asked cheerily.

Taking note of the mess which was my desk, I said, "I've been placing hundreds of depositions in chronological order since about 3:15 this afternoon." I looked into Rob's opened office where I could see from his window that it was now dark outside. "What time is it now?"

"Almost 8:15. You're still at work?" she asked, sounding surprised.

Mid-yawn, I said, "Yeah." It wasn't that late but for someone used to leaving by 6 at the latest, it felt like the middle of the night.

"Darn!"

"Tell me about it," I said dryly. Rob was away on business and Daneen had taken it upon herself to assign me work I was certain was usually done by a paralegal.

"I was gonna ask if you wanted to meet for a drink tonight. What time are you heading out?"

I surveyed the documents in front of me. "Probably not for at least another hour. And I really want to go home and go to bed after. How about brunch on Sunday? Uptown Lounge?"

"The brunch special comes with a cocktail, right?" she asked hopefully.

Smiling, I said, "I think it comes with two of them."

"Sounds good. Should we invite Caroline?"

"She's in Iceland. Her father's treat. I think it's guilt money for his delayed mid-life crisis."

"I'd let my dad marry a woman half his age if I got a free trip to Europe out of it! Er, maybe not," Bridget chuckled. "Okay, I'm outta here. Don't work too hard!"

"Tell that to Daneen."

After we hung up, I decided it was an ideal time to give my eyes a break from the papers in front of me and I logged onto Twitter for a temporary reprieve. But when the first tweet I saw was about the cover reveal for *Cut on the Bias* "by breakout new author Hannah Marshak," I groaned and quickly exited the screen. I already knew what the cover looked like and didn't need to read all of the replies about how gorgeous it was. I decided it was God's way of punishing me for daring to take a break from my real job and quickly turned back to my assignment.

Approximately 45 minutes later, I placed the box of documents in the "war room" where Nicholas and Daneen were sitting at a small table in a corner, speaking in hushed voices. I swallowed hard and cleared my throat. "Daneen?"

Looking up, Daneen said, "Yes?"

"I finished the assignment." Gesturing toward where I had placed the box, I said, "Is this a good place for it?" From the corner of my eye, I saw that Nicholas had also stopped what he was doing to look at me, but I couldn't bring myself to make eye contact. He was probably too tired to remember I no longer existed. "I'm gonna head home now if that's alright with you." Asking her permission to do something was almost as torturous as getting the cold shoulder from Nicholas.

"Did you double check that everything was accurate?"

I nodded. "Yup." I actually *had* checked the documents twice, not willing to give Daneen the satisfaction of calling me out on a mistake.

Daneen narrowed her eyes at me. "Are you sure? We're working really hard here and it is imperative we all give 110 percent."

As I opened my mouth to use what was left of my patience to placate Daneen, she added, "Even the secretary."

At that, Nicholas' head whipped around to look at Daneen but he quickly brought his attention back to the papers in front of him.

Running a tired hand through my hair, I nodded. "Yes, Daneen. No worries. This secretary learned how to count well before she graduated college. See you tomorrow." Hoping to be out of ear shot as soon as possible in case she asked me to do something else before I left, I turned on my heel and walked out of the office without another glance at either of them.

* * *

As I walked over to Uptown Lounge the following Sunday, my mood brightened at the thought of a girls' brunch with Bridget. Only my best friend could make me feel better about what happened with Nicholas. We'd barely had a chance to discuss it yet.

The sweet smell of banana French toast hit me in the face as I walked into the restaurant and I looked to the bar area to my left to see if Bridget was waiting for me. At the sound of my name, I looked to my right, smiling brightly at the sight of Bridget sitting at a table toward the front of the dining area. My smile faded when I saw she was not alone. But not wanting to be rude, I quickly planted it back on my face.

Standing up from her chair, Bridget opened her arms, inviting an embrace. "Hi!"

I squeezed her tight and then pulled away, my stomach now in knots. "Hi! Sorry I'm late." Turning to Jonathan, I said, "This is a surprise!"

He stood up and hugged me awkwardly. "Hey, Long."

"I hope you don't mind that I asked him to join us. He called me this morning and, well." Bridget's face turned red as she shrugged.

I sat down. As I realized I would not be able to talk to Bridget about Nicholas over brunch, my heart sank, but I forced out, "Of course I don't mind. Not like the three of us haven't hung out together before." I glanced at the menu. "You guys are getting the brunch deal, right?"

"Absolutely. Eggs Benedict and a mimosa for me," Bridget said happily. "What about you?"

"Banana-stuffed French toast, obviously! And I think I want a Bloody Mary." I turned to Jonathan. "What are you getting?"

"Eggs Benny. Same as Bridget." He motioned to her with a smile and she smiled back, her face glowing.

A match made in heaven.

We were all unusually uncommunicative while eating. What I had hoped to discuss, my fight with Nicholas, was off the table and although the big white elephant in the room was Bridget and Jonathan's budding relationship, I couldn't bring that up either. In between chews, I took sidelong glances at them, trying to decipher through their body language how far things had progressed. Bridget hadn't told me anything aside from the "sparks flying" during the first "appointment" and their plans for a follow-up. I wondered how many times they had gotten together since then. Were they officially dating? Had they kissed yet? Slept together? Bridget had always kept me in the loop before where her love life was concerned, so why hadn't she confided in me about Jonathan? Was this what I should expect for the future? Always being on the outside?

I took a sip of my Bloody Mary, practically feeling smoke come out of my ears. I had asked for it extra spicy and they had delivered. "So what's new with you guys? I feel like we haven't spoken in a while." I fixed my gaze on Bridget, hoping she would read between the lines and acknowledge that she had totally kept me in the dark.

Bridget and Jonathan glanced at each other, quickly looked away and said, "Nothing much" in unison. Then they both seemed to smile into their plates.

I swallowed hard and glanced down at the remains of my French toast. It was delicious but I wasn't hungry anymore. I felt a gnawing in my stomach and for a moment thought it might be from eating too much, but I knew better. I was hurt that Bridget had invited Jonathan as if they were already a couple without even telling me and worse, I was jealous. The idea of Bridget and Jonathan together, while incredibly unexpected and yes, sort of weird, didn't really disturb me when things were good with Nicholas. I thought back to my last night with Nicholas, when we'd had sex on my area rug and he made me believe in the existence of a G-spot. And later, how he'd wiped the tears from my eyes when I told him about Hannah's book. And then I thought back to the multitude of times over the last couple of weeks when all I wanted was a sign that he still liked me. That sign had not come and now that there was no "Nicholas and Kim," a "Bridget and Jonathan" combination felt incredibly wrong and unfair. I hated myself for drowning in self-pity when I should have been happy for my best friend.

I took a final swig of my drink, hoping our waitress would come around with our second round.

Her brow furrowed, Bridget said, "You okay, Kim? You're awfully quiet."

Smiling, I said, "I'm good. No worries." I forced another bite of French toast and looked down but I could still feel Bridget looking at me with concern which, of course, made me feel even worse. She was my best friend in the entire world, as close as family. She had always supported my relationships, and here I was pissed that she had the nerve to be happy while I was miserable. And so what that she hadn't given me the details? Maybe she felt awkward because Jonathan was my ex-boyfriend. Maybe she was just trying to protect my feelings. She was a good person, unlike me. I was a witch, and like a witch, deserved to have a house fall on top of me while wearing my favorite shoes.

I drank my second Bloody Mary as quickly as possible and told Bridget and Jonathan that I needed to get back to my apartment to work on some blog stuff. Although it was true that I was behind on my reviews, I said it mostly to justify excusing myself early. I even left before the bill came to avoid any awkwardness if Jonathan offered to pay for Bridget. His treating her would solidify them as a couple and I wasn't sure how I'd react. I threw $25 on the table and stood up. "I think that's enough but let me know if I owe anything."

"We know where you live." Jonathan joked.

Bridget stood up to hug me and as we embraced, she whispered, "Call you later?"

Fighting back tears, I nodded. "You'd better." With one last fake smile, I said, "Bye guys. Have fun!"

As I walked home, I barely resisted the urge to start crying but I forced myself to hold it together and think rationally about the situation. My romantic feelings for Jonathan were long gone as were his for me. Bridget was my best friend and more than anyone else I knew, she deserved to be happy. I would never deny her that and even though it seemed God had something against us being romantically attached at the same time, it was currently her turn and I would somehow find a way to set aside my misery and selfishness and let her shine. *Somehow*.

When I got home, I kicked off my shoes and plopped myself on the couch. I decided to catch up on my favorite blogs for an uplifting distraction. I turned on my computer before heading to the bathroom to brush the taste of tomato juice from my mouth.

When I returned to my computer, I went to my bookmarks and clicked on the *Divalicious* website. Caitlyn, the girl who ran the site, posted humorous recaps of the most popular reality shows, along with the occasional book review and author guest post. We participated in many of the same blog tours and I considered her a "virtual" friend. Reaching into the bowl of candy I always kept on my coffee table, I popped a few Smarties in my mouth and got ready to be entertained. When the home page came onto the screen and I read the title of Caitlyn's most recent blog post, *"Prosecco and Paris, getting to know Hannah Marshak, author of the fabulously fun new novel, Cut on the Bias,"* I felt my arm hairs stand up at attention and my heart rate accelerate with each and every word I read.

To the question, "What do you think it was about *Cut on the Bias* that caught the attention of an agent and publisher whereas other novels never make it past the slush pile?" Hannah responded, "Honestly? Luck. Pure and simple. I happened to send my query letter to the right agent at the right time. While I believe *Cut on the Bias* is a terrific read and I worked my butt off writing it for two years, I am well aware that there are some amazing novels out there that will never see the light of day. What makes one book stand out from the others? I don't know. You'll have to ask my agent. LOL."

I didn't know who answered the question, but it wasn't the Hannah Marshak that I knew and loathed. *This* Hannah Marshak actually came across as humble and grateful for her success instead of what she really was, cocky and entitled. Fearing I would lose my lunch if I read anymore, I quickly closed out of *Divalicious*.

Reaching into my bag to text Bridget, even though I figured she was still with Jonathan, I removed my cell phone and saw that I had a voicemail. I put the phone on speaker and listened to the message. I rolled my eyes as I heard Erin's voice.

"Hi Kim, it's me. Just calling to say hi. How are you? I saw on Facebook that Hannah posted a review of her book from the *Chick Lit and Dreams* website. It was very favorable! Was wondering when you were gonna post your review. She told me it was supposed to come out before the book was released. Time is a-ticking, sis! Okay, better go. Gerry is taking me out for an early dinner. Call me!"

"Aargh!" I tossed the phone on my couch.

I turned back to my computer and checked my email. I scrolled my unread messages and while most included the subject line, "Review Request", my eyes were immediately drawn to one from Candy Adams which read, "Review: Cut on the Bias." *Could this day get any worse?* I chewed a fingernail and opened Candy's email.

> *Hello Kimberly!*
> *I hate to be a pest, but I was wondering whether you had an opportunity to finish Cut on the Bias? The novel has been very favorably reviewed so far and Hannah is quite pleased but we're both anxious to see your review posted on the Pastel is the New Black website.*
> *Thanks, honey!*
> *Candy*

It took all of the self-control I could muster not to toss my computer across the floor. For the love of God, the world did not revolve around Hannah Fucking Marshak and neither did my life! I stood in the middle of my living room contemplating my next move and slowly, my lips curled into a smile. Chick lit readers of the world would have to look elsewhere for a review of *Cut on the Bias*, but if they wanted to "get to know Hannah," I would gladly make an introduction. Needing fresh air, I decided to go to Starbucks to write my masterpiece. I put my shoes back on, tossed my mini laptop in my oversized handbag and headed out of my apartment.

Chapter 24

"The truth about Hannah Marshak

*If you're a fan of chick lit, which I am guessing you are if you're reading my blog, you might have heard some buzz about the upcoming release of "Cut on the Bias," the debut novel of author Hannah Marshak. It seems I can't even log onto my computer these days without reading an advance review or guest post by Ms. Marshak. If, like me, you've read these posts, you are probably under the impression that Hannah Marshak is your average girl-next-door who just happened to get a publishing deal. Maybe Hannah reminds you of a friend from your days back in summer camp or an old classmate. As someone who actually walked the same halls as Hannah in junior high and high school, I'm here to tell you that she's not your "average girl" and you would **not** want her living next door or even in the same zip code. Here's why:..."*

AFTER SHARING SOME of Hannah's most evil machinations from our high school days, I typed the conclusion, *"So in closing, while Jacqueline Milano, the main character of "Cut on the Bias," might be a heroine to root for, Hannah Marshak, the woman who created her, is not."* I leaned back in my chair at Starbucks and quietly clapped my hands. *Magnifique.* I set my blog to have the post go live at 6 the next morning and took a sip of my vanilla latte.

Was it professional of me to air Hannah's dirty laundry? Probably not, but if she was going to withhold her true essence from her potential readers, someone had to set the record straight. *Pastel Is the New Black* was my blog and I could post whatever I wanted. If, armed with the knowledge that Hannah was a two-faced, manipulative, lying attention whore, people still wished to spend their hard earned money on *Cut on the Bias*, so be it.

Happy to get that out of my system, I perused the other chick lit sites on my blog roll, with the exception of *Chick Lit and Dreams* since I did not want to read the great review of *Cut on the Bias* that Erin had mentioned. When I was finished, I logged onto Facebook to see what was going on in the "real world."

Caroline had posted pictures from her trip to Iceland and I commented that I hoped she was having a great time and couldn't wait to hear all about it. I "liked" Denise Porter's status that it was her fourth wedding anniversary, and I laughed at the video Jonathan had posted about the SNL skit spoofing *Fifty Shades of Grey*. I continued to scroll, mumbling, "boring, extremely boring, same ol'" and was about to log out when I saw in the news feeds' ticker that Nicholas Strong had been tagged in Daneen Barnett's picture. Feeling my heart practically beating out of my chest, I took a deep breath and double clicked on the picture.

Staring back at me was a smiling Nicholas, dressed in a well-fitted dark suit. He held a drink in one hand while his other arm was around Daneen's slim waist. Stunning and long legged in a dark purple evening gown, Daneen grinned as if she held the winning lottery ticket. From where I sat in my uncomfortable wooden chair in Starbucks studying the photo of Nicholas with his arm around her, it looked like a huge jackpot.

I covered my face with my hands as I tried to wipe away the visual of them socializing with other power couples at whatever event they had attended or worse, dancing cheek-to-cheek at a wedding of one of Daneen's friends or family members. I wondered if Nicholas had let her wear his suit jacket to stop her from shivering while they stole secret kisses outside.

I closed my eyes and let the implications of the picture sink in. I was being silly. Posing for a picture together did not mean they were an item. The fact that Nicholas hated me didn't mean he had immediately jumped in the sack with her! I opened my eyes and returned my focus to Facebook. Daneen had tagged Nicholas in two more pictures and I let out a joyous exhale when I saw Lucy and a few other lawyers from the firm in the other ones. It was a work function after all.

But why were Nicholas and Daneen next to each other in every single picture?

"Well, if it isn't Kimberly Long."

I looked up to see Hannah Marshak staring down at me with her huge topaz eyes. With my luck she had psychic ability in addition to writing talent and had come here to guilt me out of posting her "unauthorized biography" on my blog the next day.

"What are you doing?" she asked, nodding towards my laptop.

I turned it away from her and was about to say it was for my blog to see if she'd start kissing my ass again when I noticed them. "Nice shoes," I said dryly, pointing to the identical shoes I had worn to the reunion.

Hannah's face turned pink as she flipped her black pump to reveal the bright red sole. "Yeah, I realized I didn't own plain black Louboutins when I saw yours at the reunion."

I couldn't help laughing a little but since I was still reeling over the Facebook pictures of Nicholas and Daneen, it came out more like a strangled cry.

"Yeah, well I would have bought them earlier but..." With a hint of annoyance in her voice, she said, "Wait...are you crying?"

Wiping a tear from the corner of my eye, I said, "No!"

"Ha! Yes you are!"

I buried my head in the keyboard and shook it, denying the undeniable. I felt the vibration of a chair move and raised my head to see that Hannah had sat down and was studying me.

"Spill," she said.

She couldn't be serious. I was supposed to confide in her? No way. "It's nothing."

Hannah pointed a flawless red nail at me. "You don't cry easily. Believe me, I know. You and your little...well you probably don't think she's that little..."

I shot her a nasty look, still struggling not to burst into tears.

"Anyway, you're many things but a crybaby is not one of them. So what gives? It's Starbucks. Not a hospital or funeral home."

I banged the back of my head against my chair. "Fine! I just Facebook stalked the guy I was dating and he's tagged in all these pictures with a horrible girl!" *More horrible than you even.*

She narrowed her eyes at me. "Not the cutie from the reunion, is it?"

I closed my eyes and pictured the way Nicholas used to smile so wide each time he saw me. Hard to believe it was the same guy who never looked my way anymore. I opened my eyes. "Yes, him."

"What happened? He dumped you for a taller chick?" She snorted.

I shot her another dirty look.

"Joking! Lighten up, Long. If I recall, he wasn't exactly tall either."

I raised my eyebrows, alluding to her overt interest in him at the reunion.

"Right. He was sexy anyway. So who's this horrible girl?"

"They're both associates at my firm. She hated that he was with me, a measly secretary, and wasted no time when we got in a fight."

"Let me see," she said, reaching for my laptop.

I angled it towards her and pointed at the photo of Daneen smiling brightly next to Nicholas.

I watched Hannah silently study the photo until her eyes opened wide, she covered her mouth with her hand and started laughing.

"What?"

Hannah pushed the computer toward the middle of the table and took my hand in hers. I fought the urge to remove it immediately because I had a feeling she was going to tell me something important.

"Daneen?"

"Yes. You know her?" It figured. They were probably BFF. I slipped my hand out from underneath hers.

Hannah smiled. A smile that reached her eyes and the type of smile that had never before been directed at me. "Daneen's the 'Shitter'!"

CHAPTER 25

THINKING MY EARS must have deceived me, I asked her to clarify her previous statement. "The Shitter?"

"The one and only," Hannah nodded.

I scrunched my forehead. "What the fuck?"

Hannah stood up. "Come with me."

Jerking my head back, I said, "Come with you where?" I had no intention of going with Hannah anywhere lest she lock me in a closet and force me to give her book a 5-star review.

"This story requires something a bit stronger than caffeine. There's a bar around the corner. Ryan's Daughter. Come on."

"Ryan's Daughter? Isn't that a bit undignified for your taste?" Glancing at her Louboutins, I added, "Not to mention your shoes?"

Waving her hand in my face, Hannah said, "Undignified is exactly the right atmosphere for what I'm going to tell you. Now put your little computer away and come on." She paused. "Unless you're not interested in getting the dirt on your man's new woman."

My heart skipped a beat. "She's not his new woman!"

Hannah shrugged nonchalantly. "Maybe yes. Maybe no."

I sighed loudly, threw my mini laptop in my bag and followed Hannah outside into the spring air. From behind her, I called out, "What dirt?"

Hannah kept walking straight ahead, motioning with her hand for me to keep walking.

"What dirt?" I repeated.

I followed her into Ryan's Daughter where we found two empty seats at the bar. For a moment, I wondered if I was dreaming. *Or living in a Seinfeldian Bizarro World.* Bridget would die when I told her. First she would kill me for having a drink with Hannah and then she would die. But before I was murdered, I needed to know something. I turned to Hannah. "The Shitter?"

Facing forward, Hannah gave me the hand. Showing more courtesy to the attractive male bartender, she smiled and said, "Two dirty vodka martinis please. Extra olives."

Since Hannah refused to speak to me until the bartender poured our drinks, I sat there silently trying to figure out what Daneen had done to be nicknamed "The Shitter" by Hannah. Based on my own experience with Hannah, it was more likely Daneen didn't actually do anything and Hannah had simply made up a story to humiliate her. If that was the case, I'd have to empathize with Daneen and that was the last thing I wanted. I hoped no one I knew would walk in while we were together. I'd never live it down. And I had a feeling Hannah probably felt the same way.

At last we had drinks in hand and Hannah finally spun her bar stool around to face me. "Brace yourself."

"I'm braced!" I took a long gulp of my martini, involuntarily snarling from the strength of the alcohol.

Hannah let a small smile escape. "Okay. Daneen lived in my dorm freshman year. We lived in the SAE dorm and Daneen was a little..." She paused for a second as if trying to find the right word. "Let's say 'eager' to make an impression. One night she got in a bit over her head and did some drugs with the guys..."

I interrupted, "Drugs? You mean pot?" I took another sip of my drink.

Hannah shook her head. "No. I mean real drugs. Coke." She took a small sip of her martini, her lips barely touching the glass.

My mouth opened in surprise. "Daneen? Holy shit!"

"I haven't even gotten to the shit part of the story!" Hannah laughed and took another sip of her drink.

"Okay, this I've gotta hear." I giggled and then realizing I was having fun with the enemy, sipped my martini and adopted a serious expression. "Go on."

"Anyway, as the story goes, Daneen went back to this guy Evan's room, lost control of her bowels and took a shit while having sex with him." Hannah stopped speaking and looked at me for a reaction.

"No way." *No fucking way.*

Hannah nodded. "Yes way. Hence the nickname. She transferred out of school because of it!"

I downed the rest of my martini and raised my voice. "No fucking way!" And that little bitch had the nerve to call *my* college a party school? As far as I knew, no one had ever shit in her pants while having sex at Syracuse University. Unless she became a Mormon and transferred to Brigham Young, she had no right to talk.

"Yeah. Crazy right?" Looking off in the distance, she said, "I should use that story in my next book." Then she motioned for the bartender to pour two more drinks.

"Classic."

"Next time Daneen gets in your face, subtly bring up her crapping in her pants and I guarantee she'll back down."

Smirking, I said, "*Subtly* bring it up? Sure!" As Hannah raised the martini glass to her mouth again, I noticed that her lipstick was completely intact. The girl had skills.

Hannah shrugged. "Best advice I can give you."

Feeling tipsy, I looked over at Hannah and thought to myself that this was probably the first time I had actually enjoyed myself while in her company "I appreciate the advice, Hannah." It was true. The idea of Daneen and Nicholas together didn't seem quite as bad now that I knew she had shit in her pants. I took a final gulp of my drink, noting how much better the vodka tasted after hearing about Daneen's fecal incontinence.

"Yeah, well, I hate to see another woman cry," Hannah said impassively.

I pressed a fist against my lips to contain my laughter as Hannah motioned for the bartender. Leaning her chest over the bar, she said, "Can we have the check, please?" She batted her eyelashes at him. "And one more olive too?"

The bartender's eyes flicked from Hannah's low-cut blouse back to her face. Then he reached into the container of olives and dropped two more in her glass. "No extra charge."

"Thanks, sweetie," she said.

While the two of them made googly eyes at each other, I grabbed my wallet from inside my bag and threw a twenty on the bar. Not removing her gaze from the bartender, Hannah pushed the twenty back towards me and said, "I've got this. You should save your money."

I didn't have time to be insulted before Hannah gave the bartender a wad of bills, said, "Keep it" and stood up. To me, she said, "Ready?"

I glanced at the bartender who looked disappointed. "Sure."

As we walked towards the exit, I whispered, "He liked you."

Flipping her hair, Hannah said, "*Yeah*, he did. But he's a bartender, Long."

Same old Hannah.

Drinking inside during the day always messed me up and when we exited the bar, the glare of the sun surprised me and I momentarily shielded my eyes with my hands to regain my bearings. I thought of something as we began walking towards Second Avenue. "Hannah?"

She stopped walking. "Yeah?"

Biting the inside of my cheek, I said, "This 'shitter' thing. It really happened, right? You're not just making it up?" I really had to pee and I shifted my weight from one foot to the other.

A wrinkle appearing between her eyebrows, Hannah asked, "Why would I make it up?"

Before I could stop myself, I said, "Wouldn't be the first time."

Hannah opened her eyes in surprise but then raised her shoulders in a shrug. "I save my creativity for my books these days." Smiling, she said, "And besides, when was the last time I went out of my way to make *you* feel better, Long?"

I laughed. "Good point."

"Exactly. Get over yourself." Motioning to an oncoming cab, she said, "I'm out of here. Try not to be so annoying."

"Only if you'll try not to be such a bitch!"

Hannah opened the cab door, turned to me and said, "Where's the fun in that?" Then she got in the car and closed the door behind her.

I shook my head and as the cab drove away, I practically ran back to my apartment.

When I got home, I dropped my bags at my front door and bolted to the bathroom, exhaling a sigh of relief that I made it on time. I liked to blame my small frame for my lack of alcohol tolerance but I was beginning to wonder if the aging process was causing my diminished drinking stamina. My body wasn't any bigger back in college but I sure could hold my alcohol better.

Fully dressed, I threw myself on my bed and stared at the slightly spinning ceiling, thinking about the "dirt" Hannah had dished on Daneen. I hoped I *would* find a subtle way to mention shit in front of Daneen and I also hoped she would recoil in embarrassment and maybe even resign from the firm the way she had transferred schools. Of course, I knew that was unlikely but a girl was entitled to her dreams. For the first time in my life, I actually felt indebted to Hannah. Maybe Writer Chick wasn't that bad after all. As I thought of Hannah, a fuzzy admonition zipped across my mind but I passed out before I could make sense of it.

CHAPTER 26

I WOKE UP WITH A JOLT and checked the time on my alarm clock. 5:56. *Holy Mother of God.* My scathing post on the evils of Hannah was scheduled to post in four minutes!

Dragging all of the blankets with me, I vaulted out of the bed, immediately tripping on the sneaker that was lying in the middle of my floor. Kicking the shoe out of my way, I muttered, "Fuck!" and raced to my computer. My head was pounding and my tongue felt like I had gargled with cotton balls. This was why vodka was not my drink of choice.

Although most people wouldn't be up early enough to read the article the second it posted, I had hundreds of subscribers to my blog and if it went live as scheduled, they would all get an email directing them to it. If even one person read the piece and forwarded it to someone else, it could go viral in minutes. Most of what I had written was true but I couldn't go through with it, especially after what had gone down the night before. Not to mention how unprofessional I would look. *What had I been thinking?*

My pulse racing, I pressed the power button. *5:58.* I tapped my foot impatiently waiting for the login screen. After I entered my password, I kept one eye on the time which was reflected on the bottom right of the screen until all of the various icons on my desktop finished loading. Following what felt like an entire gestational period but in actuality was less than a minute, I made my way to the dashboard of my blog and clicked on pending posts. Since *The Truth About Hannah Marshak* was the only one in that folder, I spotted it without difficulty, angled my mouse over the "delete" field and clicked. I confirmed "yes,

I want to delete this post" and finally took a much needed breath as I collapsed onto my couch in relief. Thank goodness. I closed my eyes and fell back asleep until 7:30 when my alarm clock sounded.

*   *   *

Later that morning at work, I sat back in my desk chair and read the review one last time.

> *Cut on the Bias follows Jacqueline Milano as she leaves her doting fiancé and her life in New York City behind to move to Paris in the hopes of making it big in the fashion industry. In her most vivid fantasies, Jacqueline will rub elbows, clink champagne glasses and share pain au chocolat with the fashion elite. But even her most stubborn doubts did not hint at the backstabbing and phoniness that, in reality, would derail her goals at every turn. Would the gentle but long distance support of her fiancé back in the States keep her afloat or would the loyalty and understanding she so desperately needed come from a much more surprising source?*
>
> *Cut on the Bias, the debut novel from Hannah Marshak, is well-written, extremely engaging and, at times, very humorous. The main character, Jacqueline, is remarkably believable, as most women at some point in their lives have embarked on an adventure, whether a new job, living situation, etc. and can relate to the stress involved in meeting unfamiliar people and dealing with different and sometimes hostile personalities. I felt for Jacqueline as she struggled in her strange environment and became torn between the safety she left behind and her desire to succeed in Paris and I hoped for her happy ending. With respect to the romance, I was pretty certain which man would be left standing in the end from the get go, but it was a more scintillating love triangle than most I have read recently! The end left me warm and fuzzy and perfectly fit the story.*
>
> *The only criticism I can offer is that the supporting characters could have been a bit more fleshed out as I got somewhat confused*

between Jacqueline's intern and her seamstress. Also, some
scenes were a bit repetitive and could probably have been cut out.
    All in all, this was a surprisingly good debut but I'm not
all that shocked since the author herself is quite surprising at
times. Looking forward to reading more from Hannah Marshak.
    Rating: 4 Pink Champagne Flutes.

Happy with my positive yet honest review, I posted it on my
blog, Amazon, and Goodreads, and attached the links to my
Facebook and Twitter pages. Then I sent an email to Candy Adams
letting her know that the review had been posted.

After the post went live, I felt as if the weight of a *Biggest Loser*
contestant had been lifted off of my shoulders. The moment I had
dreaded had come and gone and I had survived. I decided to pick up
a bottle of good wine on my way home and celebrate.

"Hello?"

And just like that, I was knocked out of my "life is good" bubble
as I returned Daneen's annoyed gaze. Nicholas was standing at her
side but, as usual, was pretending to read his phone. *He really needs*
to find more creative ways to ignore me. I sighed. "Yes?"

"I've been standing here for the past ten minutes!" She said,
raising her voice.

I narrowed my eyes at her. "Ten minutes? Is that right? Uh-huh."

Shoving a stack of papers in my face, she said, "I hate to pull you
away from your little blog, but Rob needs you to scan these to him
immediately, copying me, Nicholas and David."

I gently removed the papers from her hand and stood up. "No
problem, Daneen," I said sweetly. "I was actually in the middle of
reading an article about cocaine addiction in college students. Did you
know that a side-effect of cocaine is loss of bowel control? Who knew?"

Daneen's face turned ashen as she opened her eyes wide. "Uh,
I..." She glanced over at Nicholas who had stopped staring at his
phone to look at me with a confused look on his face.

"Crazy, right? I'll scan these right away," I said cheerily. I walked
away without another word and as soon as I got a safe distance away,
jumped in the air and let out a delighted yelp. "Thank you, Hannah
Marshak!"

CHAPTER 27

SHAKING HER HEAD SO FURIOUSLY, her red curls bounced all over the place, Bridget said, "No way! No fucking way!"

I nodded somberly and took a sip of my wine. "Tis true."

Bridget shoveled a forkful of Caprese salad in her mouth. "You had drinks with Hannah Marshak. A girl who probably enjoys sticking it *to* you more than she likes a guy sticking it *in* her! Unbelievable."

I chuckled. "It's nuts. I know. But I had no choice."

Bridget pressed her lips together. "You always have a choice."

Cocking my head to the side, I relented. "Okay, you're right. I *could* have chosen to not follow Hannah to Ryan's Daughter, but she was holding dirt on Daneen. It was way too tempting."

Bridget downed her wine. "*Fine.* You made the right choice. But now you like Hannah!" Shivering she said, "Blech!"

"I wouldn't say I *like* Hannah, Bridge. I just have..." I hesitated. "I have a newfound respect for her though. You should have seen the look on Daneen's face when I brought up bowel movements. And poor Nicholas."

Bridget raised an eyebrow. "Poor Nicholas?"

I frowned. "He looked so confused."

Laughing, Bridget said, "I wonder why. It's not like it was the first time you uttered the phrase 'bowel control' in his presence. I'm sure that's what you always discussed during your pillow talk, right?"

I took another sip of wine, feeling an ache in my belly at the memory of pillow talk with Nicholas. I even missed his harmonica. "So, what about you? What do you and Jonathan discuss during pillow talk?"

Blushing, she said, "We haven't had pillow talk yet. We're taking things slow."

"Oh. That's smart, I guess."

Bridget nodded. "Yeah. We don't want to rush into anything until we're sure. But he's a really good kisser!"

I nodded. "Yeah."

Her face turning even redder, she said, "I guess you knew that already."

I laughed quietly. Even though I was afraid it would make me feel worse about my own situation, I vowed to be a good friend and encourage Bridget to tell me more about her relationship with Jonathan. But first I had to get something out in the open. "Bridge?"

"Kim?" Bridget smiled.

I cleared my throat. "Can I ask you something?"

Looking at me curiously, she said, "Of course."

My voice shaky, I asked, "How come you didn't tell me about Jonathan?"

Bridget cocked her head to the side. "What do you mean? You're the one who suggested I do something about my crush."

"And I meant it! But how come you didn't tell me anything after your first 'appointment'? When I showed up at brunch, you guys were practically a couple already and it really caught me off guard." I took a sip of my wine. "Not that I wasn't happy for you, but still. I felt like an idiot."

Bridget frowned. "I'm sorry, Kim. I wanted to tell you everything and I almost did. Several times. But I knew you were upset about Nicholas and didn't want to rub it in your face."

I chewed my lip. "So, you weren't trying to keep me out of the loop?"

Bridget's eyes opened wide. "Absolutely not! You're my best friend and I want you to know everything about me. I was afraid to pour salt on the wound."

Nodding, I said, "I get it. It's just that…" I paused to collect my thoughts. "Between losing Nicholas and being abused by Daneen at work, I haven't been in the best place. Feeling disconnected from you just made me feel worse."

Bridget's eyes turned glassy. "Oh, Kim, I'm sorry. You know I love you, right?"

I smiled. "Of course. I love you too, Bridge."

Bridget grinned. "Glad we got that straight." Motioning with her head towards the bar area, she said, "A girl at the bar is staring at you."

I spun around and looked toward the bar where there was indeed a girl with a chin level bob of black hair squinting her eyes in my direction. After a brief moment, I recognized her as Sarah, Nicholas' friend from Anthony & Vic's.

I turned back to Bridget. "I know her. Sort of." I stood up. "You mind if I say hello? I'll explain later."

Bridget stood up with me. "No worries." Removing the pack of cigarettes from her bag, she said, "I'll take this opportunity to have a smoke."

Smirking, I said, "So happy to facilitate your bad habits."

Bridget winked. "One of the many reasons I love you," she said before hoofing it to the exit of the restaurant.

Following behind her, I walked over to Sarah having no idea what I was going to say, considering we'd only met once and my relationship with Nicholas hadn't exactly ended under the best of circumstances. I wondered if she knew the entire story.

She was talking to the bartender and no longer facing my direction, but turned around when I tapped her lightly on the back. She smiled wide. "Kim! I thought that was you. My eyesight isn't great. George keeps telling me to get glasses but I'm too vain. And I'm too terrified to do the LASIK surgery." Taking a big gulp of wine, she said cheerily, "How are you?"

Someone is drunk. I made eye contact with the bartender, who grinned. "Yeah, she's schnuckered," he said.

Sarah leaned over the bar and lightly swatted him. Turning back to face me, she said, "It's Tim's fault. We're in culinary school together and he keeps me company when George works crazy hours, which…'" She rolled her eyes. "Is often." Giggling, she said, "George doesn't mind because Tim is gay."

Tim shook his head. "I think the real reason he doesn't mind is because I let you both drink at my restaurant for free."

Rolling her eyes again, Sarah said, "Whatever. So how are you? I was so sad to hear that you and Nicholas stopped dating." She frowned.

I bit my lip. "Thanks. That's so nice of you to say." I figured it was the booze that was making her so enamored of my relationship with Nicholas. I couldn't have made *that* great of an impression the one time we'd met.

"We all figured it was about time he started dating again." Sarah shook her head, her lower lip still protruding in a pout.

Puzzled by her statement, I repeated, "Started dating again?"

"Exactly!"

I was thoroughly confused. I looked over at Tim, hoping for help, but he was assisting another customer. "What do you mean?"

"Nicholas is so cute! Seriously yummy, right?"

I felt that stubborn dull pain in my tummy again. Weakly, I agreed, "Yeah."

"After Amanda, we knew it would be a while before he trusted another girl but years went by and nothing." More to herself than me, she mumbled, "Bitch."

I assumed Amanda was his ex-girlfriend. "What did Amanda do?"

Sarah looked hard at me. "He didn't tell you?"

Nicholas had never told me anything about his relationship history. I shook my head, "No." I looked over as Bridget walked by on her way back to the table. I raised two fingers to let her know I would join her soon.

Sarah sighed loudly and then took another sip of wine. "They dated for years. He assumed...*we* assumed... she was the one. When he asked her to move in with him, she confessed that she was seeing someone else at the same time."

I opened my eyes wide, not knowing what to say.

Sarah continued. "And had been for almost the entire two years of their relationship."

"Holy crap," I blurted out.

"Yeah. It was her high school boyfriend!" Sarah said, shaking her head. "Bitch."

"Oh, wow," I said, still floored.

"He hasn't seen anyone else since." With a devilish grin, she said, "Well, he obviously isn't celibate or anything. Way too cute for that."

"A player, huh?" *I knew it.*

Sarah jerked her head back. "No way. But we all have needs, you know?"

Twirling a hair around my index finger, I said, "Did he...Did he ever date Mary?"

Sarah furrowed her brow in confusion. "Mary? You mean our friend Mary? She's gay, so definitely not!" She laughed and took another swig of wine. "Anyway, you were the first girl he took seriously since Amanda."

I gripped the back of her bar stool for support and repeated, "Took seriously?"

Nodding, Sarah said, "He never brought anyone out with us. Ever. Certainly not out to dinner. Until you. He really liked you." She frowned again.

Half to myself, I said, "I had no idea."

Obviously thinking I was referring to Amanda's deception, Sarah said, "I know! Who would have guessed a girl could secretly date two people seriously for two years."

I shrugged.

Flipping her hair, she said, "So, yeah, we were all so sad when he told George you guys had ended things. I still have a subscription to your blog though."

"You subscribe to my blog?" I felt a bit sick to my stomach and suspected it had nothing to do with the appetizers Bridget and I had already eaten and everything to do with how I'd misjudged Nicholas.

"Yeah! Nicholas sent me the link after George's birthday dinner. No reason I have to break up with your reviews just because you and Nicholas broke up right?" She put two fingers to her lips. "Don't tell."

I smiled softly. "Your secret is safe with me." It wasn't as if Nicholas and I were on speaking terms anyway. "Can I ask you a question?"

"Sure. I've already said too much, I'm sure." Motioning towards her wine, she said, "This shit is like truth serum."

I choked out a chuckle. "What did Amanda do for a living?"

Sarah looked up toward the ceiling as if the answer was somewhere in the track lighting. "Customer service. But I think she wanted to go back to school to be a dental technician or a physician's assistant." She shrugged. "Something like that."

Feeling like I had swallowed sour milk, I looked down at my toes and back to Sarah. "It was really great seeing you but my friend is waiting for me." I gestured toward Bridget who was now looking at me with her lips pursed in annoyance.

Sarah put her hand to her mouth. "Oh shit! I'm sorry. Didn't mean to monopolize you."

"No worries. I'm glad we ran into each other. Please tell George I said, 'Hi'."

"I will." She leaned over the bar. "Tim! Get Kim and her friend glasses of wine. On the house," she said, whispering the last three words.

"Not necessary." I said to Tim. I patted Sarah on the back and whispered, "But thanks." As I walked back over to our table where Bridget was waiting for me, the phrases "she's gay," "took seriously," "really liked you" and "customer service" swam around my brain, along with the visual of Sarah jerking her head back at my accusation that Nicholas was a player.

Crossing her arms over her chest, Bridget said, "I was beginning to think you were ditching me for Nicholas' friend. It's been..." She stopped talking and stared at me. "What happened?"

I shook my head. "You don't want to know."

Bridget leaned forward. "*Yeah*, I do."

Bridget didn't say a word as I repeated my conversation with Sarah verbatim. She just sat quietly, chewing her lower lip and occasionally nodding.

"And that about wraps it up," I said. Feeling the onset of a tension headache, I pressed two fingers against my forehead and closed my eyes. When I opened them, Bridget was looking fixedly at me. "What?" I asked.

Twirling her linguini around a spoon, she said, "I'm not sure why you're so upset about this turn of events, Kim."

"What do you mean? Were you even listening to me?" I took a bite of my pasta even though I had lost my appetite.

"Of course, I was. But everything you said implies that Nicholas really liked you. All of your concerns that you were just a distraction, that you weren't 'successful' enough, were figments of your own paranoia. That's a good thing! And your imagined competition with beach volleyball babe? Lesbian!"

"Yeah. Way to jump to false conclusions, Kimmie! Anyway, all of this would be great if we were still dating, but I hate to be the bearer of bad news, we're not. And whether or not Nicholas was embarrassed by my being just a secretary, he still made me feel that way. And he still consorted with the enemy." I mumbled, "And according to Facebook, he still does."

"Well then. I guess that means you don't like him anymore anyway, so why are we wasting our girls' night talking about him?" Bridget swallowed a mouthful of linguini and then smiled at me. "Right?"

"Right." I shook my head at her and dropped my napkin onto my plate. "I feel sick."

"I'm sorry, K." She reached across the table and placed her hand over mine.

"I was so angry at him, Bridge. But it was only a fight. I had every intention of talking to him the next morning, but he wanted no part of it. He shut me out hard." I sighed.

"Probably his defense mechanism after what his ex did."

"But I'm not Amanda. I wasn't two-timing him with my ex-boyfriend!"

Bridget chuckled. "Close enough. At least at the beginning."

"Which probably explains why Nicholas made me confirm a gazillion times after the reunion that things between Jonathan and me were really over. I wondered if he might be jealous. I kind of hoped he was a little jealous. But I never would have guessed what Amanda did to him in a million years." I took a sip of wine. "This sure was an informative night out, wouldn't you say?" I laughed even though I sort of wanted to cry.

"Never a dull moment." Bridget lifted her glass and clinked it against mine. "To another great night with my BFF!"

* * *

Later that night, I sat in front of my computer. Once I checked my email, I would get lost in a book so I could feel the main character's pain instead of mine, laugh at her missteps rather than lament my own, and cheer for the happy ending that seemed to elude me.

Among the many unread emails waiting in my in-box was one from Hannah Marshak. My first thought was that Hannah had fabricated the shitter story to secure a good review of *Cut on the Bias*. I couldn't think of an ending more befitting of the night. I clenched my jaw and opened the email.

> Hi Kim,
> I wanted to thank you for the great review. Coming from you, I'll take four stars as high praise. I'm sure your four stars are a taller girl's five stars anyway.
> JOKING, Long. Lighten up!
> Hannah

I chuckled. It turned out the mean girl had a sense of humor after all. Had I been told a mere 72 hours earlier that Hannah Marshak would elicit the only genuine smile I'd exhibit all day, I would have deemed the messenger a crack addict, but the truth was in the curl of my lips. I looked over at my closet and took a deep breath. Dismissing the thought with a shake of my head, I picked up my Kindle and flipped the on-switch. Next on my list was the sequel to a Bridget Jones knock-off I had reviewed the year before. My eyes glazed over the first paragraph but I couldn't concentrate and turned back toward my closet. I threw my Kindle on the couch, grabbed my step stool and a few old phone books, and reached for the cardboard boxes on the top shelf of my closet. I carefully stepped off the ladder and brought the boxes to my midnight blue shaggy area rug, where I sat down cross-legged. I took a deep breath, opened the first book and removed the 56 pages of the novel I'd started my senior year in high school. It was a Young Adult novel about a shy 13-year-old girl who developed special powers that allowed her to read the minds of her peers. At first she used the power to get in good with the popular kids, but later realized that some of those popular girls were not as happy as they claimed. Well, that was the intended plot anyway. I had only gotten to the part where she helped one of the cool girls barely escape being caught shoplifting to secure a coveted invite to a sleepover party. I'd begun in earnest but put it on the back burner once I started college and never found the motivation to pick it back up. In the second box was the women's fiction novel I'd started more recently. It was about a woman torn between two men: the secure "good" guy who loved her and who she loved back and the more risky, less solid "bad" guy who she also loved and who loved her back. It was not going to be one of those obvious, clichéd love triangles where you know from the start which guy is better for her. I'd read too many books and seen too many movies like that and wanted to write something more complex and unpredictable. But I'd never gotten past the outline. I had notes on at least three more books tucked away in those boxes.

To date, I had been incapable of completing a manuscript. I was one of those people who had that "great idea" that amounted to nothing. Rather than set myself up to fail again, I had given up the dream and denied that the dream even existed. Until Nicholas saw right through me. He was right. I was jealous of Hannah Marshak.

Taking the YA manuscript with me, I returned to the couch, stretched out my legs and started reading. And then I grabbed a red pen out of my desk drawer and began slashing paragraphs and writing comments in the margins. By the time I came up for air and looked at the clock, it was past 2 in the morning. I laid the manuscript on my coffee table and fell asleep right there on my couch.

As soon as I woke up the next morning, I called Rob. When his voicemail picked up, I wasn't all that surprised since it was only 7:30. "Hey, Rob. It's me, Kim. I'm sorry for the late notice, more like non-existent notice, but I need to take a vacation day. Actually, I need to take the rest of the week off. I'll be back after the weekend. If this is absolutely unacceptable, call me this morning and let me know as soon as possible. You know I wouldn't do something like this if it wasn't important. I'll explain when I get back. And, no, nobody died. Thanks, Rob. I really appreciate it." I hung up. *One call down, one to go.*

"Kim?"

"Hi, Mom." I cradled the phone in my neck while I logged onto Expedia on my computer.

"Is everything alright?"

"Everything is fine. I'm sorry to wake you!"

"You didn't wake me. I'm about to leave for Pilates. What's up?"

"I was wondering if you would mind a visitor for a few days." I ran a search for flights leaving from all NYC Airports and going to Ft. Lauderdale-Hollywood International Airport.

"Of course I wouldn't mind!" I heard her yell, "Peter! Kimberly is coming to visit!" Back into the phone, she said, "When?"

I twirled a hair around my finger. "Er, today?"

"Are you sure you're alright?"

I heard the shakiness in her voice and wanted to soothe away her concerns as quickly as possible. "I'm fine, Mom. I have a project I want to work on and I don't want to deal with the distractions of the city. I think the warm breeze of Boca Raton is exactly what I need. I'll tell you about it when I see you. You sure it's okay?"

Excitedly, my mom said, "Of course it's okay! I can't wait to see you! Will this 'project' leave you time to go shopping with your mother?"

I smiled. "I think I can arrange for that. Maybe we can do a spa day too? I can use a deep tissue massage."

My mom squealed, "Yay!" sounding more like a teenager than a 53-year-old woman.

Laughing, I said, "I'm booking my flight now."

"Good. Let us know what time we should pick you up at the airport."

"Will do." After I hung up, I booked a flight leaving LaGuardia at 3:20 pm and arriving in Florida at 6:45. It cost me $419, which I deemed a decent price considering I reserved it the day of the flight. And I had a feeling my mom would talk my dad into reimbursing at least half of the fee.

CHAPTER 28

TWENTY-FOUR HOURS LATER, I was sitting at my parent's kitchen table drinking fresh squeezed Florida orange juice.

Handing me a cup of coffee and a carton of milk, my mom said, "We just bought the Keurig last month. Do you have one?"

"Nope. Just a standard coffee pot. But if you like it, you're welcome to buy me one too." I looked up at my mother who was standing over me in a pair of black shorts and a red and white nautical inspired shirt. "You look so put together for 8:30 a.m. I feel very sloppy in comparison." I was still wearing the black yoga pants and soft pink tank top I had slept in.

My mom kissed the top of my head and sat down next to me. "This is your vacation. You're entitled. I wake up early every day. I don't want to mistake early retirement with getting old!"

I stirred some sugar into my coffee, took a sip and smiled at my mother. "You're not old."

"You bet your ass, I'm not!" she said. "So, what's this big project you're working on?"

I put down my coffee cup and took a deep breath. "I'm writing a book."

My mom didn't say anything. She just examined my face for a moment before standing up and walking over to the refrigerator.

I stared at her back, awaiting some sort of reaction. "Mom?"

When my mom turned around with a plate of fruit in her arms, she looked at me with teary eyes. Placing the bowl of fruit in front of me, she said, "It's about time."

My mouth opened but no words came out.

"You heard me," she said.

"It's about time?"

"Yes! I've been waiting for you to take your writing seriously for the past five years. This secretarial gig is a good one and Rob is a wonderful boss but, Kimberly, you're a writer. It's what you love. It's what you've *always* loved. You should spend your life doing what you love."

I swallowed hard. "But what if I'm not good?"

My mom placed her hand over mine. "You'll be terrific."

I arched an eyebrow and raised a hand in objection. "I'm your daughter. You have to say that."

Shooing my hand away, she said, "I don't have to say that! Erin is not a good writer. She has a lovely singing voice and can cut a rug on the dance floor but she can't write. And she's my daughter too!"

I laughed.

Her voice soft, my mom said, "Anyway, you're a great writer. All of your teachers said so beginning in the 5th grade. But even if you don't write a best seller, you'll never know unless you try! And I promise you'll enjoy the process. Much more than you probably enjoy making copies for Rob."

I looked down as I remembered Nicholas saying almost the same thing. Popping a grape in my mouth, I said, "It's not like I'll be able to quit my day job anytime soon."

Nodding, my mom said, "True. But I bet work will seem more tolerable because you have other passions you're following."

"That's why I started my blog."

"I know. And your blog is great. But you should write your own book," she said matter-of-factly.

"You're preaching to the converted! That's why I'm here, remember?"

My mom shook her head and smiled at me. "It's about fucking time."

My eyes opened wide. "Mom! What's with the cursing?"

Tousling my hair, she said, "We're all adults here! Now tell me about this Nicholas."

* * *

I clicked "save" and closed my eyes, feeling the tropical Floridian breeze on my face. I had only been in Florida since Tuesday night and now, Thursday afternoon, my manuscript was already 55,000 words. Granted I had written about 16,000 of them back in high school, but considering I had changed most of the original content, I was very pleased with the progress I had made in less than 48 hours. More progress than I had made in the last ten years combined, and I owed much of it to Hannah Marshak. The novel dealt with a young girl's quest to be in the popular crowd by using her special psychic powers. When I was the age of my main character, I had no desire to be in the "in crowd" and until my recent encounter with Hannah, had thought very little of the "it" girls. I still had no desire to be besties with Hannah and it wasn't as if my feelings for her had done a complete 180, but her behavior that afternoon in Ryan's Daughter and her reaction to my review made me see her as less of any enemy. It was that openness, I conjectured, that allowed me to create more three-dimensional characters for the book, something I had lacked the objectivity to do before.

A well-deserved break was definitely in order and my parent's kidney shaped pool beckoned to me as the turquoise water moved with the breeze. After I double-checked that I had saved my changes, I removed the sarong from my hips, walked to the edge of the deep end, and dove in. I swam back and forth five times, switching my strokes from the crawl to the side stroke to the breast stroke, and then I swam under water from one side to the other without coming up for air. When I lifted my face out of the water to take a much needed deep breath, I almost banged my head into my father's bare feet as he stood above me. I wiped the chlorine out of my eyes and shielded the sun with my hands. "Hey."

"Your mother wanted me to tell you that lunch is being served." He looked behind him and pointed to the patio and I could see that the table I had been writing on now had three place settings. I didn't see my mini laptop and hoped she'd put it somewhere safe.

I lifted myself out of the water and immediately grabbed my beach towel and wrapped it around my body. I knew my father preferred that I wear a one piece bathing suit, and even though I was twenty-eight years old, I still felt like I was misbehaving by running around in a bikini that did nothing to hide my 32 Cs.

A few minutes later, we sat around the table eating egg salad sandwiches and Taro Chips. As usual, my mother and I chatted animatedly while my dad read the paper and listened to our conversation with one ear.

My mom swallowed a bite of her sandwich and patted her mouth with a napkin. "Make good progress today, sweetie?"

"Yes!" I said enthusiastically. "I'm about two-thirds finished with the first draft."

My mom beamed at me. "That's amazing!" Looking at my dad, she said, "Isn't that amazing, Pete?"

My dad put down his paper and looked at me from under his sunglasses. "That is quite impressive." He patted my shoulder and went back to reading.

My mom rolled her eyes at me and we both giggled silently. My dad wasn't big on conversation. "Are you going to tell Nicholas about it?"

At that, my father put his paper back down. "Who's Nicholas?"

My mom laughed. "I knew that would get your attention. Nicholas is Kim's boyfriend."

"*Ex*-boyfriend," I clarified. "And I don't think we were ever officially girlfriend and boyfriend."

"Why is he your ex?" My dad asked.

Answering for me, my mom said, "Because *your* daughter likes to do things at her own pace and got snarky when Nicholas pushed her a bit too hard."

My dad put down his sunglasses and looked at me sternly. "Nicholas pushed you to *do* things?"

"To write a book, Dad!" I said. My face was already burning from the sun but now it was absolutely overheating. If my Dad only knew that Nicholas didn't have to push me to do other *things*. He probably thought I was still a virgin.

"I personally like the sound of the guy. Successful, handsome, and obviously intuitive when it comes to my daughter," my mom said. I had told her what happened with Nicholas and she pissed me off by taking his side.

"Oh, now she's *your* daughter?" My dad said.

"Anyway..." I said, interrupting their mock argument, "I do plan to tell Nicholas. I have no idea if he cares anymore, but I'll let him know."

"Oh, he cares," my mom said knowingly.

I shrugged. "I think he has a right to know, considering his role in making it happen. Him and Hannah, that is."

Shaking her head, my mom said, "I still can't believe you and Hannah had drinks together. Did you tell your sister?"

My dad put his paper down again. "Why would Erin care?"

"Because Erin has a girl-crush on Hannah!" I said.

My dad cocked an eyebrow. "Seriously?"

My mom and I nodded.

I hadn't told Erin that I had been out with Hannah yet, but looked forward to using it to my advantage the next time she annoyed me. I could almost see the drool collecting at the corner of her mouth.

"So when do you think you'll be finished?" my mom asked.

I had already seen the entire book play out in my mind like a movie and it was just a matter of getting it on paper. Of course, finding the right words to turn the "movie" into a book wouldn't be easy but I had a goal in mind. "I want to finish the first draft before I leave on Sunday."

"Lofty aspirations! How many more pages is that?" my dad asked, his head peeking over the paper.

"Less than a hundred, I think." I still had what remained of Thursday, all of Saturday and whatever writing time I could fit in before my flight on Sunday. Friday was a bust because my mom and I had massage appointments in the morning and shopping in the afternoon. And my parents' over-50 community had a Friday happy hour that, according to my mom, was not to be missed. "I think I can do it."

My mom stood up and began clearing the table. "I *know* you can do it!"

I smiled broadly at my mom. "Thanks for your faith, Mom!"

"Like I said, it's about fucking time."

* * *

Approximately 72 hours later, I typed "The end" right as the pilot announced we were beginning our descent into New York and LaGuardia Airport. I shut down my laptop and stored it in my carry-on bag which was stowed under my seat. My heart beat rapidly in excitement and I took a few deep breaths in and out to calm myself down. Then I leaned back against my seat, closed my eyes and fell into a deep sleep that lasted the twenty remaining minutes of the flight. When I woke up, the other passengers were busy unlocking seatbelts and checking cell phones. Feeling hazy from my deep slumber, I practically slept-walked to baggage claim before waiting on the line for a cab to take me back home.

As I sat in the taxi, my fingers firmly gripped my carry-on bag as if I thought someone would reach into the car and steal it from me. I looked out the window toward the New York City skyline that awaited me and smiled even though I felt tears brewing behind my eyelids. Inside my carry-on bag was my computer and within the hardware of my computer laid my first completed novel. In the time I had been away, I had transformed from a chronic beginner of novels to a finisher.

I couldn't wait to tell Nicholas.

CHAPTER 29

WHEN I ARRIVED AT WORK the next morning, I plopped a hard copy of my manuscript on my desk and immediately logged on to my computer to see what I had missed being out of the office for almost a week. The position of my keyboard and mouse pad had been shifted and so I knew a floater had sat at my desk, but Rob never asked floaters to do anything besides answer his phone and scan documents unless it absolutely could not await my return.

I deleted the "out of the office" and "available Rangers tickets" messages without bothering to read them and began scrolling through the remaining emails. My eyes darted up and down the list of bolded unread messages until one with the name "Nicholas" in the subject line came into my focus. I rushed back to the email and reading it more closely, saw that it said "Nicholas' going-away party." Feeling my heart in my throat, I steadied my trembling hands and opened the email.

> *Please join us on Thursday, June 21st as we bid adieu to Nicholas as he embarks on his newest adventure. Our loss is The Soap Company's gain. Destination TBD.*

I let go of the mouse, dropped my hands to my sides and leaned back in the chair with my eyes closed as I let the news of Nicholas' resignation sink in. Even though Nicholas hadn't spoken to me in over a month, I had remained comforted by the fact that we worked together. Sharing an employer came with a built-in opportunity to see each other on a daily basis and I hadn't lost hope that seeing him regularly might eventually lend itself to the possibility of reconciliation.

But once Nicholas left the firm to work with the client, the best I could hope for was connecting his phone calls to Rob or putting him through to voicemail.

I opened my eyes and squeezed back the tears just as Rob came rushing around the corner on the way to his office. When he saw me, he stopped short in front of my desk, reminding me of Kramer from *Seinfeld*. "Long!" he said. "You're back!"

I faked a smile. "You're very observant, boss man."

Pointing toward his office, Rob said, "Come in. I want to hear all about why it was imperative you take four days off with no notice." He spoke in a stern voice but I could see from his twinkling eyes that he was joking.

I stood up and followed him to his office.

"Close the door," he said. "Don't want to be interrupted from quality time with my right hand."

Already emotional over the news of Nicholas' resignation, I hoped Rob's kind words wouldn't propel me over the edge. Hannah was right. I had never been much of a crier until I started dating Nicholas. I sat down on one of Rob's guest chairs and watched him straighten out some files before leaning back in his chair and resting his feet on the desk. "So what's the story?"

"The story is that I wrote a novel," I said matter-of-factly.

Rob's eyes bugged out in surprise and he returned his feet to the ground. Placing his elbows on the desk, he leaned towards me. "You wrote a novel?"

I nodded.

His eyes still wide, Rob said, "This week?"

At last a genuine smile escaped my lips. "Yup! Well, technically I didn't write the entire novel this week since I had started it in high school, but I re-wrote it and finished a first draft while I was in Florida at my folks' house."

Rob grinned. "Kim! That is amazing."

Not used to accomplishing anything described as "amazing," I started to choke up again. "Thanks."

"But what was with the urgency?"

"I was afraid if I didn't strike while the iron was hot, I would change my mind. And I have been putting this off for ten years now already," I confessed.

Rob nodded in understanding.

I bit my lower lip. "Please don't tell anyone, okay? At least not until I've had a chance to tell Nicholas."

Rob studied me for a moment and I was afraid he was going to ask for more details. "No problem," he said.

My left leg tapping involuntarily, I said, "So Nicholas is leaving us, huh?" I cast my gaze downward for a beat, embarrassed by the thought of Rob knowing I was upset about it.

Studying me again, he said, "Yes. He got a really great offer." He gave me a sly grin. "Normally I would be pissed about losing my best associate, but since he's leaving to go with a client, it will solidify their relationship with the firm." More to himself, he said, "I guess I should make some sort of formal announcement to the squad."

I tried to summon an appropriate response but when none came, I nodded to show I was at least listening. Then I placed my hands on the chair and lifted myself up to a standing position. "I should get back to work." I started walking out.

"Long."

I turned around. "Yeah?"

"Why don't you tell Nicholas about your amazing accomplishment? I'm sure it will make his day."

Even though I wasn't so sure I agreed with Rob, I gave him a closed-mouth smile. "I will."

Before I could chicken out, I grabbed the copy I had made of my manuscript from my desk, placed it in a large manila folder and walked slowly to Nicholas' side of the floor, feeling my hands shake with each step. I hadn't so much as passed by his office since the morning after our argument, when I had overheard him laughing with Daneen.

He was reading a document with one hand scratching his head, and looked to be in deep concentration. I licked my dry lips, took a deep inhale and knocked softly on his open door.

His fingers still combing through his dark hair, Nicholas lifted his head. Looking a bit taken aback to see me standing there, he said, "Hi," but it sounded more like a question than a greeting.

I planted a smile on my face. "I heard you were leaving us." I shifted my weight from one foot to the other.

Nicholas nodded. "Yeah. I got an offer I couldn't refuse."

Attempting a joke, I said, "Is your new boss The Godfather? Did they threaten to kill you?"

He smiled and shook his head. "Nope. Not yet at least."

"Well, I'm happy for you."

"Thanks," he said with a half smile.

"You'll be missed." I cleared my throat wishing I hadn't said that.

Nicholas said, "Thanks," again, sounding every bit as uncomfortable as me. Clearing his throat as well, he said, "Did you have a nice vacation?"

Happy my four-day absence had not gone unnoticed, I said with renewed confidence, "Yes! That's one of the reasons I'm here actually."

Nicholas narrowed his eyes. "Oh?"

"You were right."

"Oh yeah? What was I right about?

I took a deep breath and exhaled before confessing, "I do want to be a writer. I've *always* wanted to be a writer." Butterflies did gymnastics in my belly as if they were training for the Olympics.

Nicholas touched his pointer and middle fingers to his bottom lip and smugly responded, "No shit," but his eyes looked sad even as the corners of his mouth curled up in a smile.

I giggled. "That's what my mom said. Well her words, to be exact, were, 'it's about fucking time.'"

Nicholas laughed but then closed his mouth and looked at me again with sad eyes. "Very cool, Kim."

"There's more," I said. "I spent the week finishing the first draft of the novel I started in high school." I placed the folder on his desk.

Running his hands along the folder, Nicholas' jaw dropped as he stared at me for a moment. At last, he smiled wide, his brown eyes reflecting what appeared to be sincere happiness. "Wow, Kim. That's really great!"

"I couldn't have done it without you," I said softly.

Nicholas argued, "Of course you could have."

Not removing eye contact, I said, "But I *wouldn't* have. Thank you."

A faint blush painted Nicholas' cheeks. "I feel silly taking any credit for such a major accomplishment on your part, but you're welcome."

"Nicholas, I'm so sorry." I paused. "For everything."

Nicholas nodded and looked down at the documents on his desk. "No worries."

There was so much more I wanted to say like, "I miss you," "I'm nothing like Amanda" and "Please forgive me" but I couldn't bring myself to go there. I already felt extremely vulnerable as it was. I motioned my head towards the folder. "I printed out that copy for you. You don't have to read it if you don't want to." I shrugged.

He smiled again. "I would love to read it, Kim. You're a talented writer and I'm sure it's terrific."

Feeling myself blush, I said, "Be kind. It's just a first draft."

Rolling his eyes, Nicholas chuckled. "I promise to give it 5 pink champagne flutes."

I jerked my head back at his unexpected reference to my blog. Embarrassed, I said, "Okay, I should get back to work. I seriously doubt Rob gave the floater any work last week, which means it's probably waiting for me." I started to turn around.

"Kim?"

I looked at him, hoping he could read my mind and know how much I still liked him. I also wished he'd call me "Kimmie" again. Practically in a whisper, I said, "Yeah?"

Nicholas' eyes met mine. "I'm sorry too."

I swallowed hard. "For what?"

Scratching his head again, he said, "Daneen's treatment of you was completely deplorable and I'm sorry I dismissed it. I should have stuck up for you."

I shrugged. "It's okay." I wished I could tell him the shitter story but figured Daneen had been humiliated enough. I also wanted something to hold over her head indefinitely.

"I doubt she'll treat you as badly once I leave."

I cocked my head to the side. "Why's that?" If he only knew that I would gladly be on the receiving end of Daneen's condescension if it meant Nicholas wouldn't quit.

"She was jealous." A film of red blanketed Nicholas' face and he smiled at me sheepishly. "I think she liked me."

I nodded. "I know…"

"And I liked *you*," Nicholas interrupted.

Not expecting to hear that, my mouth opened while I desperately searched for an appropriate response. *What about, "I liked you too. I still do." Say it. Say it!*

Breaking the awkward silence, Nicholas said, "I should get back to work." Nicholas shifted his chair, turned toward his keyboard and without looking back at me said, "Congratulations again, Kim."

As he began typing on his computer, I watched him in silence until I found my voice. I croaked out, "Um, thanks," and walked back to my desk.

CHAPTER 30

I SAT FORWARD in the passenger seat, impatient to release my seatbelt as Caroline pulled into the parking lot of Palace Spa in Brooklyn. Although it was more like a European bathing house than a luxury spa, Caroline's friend had raved about the place and at only $45 for unlimited use of the various hot tubs and outdoor pools for the day (massages were extra), it seemed reasonable enough for my limited budget. Caroline and Bridget were both stressed out over sudden growth in their careers, and between revising my novel, keeping up with my reviews and trying not to think about Nicholas' impending last day of work, my stomach was in knots. We all needed pampering big-time.

After turning off her car, Caroline looked at me and then through her rearview mirror at Bridget. "Ready guys?"

Bridget squealed in excitement as she bolted out of the car. "Everyone out of the pool! Or in our case, everyone *in* the pool!"

I stepped outside and lifted my arms in a stretch. "*So* ready!"

Throwing her beach bag over her shoulder, Caroline grinned, said, "Let's go then!" and started walking. Bridget and I locked arms and followed behind her. We looked at each other and giggled in anticipation of our afternoon of self-indulgence.

When we entered the facility, which looked more like a large warehouse than a palace, we were greeted by a young woman sitting behind a desk. My lips trembled as I glanced at Bridget out of the corner of my eye. The woman was wearing a bright pink and orange striped shirt and shorts set. I could tell Bridget was purposely avoiding eye contact with me, but her face was red and she was biting her lip.

Grateful that at least Caroline was capable of showing some semblance of maturity, I followed her lead as we showed our driver's licenses, paid our $45 fee and signed medical release forms. "Who knew European bathing houses were such serious business?" I muttered.

Bridget jabbed me with her elbow. "Shh. Don't make me laugh."

"Welcome to the spa, girls," the woman said. She could have been Megan Fox's identical twin but I couldn't see past the outfit and stifled a giggle as she handed us each a locker key. "When you walk through those doors, you'll see rows of lockers to your left. To the right is where you can get your uniforms. You are required to wear the uniforms at all times that you are not in the pool or baths.

I jabbed Bridget in her side and whispered, "Uniform?" Where were my robe and slippers?

"You guys ready? I'm so excited to go in the sauna!" Caroline said.

"Ready when you are!" I said, only slightly less excited at the prospect of my 'uniform.'

Upon entrance into the main room, I immediately stopped in my tracks at the sight before me. "Wow." The room was jam packed with women, all wearing the same heinous outfit as the lady at the front desk, which I presumed was the "uniform" to which she was referring. Many of the ladies were changing by the rows of lockers to our left and others were strewn around the room talking amongst themselves in loud but muffled voices, but they were all dressed the same. It looked more like a rec room in a women's prison than a spa. I looked to my right where we were told to pick up our uniforms. Shelves were stacked high with neatly folded sets of bright pink and orange striped shirts and matching orange pants. "Wow," I repeated, unable to form other words.

Caroline, Bridget and I slowly walked over to the shelves and requested a uniform and I could tell immediately that even the extra small was going to swim on me. I wondered who they used as the model when they sized the uniforms, maybe an extra small sumo wrestler.

Afterward, we stood in a small circle looking at each other until Bridget broke the silence. "Okay, so the uniforms would probably win worst outfit by Joan Rivers on *The Fashion Police*. Doesn't mean the baths won't feel fantastic."

I smiled at Bridget, impressed by her optimistic spirit. "True."

"Besides, we only have to wear them when we're not in the pool or baths which means we'll barely have to wear them at all," Caroline said.

I decided it was my turn to suit up and say something uplifting. "And everyone is wearing the same ugly clothes and so it's not like we'll stand out when we do have to wear them," I said. And at least Nicholas wasn't there to see me in it. *Not that he takes much notice of my attire these days.*

"True, true," Caroline said, nodding. Glancing over at the rows of lockers, she said, "So...should we?"

I shrugged. "What have we got to lose?"

"Where to first?" Caroline asked after we put on our bathing suits.

"Let's check out the hot tubs." Bridget said.

A few minutes later, I stepped into one of the heated baths and sat back in the water as the jets surrounded me with bubbles. I leaned my head against the side of the bath and closed my eyes.

"Very nice." I heard Bridget say.

"Too bad there are so many kids though." Caroline said.

I opened my eyes and noted the baths next to us, crammed with children. "As long as they stay in that bath and don't bother us, I'll be fine. I just want some peace and quiet." I felt the pressure of the jets pound against my back and neck.

"So glad the day wasn't a total loss," Caroline said, laughing. "Those uniforms had me worried. This outing was my idea."

Reassuringly, Bridget said, "And it was a great idea, Caroline. Uniform Schmuniform. No biggie." Closing her eyes, she added, "It's all good now."

I closed my eyes again, letting the heat of the water remove the tension from my body.

"So what's new with everyone?" Bridget asked.

"Work, work and more work. Although I did meet a guy on the PATH train last week. I think he might be a bit old for me, mid-forties, but he was really cute," Caroline said.

"Sounds promising," I said, opening my eyes.

Caroline laughed. "Maybe I should consider dating a *much* older man to get my dad back for marrying a woman almost half his age."

Giggling, I said, "Sounds like a brilliant plan,"

From her end of the tub, Caroline kicked one of her long legs toward Bridget. "How are things going with Jonathan? Kim told me you guys started dating!"

Her face radiating happiness, Bridget said, "Things are going well!" before ducking her head in the water. When she lifted her head, she gave me a guilty look and said, "But my bases of comparison are so stale at this point, the competition isn't exactly fierce."

Shaking my head, I said, "Don't let Bridget's nonchalant attitude sway you, she's got it *baaaad!*"

Splashing her hands in the water, Bridget smiled softly. "I kind of do." Looking at me apologetically again, she said, "Sorry."

"No need to apologize to me! I'm happy for you." And despite my own misery, I truly was, although I did my best not to think about Jonathan and Bridget getting it on. I did, however, wonder if he was more energetic with Bridget than he was with me. Someday I'd ask what he was like in the sack with her. Someday being a date in the very far-off future. "At least one of us has a man." Looking at Caroline, I said, "Maybe two of you soon!"

Frowning at me, Caroline said, "What's going on with Nicholas?"

"Ladies?"

Thankful for the well-timed interruption, I lifted my face toward the heavy-set older woman who was looking down at us from the floor. Of course, she was wearing the uniform.

"Yes?" I said.

"You're wearing bathing suits," she said, pointing at us.

No shit Sherlock. "What's the problem?" I asked.

"There are no bathing suits allowed in the baths," the woman responded.

Thoroughly confused since the lady at the front desk had said we only had to wear the uniforms when we *weren't* in the water, I said, "Huh?" When I felt Bridget kick me under the water, I turned to her. "What?"

Gesturing with her head to the neighboring baths, Bridget said out of the side of her mouth, "Everyone's naked."

I looked to my left and right and sure enough, all of the other adult bathers were sans bathing suit. Turning to face the woman, I said, "Is it okay if we wear our suits? I'm just not comfortable being naked in public."

Shaking her head, she said, "Against the rules."

Just then I felt a blast of hot water slap me in the face as a kid from one of the other baths ran by. Grinding my teeth, I said as nicely as I could, "So it's not against the rules to have children under the age of ten run around splashing everyone - in bathing suits, I might add." I gestured toward the neighboring tub which was filled with children and continued, "But it's against the rules for a grown woman to wear a bathing suit?"

The woman nodded. "Yes. These are the rules."

"Whatever!" Bridget said, removing her bathing suit top and swinging it around her head. "I'm naked now. Happy?"

Caroline stepped out of the bath. "I'm not getting naked."

"What about you, K?" Bridget asked.

I contemplated. While I would have reveled at the chance to skinny dip or soak naked with Nicholas in a hot tub, going commando surrounded by all of Brooklyn and their children was the opposite of sexy. I climbed out of the bath. "No thanks."

Slipping her bathing suit back on under the water, Bridget said, "Fine. Let's get out of here."

As I grabbed a towel from a pile in the corner, I heard a scream from behind me. Instinctively turning around to see what happened, I found myself facing a very large, very naked and very big busted woman pointing her finger at me, screaming in a language I didn't understand and pointing at my towel.

I glanced at the towel and back at the woman, trying not to notice her boobs hanging down to her knees or her '70s style ungroomed vagina. "What?" I yelled back.

She continued to scream at me and point at the towel.

"What!" I shouted back. "Did I steal your towel?"

More screaming.

With my hands on my hips, I stared her down as she continued to yell at me in some Eastern European language. "I have no idea what you're saying!" Giving her the finger, I threw the towel back on the floor and ran back to the lockers as Caroline and Bridget laughed hysterically behind me.

* * *

Forty-five minutes later, we were back in Manhattan. We were still laughing as we sat outside drinking beer and eating mussels at the Crow's Nest, the bar on the upper level deck of The Water Club on the East River. "Oh my God, what the hell was *that* about?" Caroline said.

"No clue," I said. "Maybe I stole her towel? But since she wasn't speaking English, how was I to know?"

"Did you see the rack on her?" Bridget said, her face matching the color of her hair as she tried to stifle her laughter. "Someone should have worn a sports bra when she was younger and maybe her boobs wouldn't hang so low now!"

"It was hard to notice her boobs with that '70s bush! Her husband must need a weedwacker!" I shivered at the visual.

"I thought I was gonna lose it when you gave her the finger!" Caroline said.

I dropped my chin to my face as a rush of guilt at my immature behavior swept through me. "I felt bad but I had no idea what else to do." Giggling, I said, "That place is a zoo!"

Raising her glass, Bridget said, "To the Palace Spa."

"To the Palace Spa," Caroline and I repeated, clinking our glasses together.

"Never again," we said in unison.

I took a sip from my chilled pint of beer. Smacking my lips together, I said, "Tasty!"

"True, that!" Bridget said, taking a sip of her beer.

"So what were we discussing before we were so rudely interrupted by the Hot Tub Nazi?" I bit my lip as I recalled the topic of our prior conversation.

Caroline raised an eyebrow. "I had asked about the status of the Nicholas situation."

I took another sip of beer hoping to drown my feelings for Nicholas in alcohol. "The situation is that he is leaving the firm next week and will probably fall in love with someone smarter, prettier and nicer at his new job. And taller," I added.

"He still likes you, Kimmie. I'm positive about that," Bridget said assuredly.

Feeling a knot in my stomach, I said, "Please don't use that name. It reminds me of him. Everything reminds me of him. Even the song playing on the radio right now!" Playing in the background was *Love Shack* by The B-52s, Nicholas' very first rock concert.

"Why don't you talk to him again?" Bridget asked.

"I wouldn't know what to say. I feel like we had closure when I went to his office and told him about my book. He congratulated me and turned back to his computer. He's walked passed my desk many times since and although he no longer acts like I'm not in the room, he hasn't initiated conversation either. Over and out!" He hadn't even mentioned whether he liked my book, which I assumed meant he either hadn't started reading it yet or he thought it sucked. I wasn't sure which I preferred. If he hadn't even started reading, it meant he was completely over me, but if he thought it sucked, it meant he thought it sucked. I frowned into the bowl of empty mussel shells.

"There has to be something else you can do." Bridget said.

"Well if you think of something, let me know." I swallowed another mussel and studied Caroline who was staring down at the table, seemingly lost in thought. "Caroline? Yoohoo!"

Caroline looked up, her eyes wide. "Oh, sorry. I was just thinking."

"Thinking about what?" Bridget asked.

Caroline's cheeks flushed. "This is going to sound silly, but I was thinking…" She paused.

"Thinking about what?" Bridget repeated.

"Who knows more about chick lit than almost anyone?" Caroline asked.

"Sophia Kinsella?" I guessed.

Caroline shook her head and smiled. "Nope."

"Who?" I asked.

"You!" she said, pointing at me.

Laughing, I said, "I'm flattered you think so. But what does that have to do with anything?"

"What do most chick lit books have in common?" she asked.

Raising her hand, Bridget said, "I know! I know! Designer shoes, lots of cocktails and dating stories from hell."

Immediately defensive, I said, "Not all of them! Hmm, what about humor? Female main character?"

Nodding, Caroline said, "Yes, but what else?"

I thought about the last few books I had read for my blog, including *Cut on the Bias*. Looking questioningly at Caroline, I said, "Happy endings?"

"Bingo!" Caroline said.

"I rule!" I took a bow while Bridget clapped her hands. "But what's your point?"

"Okay, this is where the silliness comes in, so bear with me," Caroline said.

Bridget and I looked at her expectantly.

"If someone, say Sophie Kinsella, was writing the chick lit book of Kimberly Long, do you honestly think she'd end it this way?"

"What way?" I asked.

"You and your girlfriends eating mussels after a comical day at a so-called 'spa' lamenting your broken heart." Caroline said.

"Hey! I resemble that comment!" Bridget said, giggling.

Waving Bridget away, Caroline adopted a serious expression. "Seriously, Kim. Is this how you want things to end with Nicholas?"

I shook my head, wanting nothing more than to feel Nicholas' arms around me again. And I missed his other parts too. "No."

"So fight for him!" she said.

Feeling my face burn, I said, "How?"

"I don't know how exactly." Caroline frowned. "But what if Rachel never told Dex to cancel his wedding to Darcy in *Something Borrowed*? Or Bridget Jones didn't chase Mark Darcy to his parents' Christmas Party and tell him not to move to the United States? Would those books have been as good if the girls hadn't fought for their men?"

Shaking my head, I said, "No way."

"Exactly!" Caroline said. "If Kimberly Long was the heroine of a chick lit book, don't you think she would pull out all of the stops with some grand gesture or something?"

I sighed. "Probably. But if I knew what to do, I'd do it!" *I'd have done it already.*

Caroline raised her voice. "Then write it, Kim. Pretend you're writing a romance novel and figure out what to do to show Nicholas how much you care."

"You *are* a writer, Kim," Bridget chimed in.

Momentarily going off subject, Caroline said, "Yeah, I still can't believe you never told me you were a writer. All that bonding over books and not a word."

I shrugged. "I was in denial."

"*Yeah*, you were," Bridget agreed. "Not to mention chicken shit. Until Nicholas brought you out of your shell."

"With a little push from Hannah Marshak. Can't let that bitch upstage me forever," I said.

Smiling brightly, Bridget said, "So glad to hear you call her a bitch again. I was worried about you!"

Caroline rolled her eyes at Bridget. "You really hate that girl, don't you?"

"The five minutes she was nice to Kim don't make up for the 500 times she wasn't. Five minutes notwithstanding, a leopard doesn't change its spots," Bridget said.

"Too bad, I thought maybe me, you, Hannah and Plum Sheridan could go out for drinks together," I teased.

Bridget didn't respond except to subtly scratch her nose with her middle finger while looking at me.

I laughed and turned to face Caroline who said, "So what do you say? Now that you completed your first novel, think you can write your own happy ending?"

The three of us sat in silence for a moment letting Caroline's idea sink in. She made it seem as simple as "four plus four equals eight."

Finally, I turned to Bridget. "What do you think Bridge?"

"Do you want another shot with Nicholas?" she asked.

I nodded solemnly. "Abso-fucking-lutely."

Bridget looked at me, her green eyes watering. "Then not to get all Miranda Hobbs on you but..." Placing her hand over mine, she said, "Go get your man!"

CHAPTER 31

THAT MONDAY, I was finalizing my 3-star review of *Better Luck Next Time*, a romantic comedy that could have been more comedic if the author hadn't utilized every chick lit cliché in the book, from the gay best friend, to the shoe addiction, to the evil boss, when I received an email with the subject line, "Nicholas' Farewell" from Lucy. I had been cautiously awaiting this email for the last two weeks. All too aware that time was running out for devising a plan to get Nicholas back, I was both excited for an opportunity to be in the same room with both him and alcohol (aka "liquid courage") and dreading the close of the night when I would probably never have an excuse to see him again. About to open the email, my phone rang. Still looking at my computer screen, I picked up the phone, "This is Kimberly." I clicked on the email.

"This is Erin!" my sister mimicked.

I instantly wished I had looked at my caller ID before picking up. "Hi," I responded dryly.

> *The time is quickly approaching to bid farewell to Nicholas as he embarks on his next legal adventure. We'll miss him but can be comforted knowing he will have an endless supply of soap to keep him smelling good.*

I closed my eyes and inhaled through my nose, trying to conjure up Nicholas' scent from my memory. Sweet like gingerbread.

"Hello?"

I opened my eyes. "Oh. Sorry, Erin. I was reading an important email when you called. Got distracted. What's up?"

"I saw your review of Hannah's book."

"You just read it now?"

Erin let out a deep breath as if exhausted. "I'm furnishing our living room and have been so preoccupied that I hadn't been on Facebook in a while. I was on Hannah's page and I saw the link to the review."

I wasn't going to tell her that the review was also posted on her very own sister's blog. God forbid she got a subscription. Even Sarah, Nicholas' friend, had a subscription but not my own sister. I continued reading the email.

> *Please join us this Friday night directly after work. We've rented the back room of Iggy's on 2nd Avenue between 74th and 75th for happy hour.*

The Upper East Side was kind of far away from the office, but whatever. At least it was close to my apartment.

"You liked the book, huh?" She said knowingly.

"Yeah. It was a solid debut novel. Hannah is a good writer," I admitted. I was still in shock that I could say that without instantly vomiting in my mouth.

"I told you so!"

I rolled my eyes. "Yeah. Hannah's not all bad. She had me laughing out loud when we went out for drinks."

I heard Erin gasp. "Wait... What? You had drinks with Hannah? When? Where?"

I remained silent, but smiled as Erin continued with her barrage of questions.

"Do you think you'll have drinks again?"

Unlikely. "Probably." I smiled again.

"Maybe I can come along! I'll take the train in and stay with you?"

"Maybe. Maybe not. We'll see." I was probably going to hell but it would be worth it.

> *The person with the best Karaoke performance will drink for free! Who are we kidding, drinks on the firm for everyone of course.*
> *See you there.*

"Erin, I gotta go." I hung up.

Karaoke, huh? *Interesting.*

CHAPTER 32

I STRAIGHTENED OUT my form-fitting T-shirt so that the words "Penny Lane" fell across my chest and took a deep breath before entering Iggy's. I declined heading there with the folks from the office so that I could run home and change first. I felt like such a dork wearing the shirt and wondered if Nicholas would even notice it. He was such a Beatles fan he might not make the connection to the jingle he had written after the first time we had sex. Who was I kidding? The second he saw me, he would know it was no coincidence. It made no difference since my feelings for him would be obvious to everyone by the time the night was over anyway. *Assuming I don't chicken out.*

The narrow front area of the bar was pretty empty for a Friday night and the bartender glanced at me as I walked in. I pointed to the back area. "Here for the party," I said and kept walking. I paused for a moment before heading in and made a quick decision to pretend this was like any other happy hour I had attended with my colleagues. I would politely say "hi" to Nicholas and then socialize with the others until it was *time*.

Walking into the room, I whispered to myself, "You can do this."

"Kim!"

I turned left toward the sound of my name and faced Lucy. Her cheeks were flushed and her blonde hair fell loosely across her shoulders. I almost didn't recognize her.

"Where have you been? I'm almost finished with my second Appletini!"

Her more relaxed demeanor made much more sense once I noticed the almost empty martini glass in her hand. "Sorry I'm late. I had to run an errand first." At that moment, the crowd parted and I saw Nicholas in the back of the room. He had also changed—into dark blue jeans, a brown T-shirt and his Converse sneakers. He was talking to Rob, whose back was to me, but his eyes met mine and I smiled softly in his direction to disguise the trembling in my stomach. I felt every muscle in my body tense and wondered if he could read my shirt from across the bar. I took a step in his direction, opting to get the initial awkwardness over with. I hoped he would react positively to my being there and help instill the confidence I needed to go ahead with The Plan. *If not, there was Plan B: shots.*

"I'm going to get another drink." Motioning to my empty hand, Lucy grabbed my arm. "Looks like you need one too. Come with me!"

Following Lucy to the bar, I glanced back at Nicholas over my shoulder. He was still talking to Rob.

"What are you drinking?" Lucy asked.

I watched the bartender as he prepared another Appletini for Lucy. "I'll have what she's having."

Grinning, Lucy said, "Good choice."

The bartender smiled at me and I shrugged, smiled back and mumbled, "I certainly hope so."

Taking a sip of her drink while the bartender prepared mine, Lucy said, "Are you gonna perform later?"

Suddenly I felt like the temperature in the room had risen by ten degrees. I knew I had to get a grip if I was going to survive the night. Feigning nonchalance, I said, "We'll see. Maybe!" I grinned at Lucy as if I was no more vested in this night than anyone else in attendance. "What about you?"

"There's no way I'm singing alone but I'd do a duet. Maybe we can do one together?"

"Maybe!" I picked up my drink. To the bartender, I said, "Thanks" and took a few sips before peeking back into the bar. Nicholas was talking to Daneen, who I no longer considered a threat thanks to Hannah. "I feel rude. I should probably say hi to the guest of honor."

"Of course!" Lucy said, waving me away. "I'll come find you later. Maybe we can sing something fun like *Don't Stop Believing.*

Grinning, I said, "Well if you want to sing that one, you're probably gonna have to be among the first performers. It's not exactly the most original choice." *Unlike mine.* "Okay, I'll see you later."

Leaving Lucy behind, I walked through the crowd nodding "hello" to my colleagues as I made my way over to Nicholas. When he saw me, he stopped talking to look at me and when Daneen saw Nicholas look at me, she stopped talking and looked at me too. I felt like a science experiment. Standing taller, I smiled and said, "Hi guys!"

"Hi, Kim," Daneen said. "I'll see you later, Nicholas." I smiled as I watched her walk away. Her treatment of me had gotten considerably better after I made the bowel movement comment. She even addressed me by name.

"What was that about?" Nicholas asked.

I touched my finger to my chin. "What do you mean?"

Nicholas looked over my head to where Daneen was now talking to Rob. "Daneen's being sort of nice to you. What happened between you two?"

Attempting to flirt, I raised and lowered my eyebrows. "Maybe I'll tell you someday."

Not taking the bait, Nicholas simply said, "Okay" and glanced over my shoulder.

He looked around the room, turned to see what was going on behind him and then back over my head. It was obvious to me that he was avoiding eye contact. I cleared my throat. "So, I just wanted to stop by and wish you the best."

Finally he looked at me. "Thanks, Kim. I appreciate it." Glancing at my full drink and down at his almost empty glass of beer, he said, "I need a refill." Then he patted me on the shoulder, said, "Enjoy the open bar," and walked away. As I watched his back get farther away, I felt my spirits plummet. He hadn't even noticed my shirt, something he surely wouldn't have missed had he even glanced at my chest.

Not exactly the confidence boost I was hoping for.

*   *   *

My body shaking with laughter, I wiped the tears from my eyes as Tina the mailroom clerk shook her booty to *Baby Got Back*. I had been at the bar for over an hour and with alcohol now coursing through everyone's veins, the Karaoke portion of the night had begun. So far,

two associates, one white and the other African American, had sung
Ebony & Ivory; One of the secretaries sang *Nine to Five*; and, as predicted,
the first performance was *Don't Stop Believing* from two guys and one
girl in Accounting. I turned to Rob standing next to me. "I'm truly
impressed with the showmanship of my co-workers! No one has made
a fool of himself yet."

Rob raised an eyebrow in doubt. "The night is still young, Long."

As I laughed with Rob, I quietly wished for someone to give a
horrible performance soon so the ice would be broken.

Gesturing towards the stage area, Rob said, "You getting up there?"

I took a sip of my drink, only my second as I was pacing myself,
and watched Nicholas give Tina a high-five after her performance.
"Eventually, yeah."

Widening his eyes, Rob said, "Really? Well, don't wait too long.
That I've got to see."

"Keep your expectations low, Boss Man!" I joked.

After the applause for Tina died down, the DJ walked over to the
microphone and I wondered who would be up next. I hoped whoever
it was would kind of suck since so far the night was turning out to be
like an audition for *America's Got Talent*.

Pointing at Tina who was standing over to the side as Nicholas,
smiling brightly, wrapped his arms around her in a congenial hug,
the DJ said, "That will be a tough act to follow but I'm confident!
Next up, we have the Twenty-Fours singing *It's Raining Men* by The
Weather Girls!"

A giggling Lucy ran to the front of the stage followed by Patti,
Belinda and Joanne, the other secretaries on my floor. As the music
started, the four girls awkwardly shared two microphones and began
singing, *"Hi' - we're your weather girls. And have we got news for you!"*
in very off-key and unharmonious voices.

Finally, we have bad singers in the house!

Leaning down and burying his head in my shoulder, Rob muttered,
"Lucy is scaring me."

Laughing, I pushed his head away, "No hiding! Gotta support a
member of the Squad."

Rob stood up straight and looked at me. Then he slowly curled
his lips into a smile. Suddenly, he yelled towards the stage, "Aren't you
missing someone up there?"

Not knowing what he was talking about, I gave him a questioning look as he stared towards the stage and cocked his head in my direction.

Feeling my whole body freeze, I punched him lightly in the arm. "No!" I wasn't ready yet.

Rob shrugged. "Okay. But I'm not leaving until you get up on that stage."

Groaning inwardly, I mumbled. "No worries."

After the girls finished singing, I walked over to the DJ as discreetly as possible and looked through the song book. After I confirmed that my song was there, I filled out a song request form and handed it to the DJ, a long-haired guy who looked to be about my age and probably never heard of the song.

Wearing black jeans with holes in both knees and dark chest hair peeking out of a very worn T-shirt, he looked at the form and back at me. One eyebrow cocked, he said, "Interesting song choice."

Not surprised by his reaction, I smirked. "Yeah, I bet it's not that popular among twenty-something Upper East Siders."

Smiling at me, he said, "You'd be surprised by some of the song choices of yuppies. But I don't think I've actually seen this particular song done before."

"Well, unless I chicken out, tonight might be your lucky night."

"Looking forward to it." Scanning the form again, he said, "Break a leg, Lil' Kim."

"Thanks!" I started to walk away but thought better of it. "Er, about how many performances before mine?"

I chewed my lower lip as I observed him count the forms until he looked back at me and said, "Six."

I took a deep breath. If my heart beat any faster, I was afraid it would jump out of my chest and knock the poor guy over. Sneaking away to the bathroom, I chanted, *"I can do this. I can do this."*

Squatting over the toilet bowl, I texted Bridget. "Just gave the DJ my song choice. I think I'm gonna have a heart attack." I contemplated staying in the bathroom until my name was called until I heard a knock at the door. *Damn dive bars with single stall women's bathrooms!* I called out, "Almost done!" ran my hands through my hair and blotted my lips with some more gloss as I reminded myself of Caroline's words. "Pretend you're a heroine in a chick lit book." Bridget Jones would totally do this. She'd make a complete ass out of herself but she'd do it and she'd get the guy. And I, Kimberly Michelle Long, would also get the guy!

With somewhat renewed confidence I prayed would not betray me in the twenty-third hour, I walked out of the bathroom and smiled at the firm's real estate paralegal, Ellen, who I had met on exactly one occasion and who would now be witness to what might turn out to be the most humiliating night of my life. Or the most romantic, I thought as I remembered how Caroline's face lit up when she encouraged me to go for it.

I was standing in the back pretending to listen to the performance on stage, a rowdy rendition of *Living on a Prayer* when my phone beeped. Bridget.

"You can do this!" Since she knew me better than anyone, I wasn't surprised she used the same words of encouragement I had used on myself.

I texted back, "From your lips! Wish you were here for some in-person moral support ☺" and put the phone back in my pocketbook.

I was torn between wanting to get the damn thing over with and wishing the performances ahead of mine would go on indefinitely but when I saw the DJ grab the microphone from the guys in collections who sang *The Lion Sleeps Tonight* and search the crowd, I immediately knew he was looking for me. I slowly walked closer to the stage and waited.

Spotting me, he said, "There she is! Come on up Kim. Singing *Don't it Make my Brown Eyes Blue* by Crystal Gayle is your very own Lil' Kim!"

The crowd all looked left and right as if expecting to see the real Lil' Kim but as I approached the stage, the chuckling started as everyone got the joke.

The DJ handed me the mic, winked and said, "Break a leg!"

I felt my body shaking in fear as I took the microphone and faced the crowd. I saw Rob first and he gave me the thumbs up sign. David smiled wide at me. And then Lucy clapped her hands together, "Yay, Kim!" I saw the smiling faces of almost everyone in the Squad as well as a scowling Daneen but I didn't see Nicholas anywhere. I panicked that he had left or was in the bathroom until I spotted him and panicked some more. And then suddenly, from the back of the room, I heard, "Knock 'em dead, Kimmie!" and a loud whistle and saw Bridget and Jonathan in the back of the room clapping their hands in encouragement. I spied Nicholas turn to face them and look back at me in confusion as I mouthed, "thank you" to Bridget and Jonathan. *I was ready.*

CHAPTER 33

SPEAKING SOFTLY INTO THE MICROPHONE, I looked directly at Nicholas and said in the most unshaky voice I could muster under the circumstances, "This one's for you, Nicholas," and without awaiting his reaction, motioned for the DJ to start the song.

As the first few notes played, I took a deep breath in the acknowledgment that by the time I left the stage, it would all be over, and started singing, *"Don't know when I've been so blue. Don't know what's come over you."* Even though every molecule in my body was begging me to look elsewhere, I kept my gaze on Nicholas. His expression gave away nothing except perhaps shock. And maybe a little embarrassment. But I carried on. I had to. *"I'll be fine when you're gone. I'll just cry all night long."* The room was spookily quiet, yet I couldn't hear a word that was coming out of my mouth. *"I didn't mean to treat you bad. Didn't know just what I had. But honey now I do."* Nicholas was still staring at me, his mouth slightly open in a half smile. Although the half smile might have been wishful thinking on my part. Did he even know who Crystal Gayle was? He'd never mentioned a love of country music, certainly not country music from the 1970s. *"And don't it make my brown eyes blue."*

When singing directly to a practically stone-faced Nicholas became unbearable and I needed to connect with someone more encouraging, I shifted my gaze to the back of the room where Bridget stood with Jonathan. They smiled at me and Bridget gave the thumbs up sign and mouthed "awesome," offering the positive reinforcement I craved. I could tell from Bridget's expression that she meant it since she had a horrible poker face. As the song began inching towards a close – at last - I raised my voice in the knowledge that the worst was over and there was no going back. Smiling down at Rob and David, I sang the chorus, *"Don't it make my brown eyes. Don't it make my brown eyes."* Pumping his fists in the air, Rob joined me singing, *"Don't it make my brown eyes blue!"* until little by little more people joined in, chanting, *"Don't it make my browns eyes. Don't it make my brown eyes."* As my solo turned into a sing-a-long, I almost forgot why I was up there and enthusiastically finished the song. When I was done, relief washed over me and I took a proud bow as my co-workers gave me a rambunctious round of applause. And then I remembered that the song was over, but my performance wasn't.

My smile instantly faded as I turned to face Nicholas, fearing he was not the slightest bit moved by my grand gesture. As I walked toward him, praying my shaking legs would not fail me, I noticed that most of the room was taking turns looking from me to him in fascination. Since we'd never made our relationship public, I appreciated their confusion as to why I dedicated a love song to him, but I tried my best to tune them out.

"You rock!" said Lucy. "Must toast your performance with a shot."

"Um, sounds good. Maybe later!" I responded as I continued on my way.

"Nice job, Long!" Rob said, slapping me on the back as I walked past him.

"Thanks," I said without looking at him.

Blocking my path, David said, "I had no idea you could sing!"

I looked past his head at Nicholas. He was mere inches away but I feared it would take me an hour to reach him if people kept stopping me.

Trying to find that fine line between nipping the conversation in the bud and being rude, I smiled at David and said, "I have many talents!" and kept walking before he could respond.

Finally, I stood before Nicholas with only a wall of tension between us.

CHAPTER 34

HERE GOES NOTHING.

I clasped my hands behind my back and looked up at him. Smiling shyly I said, "So... that was scary."

Nodding, Nicholas gave me a closed-mouth smile. "I'm sure."

I waited a beat for him to say something else but when he didn't, I realized he wasn't going to make this easy for me and I let out a deep breath before speaking again. "I'm assuming my song got the point across but just in case you missed it, my brown eyes have been blue since you slammed my door and walked out. I really messed up, Nicholas. But..." I looked down at the dirty floor for a second. Swallowing hard, I looked back at up at him and I said, "I'm sorry. I still really like you. I mean, *really* like you. The things I said..." I shrugged. "Well, most of them were because of my own insecurity. I didn't mean to take it out on you. Can we try this again or is it too late? Do you hate me?" I stopped talking and took what felt like my first breath in days.

Nicholas continued to stare at me but didn't say anything. I swallowed hard again, trying to read his mind. *Say something!*

Finally he spoke. "I don't hate you, Kim." He frowned and shifted his eyes to the ground but quickly back at up at me. "I actually think you're pretty amazing. Despite the fact that you never seemed to think of yourself that way *or* recognize that I felt that way about you. I did. I do." Scratching his head, he said, "I even wondered what you saw in me – a workaholic, boring attorney."

I whispered, "You're the whole pack..."

Nicholas raised his hand to stop me. "Please, Kim. Let me finish."

Taken aback, I said, "Sorry. Go on."

"As I was saying, I think you're pretty terrific. You made me angry but in hindsight I could see how my actions could be misconstrued."

I smiled. My pulse was still racing uncontrollably but we were off to a good start.

Nicholas continued, "But trying again? I don't know. Things are different now."

"Different how?" I noted the crack in my voice and silently cursed my inner pubescent boy. Was he seeing someone else already?

"When we dated before, you were just Rob's assistant and part-time blogger. Now that you're giving this writing thing a go, I'm not sure it could work." He shrugged.

My jaw dropped. "What? You're the one who encouraged me to write!"

Nicholas raised his palms in the air. "It might be too much for me. Between working for Rob, your blog and this new writing venture, I just don't see how you'd have room for me in your life and I think I might need a girlfriend who's well, less ambitious."

I balled my hands into fists as anger consumed me. "You must be fucking kidding me!"

Nicholas looked from side to side awkwardly, turned back and gave me an apologetic frown.

I felt Bridget's presence behind me but knew if I turned around, I would break out into tears. It was one thing to cry *over* Nicholas but crying in front of him was an entirely different animal. I might have actually been too angry to cry. "Unfucking believable," I said looking at him in disbelief. "You must be kidding me," I repeated. Caroline and Bridget had promised that Nicholas still liked me. This was nothing like the end of *Bridget Jones's Diary*.

I squeezed my eyes holding back the tears and forced myself to face Nicholas one more time. "Okay, then."

Nicholas shook his head and slowly smiled. "Yes, Kimmie. I'm kidding you. I'm sorry, I just couldn't resist." Inching closer to me, he took one of my hands in his and looking deep into my eyes said, "The truth is my brown eyes have been seriously blue too. I'm crazy about you."

Still too angry to digest the magnitude of what he'd just said, I removed my hand from his and punched him in the arm, "You suck!"

Grabbing me to him, Nicholas kissed me hard until I felt my legs practically float off the ground. Releasing me, he said, "Yup. Take me or leave me."

Gazing up at him, I stood on my tippy toes and wrapped my arms around his neck.

"I'll take you," I whispered in his ear. Placing my lips softly against his, I kissed him again. I didn't care that practically the entire firm was watching us in a drunken stupor. When I pulled away, I touched my fingers to his freshly shaved jaw and whispered, "You look so clean cut."

Nicholas touched his hand to his chin and whispered back, "Yeah. Trying to look professional for the new job. You hate it?"

I smiled. "Sort of. But if I have to take you as you are, I guess that includes facial hair or lack thereof, huh?"

"I promise not to shave on the weekends and, who knows, once I get comfortable there, maybe I'll let my lazy shaving habits take over again." Squeezing my hand, he said, "Deal?"

Squeezing back, I said, "Deal," reached up and kissed him again.

"Is it okay to interrupt this romantic moment yet?" said a smiling Bridget in a mock impatient voice.

Embracing her fiercely, I said, "I can't believe you showed up. Thank you!"

"You said you wished I was here so of course I showed up! And besides, you said you thought you might have a heart attack and I was worried." Poking Nicholas lightly in the arm, she said, "I'll have you know that despite her flawless performance, Kim here was scared shitless to sing in front of you."

Nicholas gently patted my back in small circles. "She was fantastic." Then he looked at me like he was picturing me naked. "Nice shirt by the way."

Remembering what *he* looked like naked and more than a little eager to see him sans clothes again, I felt myself blush. "Thanks." Locked in a staring contest, I momentarily forgot where I was until I remembered that Nicholas and Bridget had never met before. "By the way, this is my very best friend Bridget. And you remember Jonathan, right?" At least I thought it was Jonathan. This guy had perfectly coiffed brown hair. I was dying to know how Bridget convinced him to cut his mop. But first things first.

As I searched Nicholas' face, afraid he might get the wrong idea as to why Jonathan (or his freshly groomed doppleganger) was in attendance, Nicholas reached over and shook his hand. "How's it going?"

"Bridget and Jonathan are dating," I said.

His polite smile turning into an all-out grin, Nicholas said, "Oh!"

Although he was unaware I knew about his ex-girlfriend's duplicity, I squeezed his hand again in quiet understanding. "Yup. And they make almost as adorable a couple as we do."

Nicholas winked. "Almost."

CHAPTER 35

FLAT ON MY BACK, I looked sideways at Nicholas who was propped on one elbow facing me in bed. "I missed you," I said. It was later that night, close to morning actually, and we were taking a much needed rest from our late night of marathon make up sex.

Nicholas ran his hand over my belly. Although his touch was warm, I shivered from the sensation. "I missed you too, Kimmie," he said.

"I was so afraid I'd never see you again after you quit." The prospect still hurt my stomach and I swallowed hard. I felt the need to memorize his face in case the entire night had been a dream and we hadn't actually gotten back together.

"I'm glad that didn't happen."

"Me too," I smiled at him.

"I probably would have made some excuse to see you again anyway," he said.

"Probably?"

Nicholas nodded. "I would have. But I'm glad I didn't have to wait that long. I still can't believe you sang for me. That was something."

"I had to write my happy ending!" I made a mental note to thank Caroline as soon as possible. Well, as soon as Nicholas and I were capable of keeping our hands off of each other for more than twenty minutes at a time. As Nicholas inched closer to me, I had a feeling it would be a while.

Nicholas kissed my forehead softly and pulled back to look at me. "I saw your review of Hannah's book by the way," he said,

"You did?"

Nicholas nodded. "Yeah. I was really proud of you."

I smiled softly and whispered, "Thank you. It was the right thing to do."

"It was. And I knew you'd figure that out eventually."

"But you stalked my website to make sure, huh?"

Nicholas chuckled. "No, I stalked your website to make sure you weren't bad mouthing your ex-boyfriend."

As I tried to disguise my glee that he had considered us "boyfriend and girlfriend," Nicholas added, "Actually, I stalked your website because I missed you."

Feeling my nerve endings tingle, I said, "I missed you too."

"I guess it's safe to say that we missed each other, huh?"

I reached over to pull him closer to me. "Yup."

Hovering over me, he said, "By the way, I loved your book." He leaned down and began kissing my neck.

I quickly sat up. "You did? I was afraid you hated it!"

"Not even a little bit!"

"What did you like about it? Tell me! Tell me!"

Nicholas laughed. "I promise to give you my thorough review later, but first things first." He flipped me onto my back again and smiled down at me. "I'm not quite through reacquainting myself with your hot body."

I reached up and touched my fingers to his face, happy to see some stubble sprouting already. "That's good cuz I'm not through reacquainting myself with yours."

Nicholas leaned down as if to kiss me but instead began singing, "*Kimmie Long was in my pants.*" He stopped.

"What? You forgot the words?" I joked.

Nicholas shook as head. "No. I just thought of something."

"What's that?"

"Kimberly Long and Nicholas Strong."

At the sound of our names together, I smiled. "What about us?"

"*Strong* and *Long*. Our last names rhyme!" Nicholas said laughing.

I slowly repeated, "Strong and Long" and nodded. "You're right. Our last names totally rhyme. I'd never thought of that!"

**OTHER NOVELS BY
MEREDITH SCHORR**

A STATE OF JANE

*JUST FRIENDS
WITH BENEFITS*

**Keep reading for a sneak
peek at *A State of Jane*!**

PREVIEW OF
A STATE OF JANE
BY MEREDITH SCHORR

HOLDING THE PHONE AGAINST MY EAR with my shoulder while I painted my toenails with OPI's *That's Hot Pink*, I said to my sister, "Wish me a happy anniversary."

"Happy Anniversary, little sister." Claire was only seventeen months older than me, practically my Irish twin, but she always insisted on referring to me as her "little sister." "May I ask what anniversary you're celebrating?"

"My first one. And hopefully my last."

Claire replied, "Clarify."

"My first anniversary as a single person. It's been exactly a year since Bob and I broke up and I'm officially ready to fall in love again." I looked toward my computer screen where my eHarmony profile was twenty-eight percent completed.

Claire snorted. "Says who?"

"I've done extensive research online and my score on several questionnaires clearly indicates that I'm emotionally available for a new relationship."

A hint of doubt in her voice, Claire questioned, "Cuz it's been exactly a year?"

"Precisely. Three hundred and sixty-five days!" I was not going to let Claire's teasing get to me. I knew by waiting a year, I'd be less likely to waste my time in a rebound relationship.

"Only you would actually think a few days give or take would make a difference," Claire said, giggling.

"Ha ha, Claire. Laugh all you want. Laugh all the way down the aisle you'll walk down as my matron of honor!"

Still laughing, Claire asked, "So who do you intend to have this new relationship with?"

"Someone amazing! I just have to find him. Could be anywhere – eHarmony, subway, bar, work. In fact, a new set of first-year associates is starting this week!" I bit my lip. "Although if they started law school right after college, they might only be twenty-five." Not everyone worked as a paralegal first like me.

"And that's a problem because?"

"I'm twenty-six! I'd rather date someone older. Or my age." Thirty would be perfect since men matured less quickly than women. A four-year age difference might mean we'd be ready to settle down at the same time.

"It's a one year difference, Jane. Keep your options open."

"They are open!"

"Whatever you say."

I blew on my toes, willing the polish to dry faster. "I hate when you do that, you know."

"Do what?" Claire asked innocently.

"Dismiss me."

Claire sighed loudly. "You're not in high school anymore, Jane, and guys in New York are not gonna fall at your feet." Laughing, she added, "Except the really short, nerdy ones with balance problems. Just don't expect to meet Dr. Right who looks like Eric Bana. It ain't easy and you've got lots of competition."

When I met Bob the summer between our sophomore and junior years in high school, we were co-counselors for the same group of seven-year-old boys. We became good friends but when I told Claire I had a crush on him, she said I'd never have the guts to make a move and should just use his friendship as practice for talking to guys. "As always, thanks for the uplifting pep talk. And it's not as if guys fell at my feet in high school either. Bob was my first boyfriend, remember?"

Softening her voice, Claire said, "Sorry if I sounded mean. You're a definite catch, sis. You're just naïve and I don't want you to be unprepared. You understand, right? Just go in with no expectations, OK?"

"OK," I said softly. I had hoped Claire would share my excitement, not give me unsolicited advice.

Her voice brighter, Claire said, "So, you do realize that you'll need to actually go on dates, right? Which means no more back-to-back episodes of *The Barefoot Contessa* and *Iron Chef* on The Food Network on Saturday nights."

"It's not like I'm a hermit, Claire. I just wanted to make sure I gave myself enough time to move on after a nine-year relationship." The fact that I broke up with Bob and not the other way around didn't make the split any less traumatic. Well, probably not *that* much less traumatic anyway. On a positive note, I'd learned a lot of new recipes over the past year. "Anyway, I'm ready now."

"I'm sure you are. Just please don't expect things to be as easy as they were when you met Bob. The dating world post-millennium is an entirely different animal and you're dealing with experienced men, not innocent boys. It might not be as easy to meet another Bob. Just ask Pin Cushion."

Pin Cushion was my sister's nickname for my far from virginal roommate, Lainie, and she was the last person I'd ask for relationship advice. Birth control advice, maybe.

"I'll just be myself and things will happen. Just like they eventually did for you."

Claire let out a deep exhale. "Eventually is the operative word. And now we can't make a baby to save our lives."

I remembered when Claire had dyed her dirty blonde hair jet black when she dated a drummer in college and how she gave up meat when she dated a vegetarian. She wound up married to Kevin, another high school teacher from the suburbs who, ten times out of ten, also chose cheeseburgers over tofu and soy milk. They were a perfect match, but baby making had proved to be challenging. "It will happen when it's supposed to, Claire. I truly believe that." Secretly, I wished it would happen already since I couldn't wait to buy cute baby clothes for my little niece or nephew.

"My advice to you – take your own advice. It will happen when it's supposed to happen. Don't look at every guy as the potential 'one.' "

"Not every guy, Claire! Just the single, handsome, ambitious, generous, funny ones!" Just then, a message popped up on my computer that my session on eHarmony was going to timeout if I remained idle for another sixty seconds, so after I told Claire I loved her and would cross my fingers that she didn't get her period that month, we hung up and I finished my online profile. I couldn't wait to be matched with someone with whom I was compatible on twenty-nine dimensions!

ACKNOWLEDGMENTS

It did not take a village to write *Blogger Girl* but I had a whole lot of help:

My beta reader, Natalie Aaron—calling you a "beta reader" might be the world's hugest understatement. How many beta readers mark up every single page of the manuscript? How many beta readers talk through the comments over a two-hour phone call? And put up with constant follow-up emails? While I was initially horrified at the prospect of making so many edits, I can sincerely say that your comments made *Blogger Girl* SO much better. A world of thanks for all of your help and support, your amazing eye for details and your brutal honesty. I also want to thank you for your humor and your snark and for simply "getting" me. You are so incredibly talented. Please please PLEASE write another book.

My editor, Gabrielle Roman – I truly thought *Blogger Girl* was almost finished when it made its way into your talented hands. Oh, how you proved me wrong. Once again, your brilliant feedback helped me take my work to the next level. I cannot wait to work with you on my fourth novel.

My fabulous publisher, Booktrope, and all of its "cool kids" – I am so happy to be a member of the Booktrope family. You guys are terrific. My Book Manager, Beth Bacon—you amaze me with your ability to think outside of the box and I just know we will work well together. Loretta Matson, my fantastic cover designer—you worked tirelessly on the cover and I'm sure there were times you thought we'd never be satisfied. I, however, always knew you'd create the perfect cover for me. And you did. And Heather Ludviksson and Jesse James Freeman—I know I sometimes send you guys a million emails but it's only because you are both a wealth of information. Thank you for patiently answering each and every one of them.

My fellow Chick Lit Goddesses – Only fellow authors can truly understand the highs and lows, pleasure and pain, and rewards and frustrations associated with being an author these days and I am so lucky to have found you all. Thank you for consistently reminding me why I love being a writer and for making me laugh until my tummy hurts on a daily basis with your witty posts. Special shout-outs to Samantha Stroh Bailey and Francine LaSala. I love you guys so much. Thank you for being so talented, so funny, so supportive and so uniquely "you." You inspire me to be a better author and a better person – I cannot wait to plan Book Buzz 2014 with you.

My friends – I have the best friends in the world. I really do. Without my wonderful friends, I'd probably lock myself in my apartment and spend all day writing, blogging, tweeting or posting updates on Facebook. Thank you for encouraging me to go out, eat, drink and be "Meri." Honorable mentions to Ronni Solon, Jenny Kabalen, Abbe Kalnick, Shanna Eisenberg, Megan Coombes, Deirdre Noonan, Anne Lekow, Jason Shaw, Hilda Black, Jennifer Jacobs, Julie Marie Shinkle and Shannon Labetti.

My Family – Thank you for your unconditional love and support and for purchasing multiple copies of all of my books. Special thanks to my mom, Susan, for being my biggest muse and for repeatedly expressing how proud she is of me. The feeling is mutual. Also, eternal gratitude to my sister, Marjorie, for being my first beta reader and my best friend in the entire world.

Book Bloggers – Wow. I cannot say enough about you guys. There would not be a *Blogger Girl* without you! Thank you for doing what you do and for doing it so well and with such grace. Special shout-outs to Samantha Robey, Melissa Amster, Laura Chapman, Michelle Bell, Stephanie Territo, Ashley Williams, Isabella Anderson, Julie Valerie and Kaley Stewart for inspiring me regularly, but I love you all!

Dedication – I'd like to dedicate *Blogger Girl* to Alan Blum. Your friendship means the world to me. Without your encouragement, support, extensive comic relief and mini therapy sessions, I could not write one, much less three, novels. Your faith in me gives me faith in myself. The world threw you an unexpected and unwanted twist this summer but I hope by the time you read this dedication, you have emerged victorious. The world is a better place because you are in it. I love you and cannot wait until you're back at work where you belong.

PRAISE FOR
BLOGGER GIRL

"Meredith Schorr is such a witty author that brings heart and humor to every story she tells. Her characters are always a delight to get to know and this book was no exception. There are well developed supporting characters that don't overpower the main story of Kim and her journey. I love the strong friendships that Meredith writes about in her novels and a love interest that will make you smile. I just flipped back through "*Blogger Girl*" again to see if there was anything that I would say I wish was different and absolutely nothing. This was a solid book from start to finish, highly entertaining and difficult to put down. Even the books that are reviewed within the book were compelling. And you will never think about The Beatles "Penny Lane" the same again."

—Michelle Bell, book blogger
and founder of Michelle's Book Nook

"Meredith Schorr's delightfully flawed heroines have never failed to charm me, and *Blogger Girl's* Kimberly Long joins Jane (*A State of Jane*) and Stephanie (*Just Friends with Benefits*) in a special place in my heart. I really connected with her, especially, I hate to admit, over the frustration of seeing her high school nemesis thrive while she floundered. A great character. So very human and full and dimension. A satisfying and enjoyable read!"

—Francine LaSala, author of *The Girl, the Gold Tooth*
& *Everything* and *Rita Hayworth's Shoes*

"Like Sophie Kinsella, Meredith Schorr's stories seem effortless. This is the third book that I've read by her, and she is one of my favorite authors. *Blogger Girl* is delicious chick lit – a smart, hilarious, action-packed novel with characters who jump off the page and into your heart. With a fresh and contemporary look at the inside world of book bloggers, *Blogger Girl* made my heart pound with every page. I tore through this book and often laughed so hard that I had tears. An excellent novel that is a must read for anyone who loves a funny, heartwarming and relatable story."

—Samantha Stroh Bailey, author of *Finding Lucas*

MORE GREAT READS FROM BOOKTROPE

A State of Jane by **Meredith Schorr** (Contemporary Women's Fiction) Jane is ready to have it all: great friends, partner at her father's law firm and a happily-ever-after love. But her life plan veers off track when every guy she dates flakes out on her. As other aspects of Jane's life begin to spiral out of control, Jane will discover that having it all isn't all that easy.

Thank You For Flying Air Zoe by **Erik Atwell** (Contemporary Women's Fiction) Realizing she needs to awaken her life's tired refrains, Zoe vows to recapture the one chapter of her life that truly mattered—her days as drummer for an all-girl garage band. Will Zoe bring the band back together and give The Flip-Flops a second chance at stardom?

Caramel and Magnolias by **Tess Thompson** (Contemporary Romance) A former actress goes undercover to help a Seattle police detective expose an adoption fraud in this story of friendship, mended hearts, and new beginnings.

Grace Unexpected by **Gale Martin** (Contemporary Romance) When her longtime boyfriend dumps her instead of proposing, Grace avows the sexless Shaker ways. She appears to be on the fast track to a marriage proposal… until secrets revealed deliver a death rattle to the Shaker Plan.

Ties that Bind by **Heather Huffman** (Contemporary Romance) Kate has moved to San Francisco and gotten herself hired by the man she suspects to be her dad. Soon, she will have to confront the decisions of her past to find out whether she can love the man who gave her up, the man who loves her, and even herself.

Work in Progress by **Christina Esdon** (Romance) Psychologist Reese Morgan refuses to let go of a childhood trauma. When she meets a handsome contractor, Josh Montgomery, she wonders if the walls around her heart can be knocked down to let love in.

Discover more books and learn about our
new approach to publishing at **booktrope.com**.

CPSIA information can be obtained at www.ICGtesting.com
Printed in the USA
LVOW08s0906120214

373379LV00001B/124/P